Dear Reader:

Thank you for picking up this copy of *Daddy by Default* by Pat
Tucker. Pat is a phenomenal storyteller and it is a pleasure to now
have her as a part of the Strebor Books family. The main topic of
Daddy by Default intrigued me because, as much as I hate to admit it
being a female myself, there are a lot of men in the universe raising
and supporting kids because they were bamboozled by trifling
females. There are those women who see their children as "paychecks" and even plot to have kids in order to have an influx of
monthly funds for eighteen plus years.

The *Maury* show often has episodes packed to the brim with women
who state that they are "one million percent sure" that men are the
fathers of their children, only to end up being embarrassed when the
DNA tests prove the opposite. Some of them end up testing eight,
nine, or even twelve men, searching for the one man whose sperm
created their offspring. It is really sad. And while it is easy for a lot of
us to blame the men for playing craps with their penises on a regular
basis, some women see that as a great opportunity to flip the script.

I hope that you enjoy *Daddy by Default* and that you will also pick
up Pat Tucker's next novel, *Football Widows*, about the activities of
football coaches' wives while their husbands are hard at work and
traveling to away games. As always, thanks for supporting the authors
that I publish under my imprint, Strebor Books. All of us truly appreciate your support. If you would like to contact me, please email me
at Zane@eroticanoir.com.

Blessings,

Zane

Zane
Publisher
Strebor Books International
www.simonandschuster.com/streborbooks

ZANE PRESENTS

DADDY
By DEFAULT

ZANE PRESENTS

DADDY *By* DEFAULT

A Novel

PAT TUCKER

STREBOR BOOKS

NEW YORK LONDON TORONTO SYDNEY

Strebor Books
P.O. Box 6505
Largo, MD 20792
http://www.streborbooks.com

ISBN 978-1-59309-313-6
LCCN 2010936659

First Strebor Books trade paperback edition November 2010

Cover design: www.mariondesigns.com
Cover photograph: © Keith Saunders/Marion Designs

10   9   8   7   6   5   4   3   2

Manufactured in the United States of America

For information regarding special discounts for bulk purchases,
please contact Simon & Schuster Special Sales at 1-866-506-1949
or business@simonandschuster.com

The Simon & Schuster Speakers Bureau can bring authors to your live event.
For more information or to book an event, contact the Simon & Schuster Speakers
Bureau at 1-866-248-3049 or visit our website at www.simonspeakers.com.

ACKNOWLEDGMENTS

I'd like to thank God Almighty first and foremost. The greatest appreciation goes to my patient and wonderful mother, Deborah Tucker Bodden; my number one cheerleader and sister, Denise Braxton; my new brother-in-law, Tavares. Thanks to my stepfather, Herbert, for keeping my mom happy; and Lydell R. Wilson, thanks for your patience, love, and support.

I'd like to thank my handsome younger brother, Irvin Kelvin Seguro, and his fiancée, Amber; the two best uncles in the world, Robert and Vaughn Belzonie; aunts Regina and Shelia; my older brother, Carlton Anthony Tucker; my nephews, nieces, and the rest of my supportive family.

We don't share the same blood, but I love them like sisters: Monica Hodge, Marilyn Glazier, LaShawanda Moore, Lee Lee Baines, Tameka Brown, Kevina Brown. My love and thanks to Keywanne Hawkins, Desiree Clement, Yolanda Jones and the rest of the most exquisite ladies of Sigma Gamma Rho Sorority Inc., especially my sisters of Gamma Phi Sigma here in Houston.

And this too shall pass: it's what people tell you when you're going through the storm, but very few are there to remind you to keep your head held high. I know I'm blessed because I am surrounded by friends who really know me and accept me just the way I am. ReShonda Tate Billingsley—who is able to tell me what I'm thinking and somehow says what I'm about to say! Thanks for your constant support, listening ear, and faith in my work, and Nikki Turner for her continued support.

Many, many thanks to Alisha Yvonne, Markisha Sampson, Major Logan, Robyn Cuffee, Ron Reynolds, Marlo Blue, Edel Howlin, Julie Sowchuck, Nick Alvarado, Afshar Karat Bobby Modad—you guys make my days easier so that I can focus on writing at night! Charles Dixon and LaKeisha Madison.

Special thanks to my super agent Sara, my publicist the terrific Tasha, and a world of gratitude to my new Strebor family, Charmaine, and Zane for having faith in my work.

My deepest gratitude goes out to you, the reader. I know you have many options out there. I'm so honored that you picked up my book. My hope is that you enjoy this story so much that you tell a friend or two about it. (Spread the word—not the book.) Support Black Authors and remember: books make great gifts! Look out for my next novel, *Football Widows*.

If I forgot anyone, charge it to my head and not my heart. I hope you enjoy the story. Regardless of whether you do, please drop me a line at rekcutp@hotmail.com or sylkkep@yahoo.com.. I'd love to hear from you.

Warmly,
Pat

I never knew there were states where men are given a deadline to question paternity— if they miss that deadline, guess what?

ROXANNE

Goosebumps rose on my arms and legs. The hairs that stood up on the back of my neck were nothing compared to the chill that touched me to the core. Even at twenty-nine years old I still wasn't comfortable being in hospitals. I never liked the cold and impersonal feel you got while in there. You always knew bad news was hot on your heels, and this time was no exception. I watched my husband pace the area inside the small exam room as we waited for the doctor to come back. I sat at the very edge of the table with my legs dangling.

"You okay?" he asked again, for the umpteenth time.

I simply nodded. My voice had left long ago. I wasn't all right, but his was a rhetorical question. I laced my fingers together and placed my hands in my lap.

"What's taking so damn long?" I muttered nearly to myself. I cringed at the thought of what was to come.

Parker sighed. His broad shoulders slumped. His smooth, chocolate-colored skin seemed to lack its normal glow. I could see the stress etched into his features. Bags had formed beneath his hooded bedroom eyes; his pink lips looked pinched. Parker was in need, but how could I comfort him when I needed comforting myself? I wanted to curl myself into a ball and holler until I woke from this nightmare.

By the time the doctor came back into the room, I had already braced myself for the worst. He was a tall and thick man, of Asian descent; although I couldn't pinpoint which ethnic group. The sad look in his slanted eyes gave him away before he even spoke. Although I was prepared for his diagnosis, the actual words made my pulse slow.

"Mister and Missus Redman, there's really no easy way to say this," he began, and cleared his throat.

Parker came and stood next to me. He grabbed my hand, but I barely gave it to him. I started swallowing back tears and fought against the bile churning in the pit of my belly.

"...so our estimation is the baby died at ten weeks," I heard him say.

Despite his attempt to handle me, us, gently, his words were still as lethal as a machete that sliced through my chest and punctured my heart. How could my baby have died and I not even know it? I shivered at the thought of what was to come next. We'd been down this road before, but despite that, nothing prepared us for this, for the heartbreak that followed.

"...a D and C," the doctor was saying now, but I kept hearing the heartbreaking words that had once again changed our lives.

...the baby died at ten weeks.

My head hung low, and I couldn't even attempt to suppress my sobs, which grew louder. Last time, we didn't make it out of the first trimester either.

"It's gonna be okay; we'll make it through this," Parker assured me. He stopped short of saying, "just like before." His voice was soft, soothing, but not enough to ease my pain. I felt Parker's massive hand rubbing my back as I buried my face into his chest and cried uncontrollably. I felt myself gasping for air as I sat, completely overwhelmed by emotions.

"I, um, if you guys don't have any questions..." the doctor mumbled.

Parker continued to rub, as my shoulders convulsed.

"Why don't I give you some time alone? I'll leave a prescription at the nurses' station." The doctor took a few steps, then stopped at the door and turned back to us.

"If you all have any questions, anything at all…" the doctor's voice trailed off.

I felt Parker move; he must've nodded his response, because I didn't hear anything else. Then I heard the door open and close.

The last time Parker cried like that was the last time we went through this. I couldn't wrap my mind around why, or even how, we were going through this again. What a way to spend a Friday evening. For us, summer was off to a horrible start.

"Let's go home," he mumbled, sniffling back his own tears. He scooped his arm around me and we headed out of the exam room. We stopped long enough to pick up the prescription. The doctor left, then we headed out.

I don't even remember being led out of the emergency room and into the parking lot. I stood by, watching, as Parker gave his keys to a parking attendant. I was in a fog as he helped me into the car and fastened my seat belt.

"We're gonna make it through this," he assured me again as he threw the truck into gear and took off.

"Again," I emphasized, seething. Tears pushed their way through and I started crying all over again. What had we done to deserve this, *again*? I didn't understand.

Friday night traffic was a bit light and I was glad, figuring we'd make it home quickly. After we'd been on the road a while, I said, "I know you're gonna get tired of this, Park. I know how badly you want kids—just as badly as I do. We've been married for three years now and this is our third mis…" I couldn't bring myself to finish.

He reached over and touched my hand; I couldn't stop trembling. This wasn't fair to him; I saw how he watched his friends and their sons, and even his best friend, James, with his daughter. I noticed the longing his eyes couldn't hide and I felt awful. It wasn't his fault that I couldn't carry a pregnancy through full-term. Why should he have to suffer, too?

"Hey! We're in this together," he said, squeezing my hand.

I wanted desperately to believe him, his words, but in my heart of hearts, I realized that with each failed pregnancy, I was losing a small piece of him.

"What now?" he blurted. That's when I looked at him and noticed his narrowed eyes focused on the rear view mirror.

"Great!" he snarled as he steered the truck over to the right shoulder of Highway 59.

I turned my head to see the red and blue strobe lights announcing the police cruiser that was pulling us over. My cell phone rang. The caller ID showed Serena Carson, my closest friend. I figured there'd be time to call her later, so I let voicemail answer.

Once at a complete stop, Parker put the truck in park, turned down the radio, and turned off the ignition. We sat for a long moment and I wondered what was taking the officer so long. Parker's eyes remained locked on the rearview mirror. His jaw tightened, and I tried to be patient.

"What's he doin'?" I asked, frowning. I wasn't in the mood for this. I needed to be home.

Parker shook his head. "Ain't no tellin'. Running the plates, I'm sure," he said, half lifting a shoulder. He seemed frustrated, too.

"Great! I'm ready to get home and we're sitting here like some common criminals," I sulked. "What did you even do?" I asked as other vehicles zoomed past us.

"I guess I musta been speeding or something, but it's gonna be fine." Parker tried to reassure me as he reached for my hand again.

I turned my head. Now the officer was stepping out of the cruiser and heading for Parker's side of the truck.

"I'll make it quick; take my ticket and get you home," he promised. He took my hand to his lips and kissed it softly.

"Driver's license, registration and proof of insurance, please," the officer said sternly, the moment Parker lowered the window.

"What's the problem, Officer?" Parker asked as he reached for his wallet and the insurance and registration papers I had already pulled out of the glove box.

"Do you know how fast you were going back there?" the officer asked as he took the papers and license from Parker's hand.

"It doesn't matter; I'll just take the ticket so we can go. We've had a very stressful evening. My wife's tired and we're ready to get home," Parker explained.

"That doesn't give you the right to break the law. I'll be right back," the officer said firmly, before he spun on his heels and made his way back to his cruiser.

✪ ✪ ✪

It felt like an eternity had passed, sitting there, under scrutiny. I wanted this to be over so I could go home and mourn our loss in peace.

Parker must've been reading my mind because it seemed like he also started getting restless, shifting in his seat and checking the rear view mirror every so often.

"What's takin' so damn long?" I wondered aloud. When I turned, I saw the officer looking at our car, then talking into his radio. My stomach began to twist into knots.

Parker shrugged his shoulders and sighed. He glanced into the rear view mirror again, then reached for me.

"I'm sorry 'bout this, babe," he said sincerely.

We didn't have to wait long for the second biggest shock of the evening.

The officer walked back to the vehicle and said, "Mr. Parker, I'm gonna need you to step out of the vehicle, and keep your hands where I can see 'em."

"Huh?" Parker sat with a bewildered expression on his face.

"Sir, I'm gonna need you to step out of the vehicle, and keep your hands where I can see 'em," the officer repeated his request slowly.

When I noticed his hand on his taser, my heart thudded loudly in my ear. I didn't want an incident; we'd already been through enough.

"What's going on?" I lowered my head, trying to see the officer through the driver's side window.

"Ma'am, please be quiet," the officer said.

Parker hadn't moved. He sat with a dumbfounded expression on his face.

"Ah, Officer, I thought I was getting a ticket for speeding. I told you my wife and I..."

"Sir, I'm not gonna ask again. I need you to slowly get out of the vehicle, and keep your hands where I can see 'em!" This time he spoke with such firmness, ice raced through my veins. What was this about? Parker shook his head as if he couldn't comprehend.

I was thunderstruck. I didn't understand what was going on either.

"Honey, I'ma just do what he's asking. Ain't no need to get upset. I'll get out, talk to him and we'll be on our way real soon."

I nodded, agreeing with his decision, but something didn't feel right. Why would all of this be necessary for a doggone speeding ticket? It simply wasn't adding up.

Parker eased out of the truck slowly, as the officer stood back. They made their way to the hood of the truck.

"Is your name Parker Delewis Redman?" I heard the officer ask.

"Ah, yes; what's this about?" Parker asked.

"Does your wife have a current driver's license?"

"Of course!" Parker said.

"Mr. Redman, you're under arrest. I'm gonna need you to turn around and put your hands on top of your head."

"Under arrest? What'd I do?"

By now, I had opened the door and stepped out of the truck, but I stayed on my side of the vehicle.

"Officer, what's going on?" I asked.

"Ma'am, I need you to get back in the vehicle. Mr. Redman, you are under arrest for delinquent child support. Look, I don't want to do this, but I'm only doing my job," the officer finally admitted.

For the first time since he'd pulled us over, I started calming down. This was definitely a mistake, but I needed to understand what was going on.

"Child, what? Oh, you definitely got the wrong man. That's got to be a serious mistake," Parker said, as he was being handcuffed.

"Sir, I have a warrant for your arrest. Records show you owe more than forty-five thousand dollars in back child support payments."

Parker's eyebrows bunched together and we both shook our heads at the foolishness. Here we were, trying to deal with yet another miscarriage, and now he was being arrested for being delinquent on child support payments? If it wasn't so serious, I'd laugh at the sick irony.

"Officer, I swear, this is some kind of misunderstanding. You're making a huge mistake. I don't have any damn kids! Ask my wife. I may have been speeding, but it was only 'cause we just found out she had another miscarriage. We don't have any kids," Parker said, trying to reason.

What he said made my heart sink. Yes, it was *another* miscarriage, but did he have to say it like *that*? However, it seemed to give the officer pause, because he slowed and looked over at me.

"He's telling the truth. We've been married for three years; no children, I promise you that," I confirmed softly. Again, I started to cry.

The officer's face softened a bit, his green eyes showing sadness. Then he cleared his throat and said, "Well, if this is a mistake, we'll clear it all up down at the station, but for now, I have to take you in." He'd turned his attention back to Parker.

"For not paying child support?" Parker asked as if he was trying to get clarification.

"That's right. Again, I'm just doing my job. If this is really a mistake, you're gonna have to clear it up with the judge." The officer looked at me. "But to avoid having the vehicle towed, Ma'am, you can drive it home," he tossed my way like it was some sort of consolation prize.

My head was spinning as I stood on the side of Highway 59 watching helplessly as my husband was being hauled off to jail.

This was an absolute mistake because there's no way in hell Parker has a child.

JAMES

I pulled up into my old driveway and was shocked to see Serena's Mercedes parked there. I wondered if I should turn back, although I knew I couldn't.

"Aw, shit, Dawg, I need to go," I said to my boy as I pulled up behind my soon-to-be ex-wife's SUV. "I'll holla' at you in a minute."

I pressed the button on my Bluetooth to end the call and sat, thinking for a moment. It's not like she's the one who moved out, but I came by the house during lunch intentionally. I was hoping to avoid her. Unfortunately, my timing was off. I didn't feel like dealing with any drama, but I had no choice. I'd forgotten some important papers in my old office. I turned off my ignition, took a deep breath and got out of the car, forcing myself to think positive thoughts.

"Maybe she's sick or something, and won't feel like sparring today," I mumbled. One could only hope. Serena the Sicko, my nickname for her, was explosive, if nothing else, and it didn't take much to set her off. Once you rubbed her the wrong way, there was no turning back. I had been on the wrong end of her fury one too many times and I knew firsthand how volatile she could be.

At least she was keeping up with the yard work, I thought, as I took in the perfectly manicured lawn. I strolled up the shrub-lined walkway, still hoping for the best.

We decided to divorce a couple of weeks after I left home in late February. It had been nearly three months since I'd moved out of our two-story brick house, and I hadn't regretted it one bit. If it weren't for our six-year-old daughter, Semaj, who had sickle cell anemia, I would've wrapped our marriage up long ago. The disease made her so sick, sometimes I wished I could've traded places with her to take the pain.

Then there was Serena's eleven-year-old son, David, from a previous relationship. We were working on getting close, but Serena even made that hard. It was almost like she was intentionally sabotaging my relationship with him. Truth be told, I had been tired of Serena's foul mouth, nasty attitude, and bullshit long ago, but hung in there for my girl.

I wanted to show my daughter what a real man was supposed to be like, teach her that her daddy should be the mold that others should try to live up to. Serena and I had been married for eight years, but if I had to be honest with myself, I'd say our marriage was really dead about three years ago. That's when this chicken-head I had a fling with had busted me out by showing up at our front door. Well, let's just say that was the last straw for Serena. She was quick to toss my ass out, like used bathwater.

At first, I was pissed about being caught. Again, I never wanted to be a failure in my daughter's eyes. But when I look back at the entire situation now, I realize that subconsciously, I was looking for a way out all along, but didn't want to leave outright. I didn't want to gaze into my daughter's eyes and have her believe that I was responsible for breaking her mother's heart. So in the end, it turned out the trick had done me a favor by showing up after all.

There was no mistaking what I was hearing as I unlocked the front door.

"Oh, yes!"

My heart fell to my feet. I stood still for a moment, but my ears weren't playing tricks on me.

"Oh, God! Oh, yes!" her voice screamed again. Serena loved as passionately as she fought. No, there was no mistaking that sound.

My heart was beating so loudly, it was like drums going off in my ears. This would be low, even for Serena's hateful ass, I tried to tell myself, although I knew she was keen for trifling antics. The closer I got to the door, the more certain there was no mistaking what I was hearing. My anger grew with each heavy step I took up toward the master bedroom, what used to be *our* bedroom.

"Yesss, right there, yes!" I heard her order.

Not in my fuckin' house! The house I still pay for!

I took the stairs two, even three at a time. When I reached the landing, I stormed past Semaj's room, her bathroom, and rushed to the end of the hall where our bedroom door was open slightly.

"Oh, God, right there." Her cries taunted me.

I stormed into the room, thinking the element of surprise was sure to startle the lovebirds. But the joke was obviously on me. They never even broke stride. They were huffing and panting like wild dogs, bodies making clapping sounds, right there in my goddamn bed!

"What the fuck is going on in here?" I screamed. That's when they finally acknowledged I was there. Serena turned and gave me the look of death.

"First and foremost, what the hell are *you* doing in my house?" she screamed, talking like she was struggling to catch her breath. Her nostrils were flaring as her light eyes narrowed and threw daggers at me. She had the nerve to use her hands to cover her bare breasts, as if I hadn't seen them before. Twisting a little more to face me, she snarled and spat in my direction, "Get the fuck out before I call the cops!"

My eyes grew wide. That's when dude tried to ease himself into an upright position.

"Hey, what's going on here?" he asked. I wasn't sure if he was talking to me or Serena.

"I got this," she snapped at him, then turned her rage back toward me.

"You sittin' up here riding a muthafucka' in my bed, our bed, and you threatening to call the cops on me?" I was trying to understand her logic. Did she not know, or understand, the heinous act she was committing?

"You ain't got no right to nothin' in this muthafucka!" She mocked me. "Remember, I tossed your ass outta here!" she screamed, pointing a warning finger at me. "Now I suggest you get the fuck out before I have you thrown out!" Her harsh words quickly turned my anger into rage.

Dude looked scared and confused at the same time. He grabbed Serena's slender hips and motioned, like he was trying to move her off his mid-section. But she jerked her body back and used her palms to shove him back onto the bed.

"I said, let me handle this!" she screamed at him again.

I didn't know what I was feeling. Serena and I were days from our divorce being finalized, but seeing her in what was once *our* bed, loving some other man, was too much. I had no way of knowing then, that this was only the beginning of a nightmare with her that would only get worse with time.

LACHEZ

I glanced at my kids in the rearview mirror and sighed. I was glad for summer break, but I couldn't wait for school to start, even though the year had just ended a few weeks ago. These damn kids were driving me nuts. It's one thing to have my own damn kids working my nerves, but toss their friends into the mix and I'm fit to be tied. It's going to be a very long summer!

"Junie," I called to my oldest, who acted like he was in a different world. He didn't look up from the hand-held game he was playing with a vengeance. I was really attempting not to get pissed, but he was trying me.

Julius Junior is twelve; his brother, Lorenzo, is ten; and my baby, Mickey, is eight. I love them all to pieces, but at times, they try my patience more than I can handle. Just like now. I'm driving to this damn appointment, and I need to make sure we're all on the same page, but instead of Junie's ass listening to me, and setting an example for his brothers, he's playing with that damn game.

"Mickey, Renzo, you guys know what time it is, right?" I questioned the two youngest.

"Yeah, Ma," Renzo answered. "We gon' tell them people how Mickey can't sit still, how you always gotta tell him the same thing over and over again," Renzo repeated like we'd practiced.

"What about the video games?" I asked.

His little head tilted to the side slightly, as if he was trying to remember. "Um," he said.

"Remember when you play with him?" I tried to lead.

"Oh, yeah, he can't play the video games because he can't do what Junie tells him he needs to, you know, to make it to the next level," he explained. Satisfied with his answer, I glanced over my shoulder and snatched the portable PlayStation game from Junie's hands.

"Dang, Ma!" he finally screamed.

"I've only been trying to get your attention for the past hour!" I replied sarcastically.

Junie smacked his lips and crossed his arms at his chest.

"I already know what to say." He pouted. I sighed and shook my head.

"You don't know what to say until I tell you what the hell to say," I scolded.

"Ma, this ain't my first time doing this. Wasn't I the one who convinced them people both you and Renzo had it, too?" he asked sarcastically. He had a point there, but I couldn't stand the fact that my twelve-year-old thought he knew every damn thing and was smarter than everyone else on the planet, including me.

"Boy, you betta watch the way you talking to me. I will slap the taste out your damn mouth. You musta' lost your rabbit-ass mind!"

He adjusted his attitude real fast when he realized I wasn't in the mood. "Now, like I said, we don't know if these people are gonna question us together or separately. I wanna make sure we're all telling the same story; you understand me?"

He answered by nodding and narrowing his eyes. I started to reach back and go upside his head, but a cop car had just passed and I didn't feel like going to jail. Somebody's always watching.

Once we got our stories straight, I pulled into the parking lot and gathered my things so we could get out of the car. We were at Memorial Herman Southwest's professional building off 59.

"Okay, boys, it's show time," I sang. Junie had lost his sour attitude since he got his video game back and I had reiterated my promise to take everyone to Chuck E. Cheese's if all went well.

We piled out of the car and headed into the building for the appointment. I couldn't stand jumping through all these damn hoops to get some more fuckin' money, but so be it.

I walked to the elevator and the crew followed closely behind. When we arrived at the right floor, we walked into the office and I pointed to a row of chairs. There were several women sitting next to children in the waiting area. Heads turned the moment I walked in.

"Take a seat and don't move," I instructed sternly to the kids.

I approached the window, which was closed, and waited for someone to open it. "My name is Lachez Baker. I have an eleven-thirty appointment," I said to the large Hispanic woman who opened the window.

"Okay, Ms. Baker, please sign in and we'll be with you in a moment. Oh, how are you paying for your deductible today?" She smiled.

I pulled out my Medicaid card and gave it to her. Her eyes looked at the card, then up at me, and said, "Oh, um, why don't you hold on to that for now?"

I had no idea what that was all about, so I shrugged and put it back in my wallet. I turned to go back to my chair and noticed several sets of eyes closely watching me. One woman in particular wasn't the least bit shy about staring. So, I took that opportunity to move my slender hips in a smooth saunter. I felt her glare move upwards from my stacked spike heels, along my fishnet-clad legs and short leather miniskirt, which I didn't even bother to tug down when it rode up my thigh a bit. Her eyebrows rose when she finally reached my low-cut rayon top. My curves and offerings up top always attracted attention from men, but this chick was freaking me out.

I twisted my neck and shot her back a daring stare when our eyes met. She finally looked away when I mouthed the word "bitch." I can't stand people who act like they ain't never seen anybody in club gear. So what? I didn't have time to change before the appointment, so sue me. What's the big deal? I took my seat next to the boys and crossed my legs, still giving her the evil eye. She was probably jealous. I was tall, slender and curvaceous, and she looked like a fat little bubble with no visible shape whatsoever.

We didn't wait long for the nurse to call my name. I got up, a bit unsure of whether or not to bring the kids. The nurse must've sensed my dilemma. She looked at me and said, "Just you and the patient being seen today."

That suited Junie and Renzo fine. They quickly rushed back to their chairs and buried their heads in that damn video game. I strutted into the psychiatrist's office, making sure to sway my hips for the benefit of my fans in the waiting room. His office was nice enough, a bunch of plaques on the wall, plants and soft music playing.

A few minutes later, the door creaked open.

"Ms. Baker?" a friendly white man greeted with a massive smile. He looked familiar, but I'd seen so many of 'em, they all started looking alike. This guy had dark skin, with dirty blond hair and green eyes. He extended his hand for me to shake.

"Yes," I answered, "and this is my son, Mickey."

"Hi there, little fella," the doctor said. "I'm Doctor Johnson. Don't worry; we're just gonna talk here today, okay? Is that fine with you?"

Mickey wasted no time falling into his little shy routine. The doctor sat behind his desk and picked up a notepad.

"Ms. Baker, I'm sure this is routine for you." He picked up a folder, flipped through it, then looked at me again. "I see both your other sons, and even you, suffer from some form of Attention-Deficit Hyperactivity Disorder. I only have a few questions. Then we'll see if we can't get some medicine to help this little guy. How's that?" he asked sweetly.

I was indifferent. I wanted him to hurry so I could get the hell out of there before lunch-hour traffic got heavy.

We spent less than an hour talking to the good doctor. He asked questions about Mickey, then asked, "Oh, how is Lorenzo doing on the new meds?"

"Well, since you ask, he's been taking Adderall for about two months, and I notice some improvement. You know, paying attention, staying in his seat, and finishing class work from summer session. But I also think he's become real mad and way too emotional at home, you know, with the other kids. Now Ren wasn't nothing like this before. Someone told me it could be that the medicine is wearing off, but what do I do? I'm afraid to ask the doctor to increase the medicine to get him through the rest of the day. He's already got enough problems getting to sleep at night. I feel like, if we increase the ADHD medication, then I'ma need to give him something to sleep and I just think that's way too much damn medicine."

"Hmm," was all the quack said. I frowned, waiting for more.

"I think maybe we need to try something different," he finally suggested. "I'll call his doctor and discuss it with him; then we'll get back to you."

I was satisfied with that.

"Okay, well, my report will be in by mid-week, and if we need to visit again, I'll call and let you know." He smiled. "Otherwise, I'll send the information to Kelly Johnson?" he asked more than he said.

"Yup, that's cool."

"Okay, I'll call if I need any more information."

I was hoping *that* call never came. I only needed his ass to sign off on the paperwork and send it to the counselor so she could do what she needed to do so I could get another check.

PARKER

I'd been in for a couple of days now, and an image kept playing in my mind like it was a movie stuck on rewind. The sight of my wife standing on the side of the road, with her face buried in the palm of her hands, made me feel like shit. I twisted my head so I could see out the back window of the patrol car. Oddly enough, even as a thirty-one-year-old man, I was still moved by my mother's voice, with her nagging reminder while we were growing up.

"Y'all bet' not ever go to jail, 'cause I ain't bailing nobody out!"

Moms didn't take no shit, and she had made it very clear to my brother and me, if we ever went to jail, we could forget about her. She used to say, "I ain't raising no jailbirds. And I don't believe in visiting no damn jails." I remember back then, the thought of not having Moms was so damn scary, that it was enough to keep Preston and me walking a straight line.

"Look, I know you hear this a lot," I said, turning in my seat. I looked at the officer through the thick glass separating us. "But I swear to you, this has got to be some kind of mistake. I don't have any kids, man," I pleaded.

It wasn't like he was gonna take me back to Roxanne and our car, but still, I felt the need to make my position known. This shit was foul, not to mention, embarrassing.

"Hey, I believe ya', Buddy, really I do. I'm sorry about what your wife is going through, but you gotta understand, I'm simply doing my job. And yeah, you're right, a lot of people claim innocence, but I don't believe you or your wife would lie about what you went through." He shrugged. "But like I said before, I'm only doing my job. You'll have to straighten this all out with the judge."

Once he said that, I eased back in the seat and closed my eyes. I had never been in trouble with the law before. The most I'd ever gotten was a traffic ticket here and there, but this, handcuffs, in the back of a patrol car? This was something else. I was taken to the Houston City Jail on Mykawa to be booked.

"Is he a threat?" a jailer asked the officer who escorted me into the processing area.

"Oh, no; he's cool," he said, looking at me as he spoke.

I was glad he vouched for me. I turned to my left and noticed a slew of people handcuffed to a bench. I assumed they hadn't gotten the same vote of confidence. One man was slouched over in a drunken stupor. Two others were struggling to free themselves from the steel bracelets locking them to the bench and another man sat there looking off into space. I damn sure didn't want to be put in the same category with that bunch.

I was ushered over to another area and told to remove all of my jewelry, which consisted of a watch, my wedding band and a silver rope necklace. I removed my wallet from my pocket and stood by as the jailer took inventory of my personal belongings.

The jailers there were pretty cool and helpful with any information they could offer. Within three hours, I was booked in, had seen the nurse, and was in a cell. Having a mugshot taken and being fingerprinted had to have been the second most embarrassing experience of my life, after being arrested. Again, my mom's words rang through my mind.

"Y'all bet' not ever go to jail, 'cause I ain't bailing nobody out!"

I shook the words from my head as I was assigned a bunk with mattress and blanket. Unfortunately for me, it would be a while before I could use the phone. So I had lots of time to sit and think.

Child support? I couldn't even remember an ex who might've had a kid from me and not told me. I was very careful, unlike my boy, James, who cheated on his wife every chance he got. I didn't get down like that.

Every time I closed my eyes, I saw that image of Roxanne standing on the side of the road, looking helpless and all alone. I knew this was nothing but a huge mistake, but I couldn't wait for my day in court. I wanted to see the judge who was gonna tell me that I had fathered a child, and then walked out on my responsibility.

When I decided to marry Roxanne, I let go of all my loose ends. I had always been upfront with her about everything. Well, not quite everything, but enough for her to know the kind of man I was.

There are some things a man should always take to his grave and yours truly was no exception. This crossed my mind as I laced my hands behind my head and thought about that phone call I'd soon have to make. I wondered *when* I'd finally get to make it.

ROXANNE

Days after Parker's arrest, my head was still spinning. It had never really stopped. I finally called Serena back and relayed the entire disgusting story to her, from the hospital to the moment she had to take another call.

I wanted to tell Serena for two reasons. First, because I needed someone to talk to. But second, Serena used to work for the Department of Health and Human Services, and was now a social worker. She knew the system and she definitely knew what she was talking about.

"Hey, I really need to take this call on the other end," she said when she clicked back after answering her other line.

"Oh, okay, well, we can catch up later," I said.

When Parker's call finally came through, I prayed he'd be telling me the mistake had been cleared up and he'd be home soon. I had been glued to the phone since I got home Friday night. Everything was still a fog.

"Babe, are you okay?" he asked the minute I pressed the button to accept the collect call. It warmed my heart that despite what he was going through, he was concerned about me. I had been worried sick about him and this mess, and here he was wondering how I was holding up.

"I'm okay; stressing over this mess. What happened? How come you're just now calling? I've been waiting by the phone for days. What happened? What'd they do to you? I—"

"Calm down; calm down. I'm fine," he insisted, cutting me off. "Let's see; well, I was basically searched, fingerprinted, and put into a holding cell. I'm calling now because I'm just getting to the phone; it's real overcrowded in here so everything is backed up."

The officers here are actually real professional and cool, but I'm sure that's 'cause I'm not acting the fool, like some of these other clowns. I told myself, they're merely doing their jobs and ain't none of 'em personally responsible for my situation. But still, I'm pissed. This has to be some kind of mistaken identity case or something like that."

I could tell he was trying to be brave for me, mostly not wanting me to panic. But I couldn't help myself.

"Okay, okay, so when are you getting out? I talked to James and he wants to know about bail."

James Carson was Parker's best friend. They'd grown up together. James and his wife, Serena, were going through a nasty divorce.

When I heard him sigh, my heart sank. I wasn't sure how much more bad news I could handle, but I braced myself for what was to come.

"Okay, I don't want you to get all worked up or nothing like that, but the officer who brought me in said since the courts aren't open on Sunday, I'll most likely be held until Monday morning. That's the earliest I'll be able to see the judge. But it's pretty crowded in here, so even that might be a bit of a stretch."

He paused and I closed my eyes, biting my lip to stop myself from crying out loud. My heart was pounding loudly in my ears. I didn't want my husband to spend days in jail for something he says he didn't do.

"Babe?" he called out to me. "You still there? You okay?"

"Yeah, I'm here. What were you saying?"

"Well, he also told me that since my warrant is a Family Court matter, I'm not eligible for bail. He basically said I'll have to wait until Monday to find out more," he warned cautiously.

Warm tears burned the corners of my eyes. And this time, I did nothing to stop the flow.

"So what do you want me to do? I don't know what to do." I regretted the words the moment they slipped from my trembling lips. I felt so helpless and useless. Despite trying to stop them now, the tears just sort of pushed their way through.

"Hey, hey, Roxy." His voice grew a bit loud. "There's nothing for you to do quite yet. We won't know anything until Monday morning. We need to get an attorney, then go from there, but that's all we can do for right now," he insisted.

I didn't respond. I sat there holding the phone and sniffling like a two-year-old.

"Roxanne?"

"Yeah, I'm here," I said.

"Okay. I want you to get some rest. I'll call you tomorrow. Tell James to call Bradshaw and ask for a referral. We're gonna need a lawyer that deals with family matters," he said. Bradshaw was a criminal attorney.

"But if this is some kind of mistake, I don't understand," I said. I wanted to ask why an innocent man needed any kind of attorney, but I held my tongue.

"That may be the case, but it doesn't change the facts. I'm stuck here because someone thinks I'm behind in child support payments."

"But how could they make a mistake like that?" I was thinking it, but I didn't really mean to ask the question in such an accusing way. He paused for a moment before speaking again.

"Wait a minute, Roxy," Parker said. "Don't tell me you think I would be capable of turning my back on my responsibilities. I don't have any kids. C'mon, you know me; I love kids. I'd never do something like this, especially to a kid."

And I did know my husband. There was no doubt in my mind about how well I knew him either. But the fact remains, he was being charged with failure to pay child support. Horrific thoughts had flooded my mind ever since his arrest on Friday. An unknown love child, a bitter ex from the past. I had barely slept, thinking all of those awful thoughts.

"Maybe an ex-girlfriend?" I questioned softly.

Parker hissed, but he didn't say anything at first. Uncomfortable silence hung in the air between us.

"I don't believe this shit!" In my mind, I imagined the frustrated look that must've been on his face, and how he would dry rub it before speaking again.

"Look, if my own damn wife doesn't believe me, I sure as hell don't see how a judge will!"

"Parker, I didn't mean—"

"You didn't mean what? What? That I've been living a damn lie all these years? That the time we spent together ain't been nothing but one big ass lie because I had some kid with an ex, didn't tell you about it, then let it mushroom into this bullshit?" he ranted, cutting me off.

"Parker, wait, you're twisting my words. That's not what I was saying. I simply don't understand—"

"Yeah, well, just think how I feel! You think *you* don't understand?" He cut me off again. Then the next thing I heard was the dial tone. I felt so sick, I cried. This could not be happening to us.

That exchange was days ago; now here I was waiting near the phone again, hoping for any news about when he'd get out.

JAMES

The only thing that took my mind off the madness with Serena was a phone call I'd gotten from Roxanne, my boy Parker's wife. Hours after I'd gotten the papers I needed for work, I stood in my kitchen baffled by what she had told me. And I thought *my* life was suddenly dogged by drama. I couldn't believe Parker was arrested for not paying child support.

"This must be some kinda joke." I chuckled, thinking this mistake would soon be cleared up. I had known Parker for years. As a matter of fact, me, him, his wife and mine, were as thick as thieves. If he had a kid, trust me, I would've known all about it.

"Look, this ain't nothing for you to worry about. I'll get in touch with a family law attorney," I said, between Roxanne's sobs.

"Oh, yeah, he told me, um," she sniffled. "Parker told me to tell you to call Bradshaw?"

"Okay, cool; I'll get on that and get a referral from him. But while I work on that, we need to start thinking about bail and what kind of money we may be talking about," I said.

She was a basket case, talking about no bail and a bunch of other shit I couldn't quite make out with all that damn crying. I wanted her off the phone, and I hoped my boy would be giving me a call to let me know what was really up.

My mind quickly flashed back to women from our past. Parker and I had done some wild things, with some pretty wild and willing women. But I knew for sure he hadn't dropped any bombs, not to mention he wasn't even the type to walk out on a kid like that. Parker loved kids. As a matter of fact, he was Semaj's god-father, although Serena the Sicko was against it at first.

But then again, Serena could be funny at times, for no damn reason. After hanging up with Roxanne, I went into the refrigerator for a beer. As I leaned against the counter, my mind went back to my own near arrest at the house nearly a week ago, fooling with Serena's simple behind.

Thinking about it now fueled the rage in me all over again. It felt like I was right back in the middle of the confrontation. I was dumbfounded by the fact that Serena had no qualms about jumping out of the bed naked to confront me.

"I told you to get the fuck out of here!" she screamed, inches from my face. "I swear fo' the life of me!"

"Serena, you need to step back," I warned, as calmly as I could.

Over her shoulder, I noticed dude scrambling around for his shorts. That's when I realized this situation was not about to get any better. I should've left then, but I didn't.

"You can't show up here whenever the feeling hits you! This is *my* damn house!" she said, her finger pointing in my face, emphasizing every word. "Oh trust, it's over for you!" she promised.

"Look, I still pay the mortgage on this house, Bitch. Until this shit is final I can come here whenever the hell I feel like it. What if it was Semaj or even David bustin' up in here instead of me? Don't you even care about your kids?" It was a weak thing to say since David was at his dad's during summer and Semaj was at day camp, but in the heat of an argument, I could never control my temper, or what came out of my mouth.

Unlike me, Serena had no problem choosing the right lethal words. I didn't doubt they sat on the very tip of her tongue, poised and ready for attack. Not to mention, her arsenal usually resulted in agonizing strikes that never missed their target.

"Oh, so now we trynta act like we got some morals and principles? Like we actually care 'bout our kids?" she hollered at me.

I stepped back, hoping to calm myself. I wasn't in the mood for this. I took a deep breath and closed my eyes.

"Oh, yeah, now you worried about your precious baby girl, but you wasn't thinkin' 'bout her or me when you was running around screwing crackheads, were you?" Still naked, Serena stood, taunting me. With her neck twisting and hands on her hips, she was fully prepared to read me up one side and down the other.

"Nah, if your nasty ass was really concerned with Semaj, you wouldna been trying to stick everything that moved, you woulda been half the man you always preaching about. Don't give me that bullshit about what you pay for and what you're entitled to. Personally I don't give a shit! Now I suggest you get your ass outta here like I said, and I hope you enjoyed sneaking in here and getting off watching me. Trust the locks will soon be changed!"

"*Watching* you? Bitch—"

I didn't even see it coming. One minute, I'm going at it with her, the next, the side of my face is stinging, and my arm is up in the air. That's when out of nowhere dude was in my face, all muscle and brawn.

"You ain't laying hands on no woman in my presence," he said.

I looked at him, confused. Me hitting her? I wondered if we were all in the same room. Did this fool not notice when Serena smacked *me* upside the head?

"Look, I think you need to bounce. This ain't 'bout to get better," he said, blocking my view of Serena with his massive frame. I heard her talking on the phone in the background.

"Look, Dawg, my beef ain't with you. This is between her and me!"

"I hear what you're saying, but this is getting out of control," he said, talking all calm and proper, like he was some kind of mediator.

I was about to go smooth off on his steroid-looking ass when I thought I heard sirens somewhere in the distance. My eyebrows flew up and I frowned a bit. I know damn well she didn't.

"Now what?" Serena's voice came out of nowhere.

"Did you…"

"You damn right I called the law on your ass! See, you think I'm playing!" she yelled, and then gave me a cynical smirk.

She was moving around the room. Now her body was covered with a silk robe, the very one I had spent hours picking out for her. She looked like the devil wrapped in fine silk. "Think you runnin' something in here? Puh-l-e-a-s-e!"

Her mouth was still running a mile a minute and the shit was starting to wear me out.

The loud booming knock on the door seemed to startle us all. Serena was first out of the room and down the stairs. By the time I made it downstairs, she had already jumped into her animated version of how I had used my key to break in on her and her boyfriend.

"I want him arrested, now!" she demanded, with a neck twist to boot.

Watching her Academy Award-worthy performance was a sight to behold.

Two uniformed officers looked at me as I walked up.

"Mr. Carson, may I have a word with you outside?" one officer asked. I eyed them both suspiciously, wondering if they had already chosen her side.

Once outside, the officer looked at me and lowered his voice.

"Your wife says you two are going through a divorce. Because of that, we don't take her claims of you breaking in seriously, especially since she slipped and said you used your key. But look, I don't think you want any trouble. We don't want to haul you off to jail, even though she says you attacked her."

"She said *I* attacked *her*?" I questioned, unable to believe my ears.

"Yes, Sir, that's what she said," he said. "I tried to explain to her that you couldn't have broken in if you used your key. I also suggested that she calm down a bit and that's when she threatened to slap *me* like she slapped you." The officer shook his head, smirked, and shrugged. "All I'm trying to tell you is, we could avoid more complications by you using your attorney to deal with her," he suggested.

"Look, Officer, I came by to get some papers. I might have stepped out of line a bit when I heard her getting it on with dude upstairs, but I didn't hit her. She hit me. I was trying to put my arm up when I thought she was about to follow up with another blow. That's when dude stepped in." I shrugged.

Neighbors were starting to come outside. I never realized how many people were home in the middle of the afternoon. This shit was downright embarrassing.

"Why don't you tell me where to find the papers? I'll go get them, and you can wait out here. That way, you don't have to deal with her again. She's pretty upset," said the officer.

I nodded. At this point, I was ready for this madness to be over with. And he was right. I didn't need to face Serena again anytime soon.

The phone shrilled and pulled me out of that nightmare. That's when I realized my fists were clenched tightly. It's such a shame how that woman brought out the worst in me.

"Serena's simple ass is nothing but trouble." I grumbled as I checked the caller ID. I jumped back when I realized my old home number was flashing up at me.

I snatched the phone from its cradle and yelled, "Hello!"

"Hi, Daddy!" My daughter's voice rang out in my ear and instantly melted my heart.

LACHEZ

"Hey, Darlene," I greeted into the phone. My voice might have sounded friendly, but I was not happy about taking this call. Darlene Baker and I weren't the best of friends, but she did call regularly to check on the boys. She lived in Victoria, about two hours south of Houston, but I was never inspired to actually make the trip down there. She had married some plant worker who was transferred there from Pasadena my last year in high school. I didn't like him, and he liked me even less, so there was no real love lost when they packed up and moved south. I stayed with my best friend Toni's family until after graduation and then ventured out on my own. I like to tell people I left home when I was seventeen, been on my own for thirteen years and ain't looked back since.

"How's everything going?" Darlene asked. But I knew she wasn't really concerned.

"Oh, everything's good," I answered, keeping it light. I never offered anything more than what she asked for. A few years ago, someone called "the people" on me, anonymously of course; claimed my kids were being mistreated. There was an investigation and all. And trust me, you don't want anybody from child protective services all up in your business. It was nothing nice.

To this day, I still think it was Darlene, after she found out about some drama with my ex, Johnny. But since I had no proof, I had to let it go. Since then, I'd made sure the kids understood if they went telling teachers and other people outside the house our business, they could run the risk of being taken away. We were a team in every sense of the word.

"Hmm, you get a job yet?" Darlene asked sweetly, but she wasn't able to hide the cynical undertone.

I rolled my eyes. I don't know how many times I had to tell her, not only did I not have a job, but I wasn't searching for one, nor did I need one. I got enough food stamps. I was on Section 8 and, with the diagnosis; I got three, soon to be four, checks. I also had my little side hustles going, so I cleared more than two thousand a month. Now, I'll admit, because I didn't monitor my money as well as I could, at times I did have to improvise, but my kids and me didn't go without and, to me, that's all that counted. Shit, I knew some working people who struggled more than me, but Darlene never wanted to hear that.

Usually this was where our conversations ended. She'd go on about how disappointed my dead father would've been if he knew how I ended up. Then she'd try to convince me to go back to school and I'd get bored and frustrated with the conversation. I'd haul off and say something way outta line and she'd have one of her "infamous" emotional breakdowns, start questioning where she went wrong with me, and I would wonder if I could've actually been adopted.

"Them kids need a good role model." She was mumbling. I had already heard enough.

"Come on with that bullshit, Darlene. You know what? Lemme get the boys," I tossed in quickly, and moved the phone from my ear. I wasn't in the mood for her shit.

"Junie, Renzo, Mickey, your grandmother is on the phone! C'mere!" I yelled. I didn't feel like talking to her anymore, so they needed to come quickly.

I eased back as one by one, my sons took turns talking to my mother on the phone. Thank God by the time it was Mickey's turn, there was a knock at the door.

"Who's there?" I asked, walking to the door.

"It's me, Terri," my neighbor answered.

Terri and her sister, Theresa, lived in our building with four kids between them. Terri was a slim redbone who didn't have a clue when it came to dressing or even taking care of herself. She wore her hair in a sloppy ponytail and always looked and smelled like she missed the shower one too many times, but she was good people as far as I was concerned.

"Hey, girl, now a good time?" she asked, her eyes trying to wander around my place.

"Yes, girl!" I shook my head, put a finger up, and left her standing at the open door. I went to get my purse. When I returned, I pulled the door close to me, so the kids couldn't see or hear what was going down. Terri slipped me a hundred-dollar bill and I gave her my Lone Star Card.

"You remember the code, right?" I asked.

"Yeah, and two-hundred cool, right?" she confirmed.

I nodded. It was chump change, but each month, I sold her use of my Lone Star card so she could use my food stamps for a small fee. The kids and I usually only used about two hundred of the four hundred dollars' worth I got each month, so it worked out well.

Terri and her sister were real cool. Every so often I had to park my car at their cousin's place on the south side when I needed some time to catch up on payments. We had a sweet arrangement, and it had been going good for three years. I was about to close the door when two other people came rushing up.

"Hey, hold up, Lachez." Gina was a smoker from around the way and Reece was her road dog. They both looked like who did it and what for, a real hot mess, but they were loyal customers.

"You got any smokes?" Gina asked, the bones in her face poking out and making her dark skin look saggy.

"Yeah, girl, lemme go get 'em. How many you want?"

Gina looked at Reece, a petite and smaller version of herself. With matted hair and dirty clothes, Reece's stench was burning my nostrils.

"Get us four each," Reece told Gina.

"Okay, eight," Gina said.

I closed my door and walked back into my room to retrieve my box of cigarettes. I pulled eight out of a pack of Virginia Slims and rushed back to the door.

"Okay, four dollars," I said.

Gina opened her closed hand to reveal some crumpled bills. I almost didn't want to touch them, but the cigarette money was what I used for the kids when the ice cream truck came around. It came in handy. Once the transaction was complete, I came back inside.

I was vexed when I realized the kids were still on the phone with my mother. Darlene was a piece of work. The reason we never really got along was because I was never good enough in her eyes. But none of that mattered anymore. The kids and I got along fine without her and my estranged brother. Between my little side hustle and help from Uncle Sam, we were doing just fine.

"Mommy," Mickey called, much to my distress. "Grandma wants you."

I rolled my eyes. If it was one of the others I could get them to lie, but Mickey wasn't there quite yet. I snatched the phone from his tiny hand and pulled it up to my ear.

"When you gon' bring my grandbabies so I can see 'em? They been out for summer for what, three weeks now?" she asked, but didn't really wait for an answer. "I bet they growin' like weeds, too. Probably wouldn't even recognize 'em."

"Maybe next time you and Bernard come this way, you'll stop by," I said, hoping that time wouldn't come anytime soon.

PARKER

After hanging up on Roxanne, I took some time to cool off. The next time I got to the phone, I made my conversation with her quick. Then, I wasted no time calling James. She had me tightly wound, and I had to get my head right. There I was sitting my ass in jail for something I knew damn well I didn't do, and she had issues. She was acting like I was hiding something. I told her ass, I didn't know anything more than what she knew, but still she wouldn't let up. All the nagging questions, an ex somewhere, a love child; I didn't know what she wanted from me.

I tried to tell myself that it was stress from her losing the baby. I was feeling it, too, but while she was recovering in the comforts of our home, I was sitting stuck in a cell.

By the third ring, James finally picked up. I heard his voice when he answered. Then the line went dead, but that was the recorded voice asking for permission to accept a collect call. And it didn't take long; a few seconds later, music to my ears.

"Dawg! What the hell you do now?" James questioned jokingly. It was so good to hear his voice.

"Aw, man, I can't even call this one," I told him. And I meant that. I tried to rack my brain, hoping to figure out how something like this could be happening to me.

"Child support, huh?"

"That's what they say, Bruh. Can you imagine?" I asked. "And not just some child support, man. These fools talking 'bout something like fifty-grand!"

"Ww-what?" James hollered. "So here's my question, if you owe somebody that much loot, how come they didn't send the law after you before now? I'm sure it's not hard to find out where you work." He chuckled.

I shrugged. "Man, this is all news to me. You know a brotha would've stepped up to the plate; no matter what. I'm not trying be no damn deadbeat dad, 'specially after what my pops put my moms through," I said, pushing thoughts of my own worthless father from my mind.

"Yeah, I feel you, dawg; I feel you. Look, this shit ain't nothing but some kind of mistake. You 'member last year, when my crazy ass cousin, Bobby, got stopped driving on a suspended license and used my name?"

"Damn, I forgot all about that," I said, remembering how pissed James was when he found out.

"Yeah, well, I ain't never gon' forget that shit. Man, it took months, but finally I was able to clear my name."

"You know, I remember that shit now. You were running back and forth to court and so forth. Bradshaw finally got that shit straightened out."

"Yeah, and it wasn't cheap either," James said.

"Say, man, you ever see Bobby after all that?"

"Nah; last I heard he was doing a bid over some dumb shit."

"Go figure."

"Yeah, I'm just glad I cleared my name," James said.

"Okay, man, so what's up? You call Bradshaw yet?"

"Yeah, it's all under control. Well, not really, but you know what I'm saying. Your new attorney is supposed to visit before you go to court. I think he's coming either later this evening or early in the morning. And look, if anybody can get to the bottom of this shit, trust me, he's the one. His name is William Smith. You remember Donald, the ol' head that works at my office?"

"Yeah, I remember him. He's the one with the drinking problem, right?"

"That's him," James said. "Well, a couple of months ago, he was arrested again for a DUI, and his ex was trying to stop his custody rights. Smith got him off, and he still sees his boys."

"Ww-hat? Is Smith a magician or a lawyer?" I chuckled.

"That's what I'm saying, dawg. He's good peoples. He ain't cheap, but he's well worth the money," James said.

I let thoughts of Donald roll around in my mind. Donald Ford was a middle-aged man who worked in James' office. He smelled like liquor at ten in the morning. Everybody knew he had a problem, but it was like the office secret nobody talked about openly. When I met him two years ago, he had already beaten something like four DUI raps and hadn't spent a day in jail. I nodded, feeling better already.

"Cool, William Smith, huh?"

"Yeah, Buddy. You'll beat this thing, and if you're lucky, maybe Smith can even get you some of your money back."

"Man, I want this shit cleared up. If we can come out like that, that's gravy, but for now, I want this mess straightened out."

"Right, right, I feel you on that; no doubt," James said, "No doubt."

I sighed.

"So, Dawg, what's it like to be in lock up?" He laughed.

"This shit ain't funny, man," I said, feigning anger.

"You meet any nice young ladies in your cell?" he cracked.

I glanced around the holding cell and had to laugh a bit myself. I knew what he was getting at.

"Nah, man, it ain't nothing like that jumping off in here. A few drunks and so forth, but like me, most of the people in here are waiting to make bail or to see the judge. And apparently that's a challenge within itself. I keep hearing that because of overcrowding, some people have been stuck here for months!"

"What?"

"Yeah, man, I'm not even sure when I'll get to go to court; apparently it's that bad!"

"Oh hell to the no! Your attorney's gonna fix that," James said.

"We'll see, but I'm not holding my breath."

"So your cellmates pretty cool or what?"

"Man, this ain't no frat reunion," I said.

"Aiight, dawg, I don't want you walking up outta there twisting your hips or nothing like that," James joked again.

"Man, get real. Besides, that's the last thing on my mind; the way Roxanne's ass is trippin'."

"Can't say I blame her though, dawg," James replied.

"Yeah, but I'm the one going through some serious shit here," I added.

"Talking 'bout serious shit," James interjected. "Dawg, I almost got myself fucked up. I woulda been in the cell right next to your ass," he said.

"Fo' real? Wait, lemme guess, that crazy-ass wife of yours?" Serena Carson was no joke at all. Nothing James could tell me was a surprise when it came to her.

"You didn't even have to ask, dawg. Lemme tell you what that broad done did this time!"

ROXANNE

I spent most of my days crying and tearing our house apart. Something wasn't right. I felt it deep in my soul. There was something about this entire mess that wasn't adding up for me. Parker swore he hadn't fathered any children, but I wasn't so sure. I went through old boxes in our garage. The pictures I found with women I didn't know, or had never seen, appeared innocent enough. There were group shots, abstract parties and so forth. But it was useless. The pictures did very little to answer my lingering questions.

"I can't believe this shit." I looked through more old pictures, but felt no closer to the truth than before I had started rummaging through everything. Frustrated and hot from being in the attic and the garage, I did what any curious wife would do. I walked into our home office, turned on the computer and started visiting various websites.

Then, I picked up the phone and called my drunk of a mother-in-law. Lord knows I had to be desperate to contact Phyllis Redman, but I had nowhere else to turn.

Phyllis was a widow still stuck in the '70s. She wore a huge bouffant curly afro with really thick false lashes and extra long fingernails. She lived in Memphis and moved around her small house in these flowery housecoats.

"Lawd have mercy!" Phyllis screamed the moment she picked up the phone. "Chile, either the good Lawd has called somebody home, or you finally done got knocked up!" She chuckled. I couldn't stand her.

"Hi, Phyllis," I said meekly. "How are you?" I called from my cell because I didn't want to tie up the house phone in case Parker was calling back. Suddenly, I wasn't so sure calling her was the best move. I glanced through a few websites that promised complete background checks for $29.95, and thought what the hell. I punched in my credit card number and information while I spoke to Phyllis.

"The real question is, how the hell are you?" She laughed again. "And why don't you tell me, to what do I owe the pleasure of this phone call while you're answering that one." I could hear Phyllis sipping, then swallowing something. It didn't take a rocket scientist to figure out she was probably enjoying her favorite pastime; sucking down Southern Comfort with a squeeze of lime on the rocks.

I rolled my eyes. "Well, Phyllis, I was hoping you could help me out with some information." I didn't quite know how to ask what I really wanted. There was no easy way to say, "Oh, I can't stand your ass, but your son has been arrested for not paying child support. Now who in his past would he have had a kid with, and hid it from his wife?"

"Where's Parker?" she quickly asked, as if she was already bored and done with me.

"Oh, um, he's out," I stammered. "I was thinking you could help me with, like I said, some information."

"Emph-hmm," she mumbled suspiciously. "And exactly what kind of information would that be?"

"I, um, I was trying to catch up with some of Parker's old friends. I'm thinking about putting something together um, for his err, our anniversary?"

"Well, chile, what is it? You can't get your story straight; either you planning an anniversary party or you not. You don't sound too sure of yourself, if you ask me," she said.

I pictured her using one of her nasty five-inch fingernails as a stirrer for her drink.

"Phyllis, what I'm trying to say is I need to know about, um, maybe some ex-girlfriends or people he was close to before me."

I closed my eyes; this was going all wrong. I couldn't seem to get my words out right. There was so much more I wanted to ask, or even say, but it was becoming obvious that I was wasting my time.

"Wait a minute here!" Phyllis balked. "You call me up outta the blue; I ain't your favorite person in the world, and I can say the feeling is mutual. Seems to me if you wanna find out some information about your husband, you'd ask *said* husband," she stated sarcastically.

Obviously I'd called too soon; the liquor hadn't settled quite yet. I should've known this wasn't gonna work. I would've been better off asking Parker myself, than depending on her.

"Didn't he used to date some girl name Jessica, Julie, or something like that?" I tried to prod her for something, anything at all.

"Girl, you must think I'm some special kinda stupid! What's the matter? You think your husband steppin' out on you?"

If I didn't have a heart, I would've told Phyllis exactly why I was calling and trying to dig into her precious son's past, but she wasn't even worth the trouble. The satisfaction I would've gotten surely wouldn't have been worth the hassle it would've caused me in the end.

"You know what, Phyllis, I'm sorry to have bothered you. I'll talk to James, or something like that." I offered.

"Oh, is that lil' man-whore still runnin' around? I woulda thought he'd be dead by now. I was certain he woulda picked up that virus from somebody. Umph, you know what they say," she said. "God works in mysterious ways."

What does one say to that? I shook my head and silently kicked myself for even thinking for a second I'd be able to get anywhere with her. Even when Phyllis wanted to run her mouth, it was never about anything useful.

"Well, Phyllis, I'll tell Parker to give you a call. You take care, okay?"

Before she could even make another sarcastic comment, I simply hung up the phone. I felt so stupid, like one of those silly women who marry a man only to later learn she never really knew him to begin with.

Calling James wouldn't get me anywhere and I knew that. I wasn't close to any of Parker's coworkers so that wasn't an option either. He worked at Reliant Energy in Corporate IT. The truth of the matter was I didn't know where to turn or what to do next.

Even if I could've found the one distant cousin he had, what would I have said? "I'm Parker's wife and, um, and I haven't laid eyes on you, or talked to you since our wedding, but I'm trying to find out if he maybe got a woman pregnant in his past that you know of?" Nothing made sense. But I had to get to the bottom of whatever was going on.

The doorbell broke my train of thought. I rushed to the door, looked through the peephole and pulled the door open.

Serena stood there. "Girl, this is a nightmare for real!" she exclaimed. Serena was a few inches taller than my five-foot-five frame. She had mocha-colored skin with light brown eyes that were very expressive. She never wore makeup and used a headband to keep her hair off her face. I led her into the house and we talked for what felt like hours. She offered up advice, what she thought I should do, and we tried to come up with ways for me to investigate my husband's past.

"I suppose the real question is: how confident are you that what he said is the truth?"

I thought about what she was asking. Parker said he didn't have any children, and a part of me wanted to believe him, but then I couldn't help thinking about the many women who years later surfaced with the surprise love child. I couldn't say 100 percent that something like that wasn't happening to us now.

Here Parker and I were struggling to have a child of our own and he was sitting in jail for a child someone claims he hadn't been supporting. I had to admit, Phyllis was right about one thing, God does work in mysterious ways.

JAMES

When I pulled up at my old house, I wondered if Serena's crazy ass had made good on her promise to change the locks. Her truck was parked in the driveway, but I didn't feel like dealing with her simple behind today. I was there to pick up my daughter. I was told they'd be home from church around twelve-thirty. My watch confirmed it was one-fifteen. I had been waiting for fifteen minutes, but I wasn't about to act an ass.

I called from my cell and told them I was outside and Serena was as nasty as ever.

"We know you out there. Hold your horses; she'll be right out!" she snarled before hanging up on me. Like I said, that was at one o' clock.

I turned on the radio and told myself there was no need to hurry anyway. I was taking Semaj downtown to the children's museum, then we'd grab something to eat before I returned her home by eight.

Just when I was getting tired of waiting, the door flew open. I watched from my car as Serena fussed with Semaj's hair and clothes. She reached down to kiss her, then stood there as my daughter walked out. I climbed out of the car to greet her at the end of the walkway.

"You bes' be back on time!" Serena yelled at me. I didn't even bother responding.

Once Semaj and I were buckled in, I took off and jumped on the freeway. After driving for a few minutes, my daughter looked up at me.

"Daddy, why you and Mommy fight so much?"

I sighed, looking into her large brown eyes. At six, I felt like my daughter had already witnessed too much for her young life. She had a brother who was nine from Serena's previous marriage, so you expected her to be somewhat advanced. Yet, I didn't like what she'd witnessed between her mother and me.

"Sometimes we both get so mad; we say things we really don't mean," I tried to explain.

"Like when I fight with David and I tell him that I hate his guts? But deep down inside, I really don't?" she asked.

"Yeah, it's something like that," I said. "But you know what? We shouldn't even talk about your mother or your brother right now; this is our time. So you should be thinking about where you wanna go eat when we leave the museum," I said.

That brought a smile to her mocha-colored face.

"Anywhere I wanna go?" she asked.

"Yup, anywhere!"

"Cool!" She giggled, then reached for the radio knob when that Chris Brown cut came on.

"This my song, Daddy," she squealed and proceeded to start wiggling in her seat.

My eyebrows inched up slightly. "What you know 'bout having a song?" I asked. "You're six!"

She kept snapping her fingers and moving to the beat.

I turned off Almeda and on to Binz Street and into the parking lot adjacent to the children's museum. It was packed, but we lucked up on a spot toward the back of the lot.

"Are you ready for a good time?" I asked.

Semaj giggled and nodded. I usually spent some time with her every Sunday. Either we went to see a movie, had lunch or dinner; whatever her evil mother would allow.

We walked into the museum and began making our way through the maze of different sections. Watching my daughter move from one area to another made me long for the times we spent as a family during the good days. Things moved quickly between Serena and me, but we were so hot for each other it was crazy. Unfortunately, it didn't take long for her true colors to shine through. I swear it's like she has ice in her veins.

Semaj and I went through the museum's massive grocery section. After we had snow cones outside and worked on a few water painting projects, I was ready to go. We'd spent close to three hours at the museum. But she was enjoying herself.

"You look tired," I said to Semaj as we sat and enjoyed the second round of snow cones.

As she sucked on the colored ice, she looked at me and said, "I had a good time today, Daddy."

"Whoa!" I held up a warning hand. "It ain't hardly over."

Her eyes lit up and a huge grin broke out on her face. Then suddenly something changed and her smile transformed into a grimace. Her eyebrows bunched together and the snow cone fell from her little hands. My heart started pounding; I knew what was probably on the horizon. I started looking around for help as fear flooded my daughter's eyes.

I jumped up and flew to her side. I took her small body into my arms and she started screaming.

"Please somebody, call 9-1-1!" I yelled.

The sound of her shrilling cries made my heart crumble. There was nothing I could do to help ease the pain.

"It's gonna be okay." I kept rocking her body as museum staff members surrounded us.

"What's wrong with her?" someone with a walkie-talkie asked.

"I need an ambulance right now!" I screamed at the woman.

After what felt like hours later, I heard the approaching sounds of an ambulance as tears streamed down my baby's face. I used this as a chance to be mad at Serena. Usually before Semaj had a crisis, which is what sickle-cell flare-ups are called, there were warning signs. Why hadn't Serena warned me? Why hadn't she told me a thing? That woman was so simple.

As the paramedics lifted her small body onto the stretcher, I told them all the necessary information.

Thank God, Texas Children's Hospital was close. As I rode with her in the ambulance, she clutched my hand so tightly I could sense her fear.

I pulled out my cell and dialed her mother's number.

"What now?" she answered nastily.

"It's Semaj; we're headed to Texas Children's," was all I was able to get out before Serena lit into me.

"What the hell did you do to my baby?"

"Serena, you need to calm down." I used the calmest voice I could muster up. I didn't want my daughter to sense anything more was wrong.

"You son of a bitch! I will go before the judge first thing Monday morning and make sure your visits are suspended. I should've known better!"

"Serena, we're pulling up to the hospital now. She had a crisis. If you can meet us at emergency, that would be great." I hung up before she could hurl anymore insults my way.

A pang of guilt gripped my heart. It had been years, to my knowledge, since Semaj had suffered a crisis. I wondered if the fighting and bickering with her ignorant mother had somehow brought this on.

Once inside the emergency room, I could hear Serena before I saw her stupid behind.

"My baby! My baby! I'm looking for my baby; she was brought in by ambulance!" she yelled as she ran up to the registration desk in the emergency room. I sat in a chair off to the side and didn't even bother approaching her. God knows I didn't want to.

"Ma'am, we need you to calm down," the young lady at the desk said softly.

"Calm down!" Serena screamed. "You don't tell me to calm down! Where the hell is my daughter? Where's my baby?" Serena looked around the room, as if Semaj might be in the waiting area.

Hoping to avoid additional attention, I walked up to her and tried to offer calm words. "Serena, the doctors are with her now. They'll be out to see us in a moment."

Suddenly, she hauled back and smacked me upside the head with her massive purse. My head started throbbing instantly. I was stunned.

"You bastard! This is all your fault! My baby is here because of you!"

I was certain every eye was focused on us.

"Mister and Missus Carson?" a voice called out to us.

Only then did we turn to see a doctor standing outside a set of double doors. "We'd like to talk to you about your daughter," he said.

The side of my head that caught Serena's fury was now burning and throbbing at the same time. I followed behind her, imagining myself jumping on her back and stomping her until she could no longer move.

LACHEZ

"Junie! Get your narrow ass behind in here now, boy!"

I get so tired of these damn kids, sometimes I wanna run away and never come back.

"Boy, if I gotta call you again!" I threatened.

"Dang, Ma, why you always gotta be buggin'?" My oldest stood in front of me with his little bony chest bare and showing.

"How many times I gotta tell your ass to wear some damn clothes around here? You ain't no man!" I said.

He rolled his eyes and shifted his weight to one leg.

"I know your ass up in there playin' that damn PlayStation! I don' told you I'ma give that shit away!"

"What, Ma?" he asked, more than a little annoyed.

I rolled my eyes back at his lil' simple ass. "You call your daddy like I told you?"

"Yeah, Ma. Can I go now?" he asked again, not even trying to hide his irritation.

"How much he bringin'?"

This lil' crumb snatcher musta been on something and I wasn't having it. He was tryin' to mess with my cash flow; he shoulda known better.

"I said, how much he bringin'?"

"He said he bringin' two," Junie answered sheepishly.

"What?" I was ready to spit fire. "Two? Didn't I tell you to tell his ass you needed at least five?"

These damn kids! Ugh! I sucked my teeth, trying to figure out how I could get the rest of the money I needed. Two hundred might as well be one; I knew the drill with Junie's ass. He was now at the age where he wanted to get his share of my hustle. Almost like a finder's fee, but what could I do? I didn't want him to catch attitude, then refuse to make the calls, so I had do what I had to do.

"You bet' not be lying to me!" I yelled, but he didn't budge. I didn't put it past Junie to lie and tell me he was only getting two when he was really get three or four. I was hip to his game, but what he didn't know was I'd been playing the system longer than his lil' ass had been alive.

When he quickly looked away, I told myself that I needed to be there when his daddy showed up to drop off the funds. If I caught his ass in a lie, I'd take my cut and get in that ass. But for now, he was free to go.

"Remove yourself from my sight!"

I barely finished before he scurried down the hall and back to the room to finish playing that damn game with his brothers.

When my sidekick chirped, I picked it up, hoping it was my girl, Toni.

"It's your dime!" I said.

"Lachez! Gurrrl, whassup?" Toni sang in my ear. She was flying way too high for me, so I needed to see what she don' lucked up on and figure out how I could get in on it.

Toni Beechum was my girl. Five-foot-five with olive skin and a dazzling smile, she was naturally pretty. Her dark features with high cheekbones and slightly slanted eyes were like a man magnet.

Even years after four kids, she still managed to keep her thick, size fourteen body looking tight. She may have been ghetto fabulous, loud as hell, but she was always down for a good time. She stayed on top of the latest *everything*. And we had a lot in common, both single mothers, trying to beat each other to Easy Street.

Just like me she had a thing for chocolate men, and also like me, she had a knack for picking deadbeats. One of her kids' fathers had been running from his child support payments for so long we joked about how rich she'd be if the state ever caught up with him.

Before she could go into the latest business, which I was sure she was planning to fill me in on, I cut her off.

"Wait, hold up! I need you to call me at the house; you ain't gon' be running up my minutes!"

"Oh snap!" She giggled. "When you get a home phone again? I thought you ran up that bill accepting those calls from county?"

"Yeah, but you know how I do," I bragged jokingly.

"No, seriously, you got a hook up or something? If so, why you holding out and shit?"

"Screeeeetch," I said. "Pump your brakes; don't go trippin'. It ain't no kinda hook-up. I put the phone in Mickey's name."

"What? Now that's old school fo' yo' ass!" she hollered. "I can't believe they still fall for that shit! How the hell a four-year-old gon' have some damn credit?"

We both laughed at that. "Girl, we even got our cable turned back on. You know me, always resourceful," I said. "But look, for real though, you need to hit me up on the landline."

I rattled off the new number and Toni called back before we ended the cell call. I snatched the phone before it jangled again.

"Now, what you know good?" I said into the phone.

"Gurrl, it's goin' down! One of the Rockets is having a private party at Sullivan's Steak House, and I got us on the guest list!" Toni squealed.

"What! You didn't!" I screamed.

"Yes, gurl! V-I-P all the way! All I want to know is if you got your gear ready?"

"Wait!" I said, my adrenaline pumping. "When is this big bash?"

"Next weekend!"

"Damn! I ain't gon' get my check by then, and you know I can't count on Julius' ass to bring the funds in time. He told Junie he was bringing a couple hundred, but knowing his cheap ass, he'll try to cut that short," I said. "I ain't even trynta step up in that mug unless my shit is tightened up properly."

"Ww-what?" Toni yelled in my ear. "So you need a loan?"

"Since when you become Big Bank Hank?" I asked, a ping of jealousy settling in. I didn't like borrowing from Toni; she was the type who acted like a little loan placed you a few levels beneath her. And even though she always talked about what she would do with the loot if her ex paid up, I had a feeling if she beat me to the punch, she'd be too busy flossing.

"I got my checks yesterday, so I got a little change."

"Umph," I responded. My mind was working overtime, trying to figure out how I could come up with an extra five hundred to get my hair done right. Fusion, the kind of weave I had, wasn't cheap.

"Can't you have Junie call Johnny?" she asked.

I took a deep breath before reacting. I was making sure she wasn't trying to jump funky with me. Toni knew damn well what had happened with Johnny, and it wasn't something I ever talked about.

"Oh, my bad, don't go getting all salty with me," she quickly added. "I almost forgot about that, but anyway, so you can't think of a quick come up?" she pressed. "I'm not trynta roll to this one alone, and you know my cousin, Shawna, is already drooling at the mouth over the V-I-P passes."

"Look, don't worry about me and mines. You say the party's going down next weekend; I'll be straight by then."

"Okay, so you straight, right?" Toni asked.

"I'm straight," I said.

"All right then, 'cause you know you gotta come correct. These are professional athletes; we talking balling out of control!" she emphasized all giddy.

"I feel you!" I blurted out, getting a bit irritated.

"Okay, I'm just saying. We can't be half-stepping up in that mug." She was beginning to work my nerves.

"Look, you know how I carry it, so don't even go there. Just make sure *you* keeping it cute, and I'll be ready to roll!" I said for once and for all.

"Cool. I'ma holla at you tomorrow then; maybe we can hit the malls for something to wear."

"Em-hm," was all I said. What about ain't nobody dropped off any damn money did she not understand?

But, as sure as my name is Lachez Baker, ain't nobody ever been able to accuse me of not being able to make a dollar outta fifteen cents and I was certain this time would be no exception.

PARKER

I was thinking about that story James told me about him and Serena. After being in jail for three days, now on my fourth, I told his ass he'd better not try her because this was no place to be. But nothing she did ever surprised me. As a matter of fact, I never really cared for her. From day one, I could see the potential for drama with Serena. I never understood what my boy saw in her, but hey, to each his own. When he up and married her after something like six months, I thought for sure he had gone and lost his mind. But she had his ass whipped, so he wasn't trying to hear nothing but those damn wedding bells.

"Visit for Redman!" a voice said, breaking my thoughts and startling me as I eased up from the bunk.

"Come again?" I asked.

"Redman, attorney visit," the jailer repeated.

"Oh, okay. Thanks, man." I got up and rushed to the door. Finally! I couldn't wait to hear what my new lawyer had to say about this madness. I wished he could get me out that day, but I didn't want to get my hopes up. I did have to admit, knowing I had someone on my side was making me feel better already.

"I'm William Smith," the big burly man said as he extended a massive paw of a hand for me to shake. I gladly accepted and smiled. His light skin was sprinkled with brownish freckles and had a red undertone. He was dressed impeccably, which to me said he had experienced some level of success in his business. I was trying to read signs everywhere I could and his appearance was a good one.

"I'm Parker Redman and I didn't do this, what they're accusing me of. I don't have any kids. This must be some kind of mistake. I need you to tell this judge they got the wrong man," I said.

"Here, why don't we take a seat?" He pulled a legal pad from his briefcase. When I sat, he cleared his throat and pressed the top of his pen. "We don't have a lot of time, so why don't you tell me everything from the very beginning?"

I sighed. "Well, it's simple really. We were on our way home from the hospital a few nights ago. I was pulled over, arrested, and tossed in jail."

Smith looked up at me like that wasn't quite what he had in mind. He hadn't even written down a single word, but I needed him to understand I didn't know anything more than what I knew when I was on the side of the road being led to a police cruiser, like I had stolen something.

"Okay, well, what do you know about these charges?"

"All I know is what the officer told me. He said he *had* to take me in because I was behind on child support payments and the Attorney General's Office had them issue an arrest warrant for me." I didn't know anything more.

"So the officer tells you about these payments and this is the first time you've heard anything about child support?"

I was trying to ignore his tone. He finally looked down and wrote something on his pad. I waited until he glanced back up at me before speaking again. I wanted to stare him dead in the eyes.

"Man, I didn't do this. This ain't my kid; it's a mistake. I need you to make sure this judge understands this. I need to get out of here, and back home," I said straightforwardly.

His eyebrows elevated, as if he was neither moved nor impressed by what I was saying.

DC Public Library

Author: Tucker, Pat.
Title: Daddy by default : a novel
Item ID: 31172073072688
Date charged: 10/30/2014, 15:07
Date due: 11/20/2014,23:59

Thank you for using the DC Public Library

"Here's what I need you to understand, Mr. Redman. These charges are serious because of the amount of support we're talking about here. It's very unlikely that the entire state of Texas, including the Attorney General's Office, have made an error like this."

My face contorted into a frown and I felt the rage building from the pit of my belly, threatening to explode.

"I said unlikely, but not impossible. We will work to get to the bottom of this, but I need you to understand it won't happen overnight," he warned.

I eased back a bit. The last thing I wanted was a lawyer who didn't have faith in my innocence.

"Okay, at least tell me this; am I getting out of jail today?"

When he didn't answer right away, my heart sank to the bottom of my feet. Smith put his pen down and looked me in the eyes.

"We're gonna do everything we can to see that you get out today, but again, Mr. Redman, I can't make any guarantees. We need to go in there and see what the judge has to say. Hopefully, she'll be in a good mood and be somewhat agreeable."

That safe answer did very little to reassure me, but looking at Smith, I could tell it was all I was about to get out of him.

"Well, if there's nothing else, Mr. Redman, I'd like to get out there and meet with your wife before court begins."

As he gathered his things and prepared to leave, I couldn't help but feel a sense of helplessness. I wanted some good news from him. Instead, I got a bunch of uncertainties.

"Just one other thing," I said.

"Yeah?" He stopped closing his briefcase and looked at me again.

"What do you mean by let's hope the judge will be in a good mood? Do you know her? And isn't she supposed to be ruling by the law and not her emotions?"

Smith sighed at that. He rose from his chair, then looked down at me. "Mr. Redman, forty-five thousand dollars is an awful lot of money. This judge doesn't even know you, has probably never laid eyes on you yet, but in this arena, where deadbeat dads are up there with murderers and society's worst, trust me, when I say she probably already hates you."

I blinked as I looked up at him, frowning. I couldn't comprehend, or at least didn't want to understand, what he was saying. I hadn't done anything, this kid wasn't mine, but I was starting to wonder whether anyone cared about that important fact.

"Keep your head up; we'll work something out," he said as he headed to the door.

I got up from my chair, but for whatever the reason, more than before, a sick feeling suddenly washed over me. It was now sadly clear that "innocent until proven guilty" meant nothing in the court of family law.

ROXANNE

By the time my husband's court date finally rolled around, I was a complete mess. Between the horror stories Serena had told me about her ex-husband before James, his string of illegitimate children, and all the worst-case scenarios that popped into my head, I was surprised I was still clinging to my sanity. I had made the necessary calls to both my job and Parker's, notifying them of the family emergency that would keep us both out, for several weeks at least. For me, it wouldn't be too bad. I was a copy editor at an ad agency and could work from home if needed. But we were probably going to have to file for a leave of absence for him.

I was nearly finished with my breakfast of a bagel with cream cheese, sliced peaches and juice when my cell phone rang.

"Hello?"

"Roxanne, it's James. I'm a few minutes out. You ready?"

I was already dressed in a smart pants suit and low-heeled pumps.

"Um…" I glanced nervously at my watch. Had I forgotten about the time we'd agreed on? "It's only nine. I thought you said ten," I said.

"Oh, I timed this all just right. I figured we'd beat the commuter crowd and be the first people down there for our time slot. I don't want to take any chances. Sorry, I shoulda' told you about that. So whassup? How much longer you need?"

"Oh, I can be ready in five," I assured him. I just needed to clean up from breakfast.

"Okay, well, I'm about five minutes away, so let's do this," he said with great enthusiasm.

James had turned into a ladies man since his separation, but deep down, I believed he was sweet. I think the thing with Serena and him had given him an impossible outlook on relationships. To me, they looked great together and made a cute couple, but one never knows what goes on behind closed doors.

He was about six feet tall, muscular because he worked out religiously, with cinnamon-colored skin, a bald head and always dressed impeccably. He was in corporate real estate, and wasn't shy about flashing his good fortune around. Despite his occasional showboating, he cared about Parker and had proven himself to be a very reliable and trustworthy friend.

Exactly five minutes after our phone call, I heard the engine of his Escalade in the driveway. I grabbed my bag and rushed out of the front door. Once settled in and buckled up, I turned to James.

"How'er you this morning?"

"Anxious. I wanna get down here, meet with this attorney, and hear what he has to say. I can't believe this is happening!"

I wasn't about to bring up the issue of whether this really was a mistake with James. I understood that talking to him was like talking to my husband; there were no secrets between the two. James was well aware of where all the skeletons were buried.

"This must be real hard for you," he said after turning to me.

I sighed. Treading carefully, I admitted, "I'm shocked, and confused as all get out."

James backed out of the driveway and when he stopped at the corner, he looked at me. "I've known Parker since the second grade. If he had a kid, trust me, I would know. Shit, I might've known before he would've," James said, almost to himself, and stepped on the pedal. "This is nothing but another one of those government fuck-ups."

I eased my head back onto the headrest and released a huge sigh. I silently prayed he was right, but I was experiencing so many emotions, I needed to try and calm myself. Parker and I never talked about this latest miscarriage; I realized there wasn't much to discuss since we'd been through this before, but it would've been nice to have him there by my side when the thoughts crept up on me. Instead this child support thing seemed like it was about to overtake our lives.

James turned up the radio and I was glad. One of my favorite songs came on and that took my mind to earlier happier times.

Once we arrived downtown at the courthouse, I was glad he'd had the forethought to leave early. Traffic was maddening, even in the commuter lane, and parking was a serious problem when we arrived. I told myself it could've been even worse if we had come any later.

"See, this is bullshit!" James said when we finally found a lot that had available parking spaces. "Coming early was the bet. They got all these damn buildings down here and not enough parking." People were scurrying in every direction on the streets of downtown Houston.

We made our way to the courthouse, and once we cleared the security screening, we were on our way to the appropriate floor. Outside courtroom 223-B, on the second floor, an older man with graying sideburns and a salt and pepper beard approached us. He actually stepped more toward James than me.

"James, my man, good to see you again."

They shook hands and James turned to me. "This is Roxanne Redman."

I smiled weakly and offered a handshake.

He nodded. "Mrs. Redman, I'm William Smith, handling your husband's case. I've visited with him this morning, moments after he was brought in; he's in real good spirits."

William Smith was a big man, with a pleasant disposition and a massive smile he wasn't shy about using.

"We're gonna get to the bottom of this mess. I don't have much time; I wanted to make contact before I head back in so I can visit with him for a few minutes more." He grinned. "You have any questions?"

I wanted to scream *yes!* I wanted to say I have tons and tons of questions, but instead I smiled and moved my head from side to side. I figured this would all be over soon enough, then I'd get my answers from Parker himself.

"Okay, well, I'll see you both after the hearing and we'll talk then." Mr. Smith smiled again.

"Is that when Parker's gonna be released? After the hearing?" I asked before he could turn and walk away.

The strange glances William exchanged with James made my stomach flip. My heart thudded, and suddenly I felt my throat go dry.

"Ah, Mrs. Redman, I believe in shooting straight from the hip. So here it goes. Realistically, your husband probably won't be getting out, unless you all are prepared to come current on the back payments and agree to whatever payment plan is set forth here today."

I blinked back tears and was dumbfounded. Pay? But this was a mistake, mistaken identity...

"But I thought—"

"I really need to run. I want to have a few words with your husband before the judge comes in," William said before turning to leave. "We'll have time to talk after the hearing," he added over his shoulder.

I turned to James, still confused. "Why in the hell would we have to pay when this isn't our debt?"

"Why don't we go inside and see what happens?" James suggested.

"Okay, but this isn't Parker's kid; you said so yourself. Why would we have to pay for something that's not even his?"

James shook his head. I realized then that he didn't know anything more than me at that very moment, but that still didn't prevent me from asking.

JAMES

I walked into my office late, after dropping Roxanne back at the house and talking with her for a bit. I didn't feel like going to work, but it was a necessity.

My weekend had been nothing but a huge roller coaster ride. Thank God my daughter was back home and feeling better; no thanks to her mother's simple behavior at the hospital. I didn't believe in hitting women under any circumstances, but damn, did she ever push me to the edge.

"I know, I know," I said the moment I saw our business manager, Pauline Dane. She'd been riding me to make some changes to the company's insurance policy for weeks. My life had been so crazy, I'd never had the chance to go get the required physical and blood work.

Pauline was an older white lady who treated us all like her beloved children. I had even confided in her about Semaj's condition and the pending divorce. She advised me to make sure that we had the best insurance set up for my daughter's healthcare. At five-feet-two, her presence wasn't very domineering, but since she handled such important aspects of the job, she was both respected and oftentimes feared.

"Come see me when you get settled, today, before lunch,"she said sternly.

"Yes, Ma'am, I'll be there in thirty."

"Make it twenty; I have a meeting." She attempted to hide the smile that was curling at the corners of her lips.

I grabbed a stack of messages from my assistant's desk and walked into my office. Flipping through the stack, I decided none were urgent and they fell farther down on my to-do list.

My voicemail button was blinking on the phone but again, I didn't feel like being bothered. I had several appointments later in the day and getting ready for those were more of a priority.

I gathered the paperwork Pauline would need, then dialed my soon-to-be-ex at work.

"Haven't you caused enough problems?" she asked in a nasty tone.

"And how are you today?" I said sweetly, just to fuck with her.

"What the hell do you want? And when are you signing the damn papers?"

"The minute I get them," I said. "But the reason I'm calling this morning is I have to make changes to my health plan at work. I need to know if Semaj is going to be carried on yours as primary and supplementary on mine?"

"Look, as long as she's covered, I don't give a damn what you do!"

"Serena, this is important. Neither of us wants her to be under-insured. It's a simple question. Are we keeping yours as her primary?"

"Yeah," she said, like she didn't want to give up the information.

"Thanks; that's all I needed. Now have a good day."

"Fuck you! Eat shit and die!"

I didn't say anything else. I simply hung up, gathered my stuff and headed to Pauline's office. Inside Pauline's office, I was prepared to have my ass chewed. Instead, she smiled when she saw me.

"James, I'm so glad you could squeeze me in."

"I'm sorry. I've been busy, with this divorce and everything else going on."

"I realize that, dear. That's why I've been trying to tell you that we need to get these things straightened out. We're about to switch carriers and they're demanding so much from us. But I'll help make it as painless as possible," she said.

"Okay, so, does it matter that my daughter has sickle cell?"

Pauline's lined face twisted. "I don't see why it should. Are you providing primary care for her?"

"No, supplementary."

"Then no, shouldn't make a difference at all. There are a series of tests the company is requiring; HIV, and any genetic disorders you're aware of."

"Nothing but the sickle cell trait. Should I tell them that when they're doing the blood work?"

"It wouldn't hurt, so they'll be aware," she said as she started banging on her keyboard. "So, your first appointment is at three forty-five. I have you scheduled to get the physical and blood work at two-fifteen."

I started laughing. "Dang, don't even trust me, huh?"

"Nope, your track record is no good with me, mister." She smiled. "You and Brown are my last two hold outs. Once I get you guys wrapped up, we're done."

I got up to leave. "Seems like I'd better keep a closer eye on you," I joked.

"Sure enough," she said, then smiled again.

When I got back to my office, my assistant was still missing in action. I decided to grab a bite before my physical so I dropped off my papers and headed out.

I looked at the address for my physical and decided it was best to grab a bite close to the location.

I hoped all was going well with Parker. I wanted to call Roxanne, but didn't feel like listening to her endless questions.

The physical took less time than I expected and I was glad to finally put it behind me. They sent me down the hall to have the blood work done and I was as good as on my way, with nearly twenty minutes to spare.

When the young lady walked in with her kit, I looked at her and said, "Oh, I need to tell you that I carry the trait for sickle cell."

She smiled, "Anything else that you know of?"

"Nah, that's my only flaw."

She pulled out her tubes and a large rubber strap. "I'll be the judge of that," she said, still smiling. "Now, roll up our sleeves; let's take a look at those veins."

Needles always made me uneasy, but I did as I was told and waited for her to tap my veins. I glanced away when she found a vein, rubbed the spot with an alcohol soaked cotton ball, and then inserted the needle.

Within minutes, she had filled several vials with my blood, working quick and efficiently.

"Is that enough?" I asked, ready to make an escape.

"Almost," she replied.

A few vials later we were done. She put a Band-aid on the prick and I was free to go. "Results will be back in five to seven days."

As I walked out of there, I hoped that I hadn't picked up anything I'd be embarrassed for my employers to find out about.

LACHEZ

"How much do you need exactly?" Drew was asking.

Drew Levin was this caramel-brown roughneck wannabe I'd been seeing for some months. He was fine as all get out, but way too stuck on himself. At first, I thought I'd hang on to him, keep him on the side. He was into running women, but had a bunch of baby mama drama going on. I wasn't trying to get all caught up in that madness. I figured I'd cash in while I could and move on.

"It's gonna cost at least eleven," I said.

"What!" he balked.

Now *that*, I was not expecting at all. I had already checked his stock, so he could afford it. Plus, he'd never struck me as being cheap. I was usually really good at reading 'em.

"Since when do an abortion cost eleven hundred damn dollars?" he had the audacity to ask. "You can't be that far along."

"Well, look, it's like this. I could get one of those bargain basement procedures, you know, like back in the day when people were hopping on kitchen tables and all, but that's not my style. I'm trynta go to Methodist in Sugarland, where the doctors know what the hell they doing."

"I hear you and all, but damn! Eleven hundred?"

"Or, better yet, why don't I have the damn baby? I ain't even really fully made up my mind yet anyway. But I already got three lil' crumb snatchers. I'm not trynta have anymore! Besides, a baby will cost you a whole helluva lot more than eleven hundred."

"Look, you don't have to go getting all emotional and shit!" he said defensively. "All I was saying is eleven hundred is a lot to pay for that procedure. It ain't like I ain't got the money or anything like that."

I hadn't read him wrong, like I thought. He had the cash. What I didn't understand was why he was trippin' like he was. This would be the end of Drew, so I figured I'd go for the gusto. Honestly, I wanted to start high and hoped to get away with at least five.

"So can I get it to you by the end of the week? Say Friday?" he asked, now using the soft tone I had grown to expect from him.

"As long as you get it to me Friday. I have to put down a deposit at least three days before the procedure," I lied.

"So you getting it done next week?"

"Yeah, Wednesday, and um, I was wondering, um, can you come with me?"

He paused.

"You know what? Forget it; don't worry about it. I'll handle it myself."

"Nah, wait!" he tried to interject.

"No, seriously; it's no big deal. I can get Toni to go with me." I tried my best to sound disappointed.

"It's just that I'd have to take the day off."

"Oh, my bad; I wasn't even thinking. That's right. You know what? Don't even worry about it. I'll get Toni to go with me. She probably ain't doing nothing anyway."

"You sure that's gon' be cool?"

"Yeah, I'll be fine, as long as you drop off the money by Friday. I wanna get this done and over with," I said softly.

"Okay, cool. And you know what? I'll throw in a couple extra dollars so you and Toni can go do something real nice together. How's that sound?"

"That's sweet, boo," I cooed.

"Cool, I'll see you Friday then. But dig it, I can't hang. I gotta drop off the cash, and then I need to bounce, aiieght?"

"No, that's cool; I understand. We'll hook up sometime next week. I should only be down for like a day or two."

"That sounds like a plan. I'll holla'," he said before hanging up.

The minute he was off the line, I picked up the phone and dialed my hairdresser.

"Hey, Vanessa, girl, what's poppin'?" I greeted the moment she answered.

"You got it, you got it. Whassup? I ain't seen you in more than a minute!"

Now, it ain't been all that damn long, but as much as she charges, she shouldn't have been surprised.

"Girl, I been out here working my jelly. You know how I do."

"Yeah, so what can I do for you?"

"Tell me you can squeeze me in this weekend." I said.

"This weekend, as in four days from now?" she balked. Vanessa stayed booked. People often made appointments with her months out; she was that damn good.

"C'mon, Nessa, I realize it's kind of short notice, but shit, I had to get my money straight before calling you up. 'Sides, I got this real hot gig to go to and you don't want me walking around looking like I do. You know how females be jocking me about my hair," I reminded her.

Five-foot-three, petite, with mocha-colored skin and gorgeous thick, long hair, Vanessa Armstrong was nothing if she was not a businesswoman. She may have been booked solid, but the thought of me going anyplace where there may be a crowd and potential clients had her seeing dollar signs. I knew her well and she was thinking about it.

"Umph, tell me 'bout this gig," she said.

"Well, I don't know much, some athlete celebrity bash, strictly VIP, nothing but first-class, so my head gotta be on tight."

"You still got my cards?"

"Girl, you know I do," I said. "But it wouldn't hurt to get more."

"Umph, well, you'd have to come real, real early on Saturday."

"Not a problem," I said. "What time, nine, ten?"

"Try five-thirty."

I waited for a moment, thinking she'd take that back, tell me she was only playing, but she didn't say a damn thing.

"Like five-thirty in the morning?" I asked. "People are actually moving around that early?"

"People who want to be fit in are," Vanessa told me.

I sucked my teeth. Was it even light outside that early? Most days, I rolled outta bed around noon, and that's only because I wanted to catch my soaps, then all the judge shows. I couldn't remember the last time I was up that early and if I was, it was because the party was still crunk at five.

"So what's up, Lachez? You coming or not, 'cause I can give that spot to somebody else if you not," she said.

I seriously doubted that, but she had me in a spot. I needed my hair done so I had no choice but to agree to her near impossible demand.

"Okay, I'll see you at five-thirty Saturday morning," I said.

"Don't play with me," she warned.

"I said I'll be there, didn't I?" I rolled my eyes as I placed the phone back in the cradle. The second I did, it rang again; it was Darlene. I wanted to ignore the call, but picked up the phone and said, "Darlene, I need to get back with you. I got company."

"But that's what you said last time and—"

"Look, I'll call you later!" I screamed and hung up before she could say anything else. I didn't even get a chance to adjust my attitude before the doorbell chimed.

"What now?" I said, getting up from the sofa. I couldn't wait for one of the kids to come get the door; they stayed glued to that damn PlayStation.

I opened the front door and looked into the dreamiest set of doe-shaped light brown eyes. Back in the day, staring at them too long almost always guaranteed I'd be giving it up.

"Hey, Lachez," my ex, Julius, greeted, the corner of his pink lips turned up in a half-smile.

PARKER

Walking back to that holding cell was probably one of the hardest things I'd ever had to do. I kept telling myself that I was close to getting out, but Smith's visit threw all kinds of confusion into my plan.

The way I saw it, I'd be out by Monday evening at the latest, but now he had me wondering about that. Then I had to go up against some male-hating judge? Things were looking grimmer by the minute.

A group of inmates were led into the courtroom. I didn't like being shackled like I was a common crook, but I had no choice in the matter. We had barely been in the courtroom for five minutes when the bailiff spoke. "All rise. The Honorable Judge Diane Brock presiding."

We stood as she strolled up to her bench and took her seat.

"You may be seated," the bailiff said.

The judge worked quickly. Before she got to my case, she dismissed one, gave a continuance on another and moved on to me. She was all business.

"The state of Texas versus Parker Delewis Redman. Mr. Smith, you're counsel, is your client prepared to enter a plea?"

It was as if the judge had absolutely no tolerance whatsoever for anything. She was an older white woman with a small frame, and a stern face with white hair that was cut in a sharp bob style. Her glasses sat at the very tip of her extremely narrow nose, as if they would fall at any moment.

"Yes, Your Honor." Smith answered firmly.

"Not guilty, Your Honor…" I said, but my attorney was quick to cut me off.

"Mister Redman tells me, Your Honor, that he has no idea why he's been arrested, and that he hasn't received any kind of notice that anything was wrong. He's basically saying he's unsure of where these charges are being derived from."

The judge tilted her tiny head forward and glanced disapprovingly at me. "Is that so, Mr. Parker?" she asked in a tone that said she wasn't buying it.

"That's correct, Your Honor," I said.

I felt like a kid waiting to learn his punishment. I tried not to take too many glances over at Roxanne and James. I was glad my boy had shown up to offer his support. But a small part of me was still a bit upset with Roxanne for the way she had been trippin' and asking all those damn questions the last time we talked. It seemed like forever as I stood waiting for the judge to say something. Instead, she turned her gaze to her left.

Suddenly, she picked up a thick folder and dropped it onto her desk. She glanced up at me as she dramatically flipped it open and changed the focus of her glare from me to whatever was in the folder. *Oh shit*, I thought.

"Umph," she said, then produced a document which she proceeded to wave around like it was the smoking gun.

"Well, Mr. Redman, I have here a summons to appear in court. It has your name on it, and it's dated a quite a few years back. This particular notice and others like it went completely unacknowledged." She frowned, waiting for a response from me.

Before Smith or I could say anything, she passed the paper to the bailiff. The bailiff gave it to Smith, who scanned it over as he held it for me to see. I shrugged as my eyes glanced over the information contained on the paper. This woman's name may as well have been written in French because I didn't know *it* nor did I know *her*.

I was bewildered, struggling to remember women I had come in contact with, trying to make this name register. But when I couldn't, and it didn't, I felt my anger threatening to explode. This was crazy! How could this be possible?

It was all here in black and white, and there had been notices sent to several of my previous addresses, but long after I had moved. I tried to wrack my brain, but I didn't know anyone by that name, and I couldn't will myself to make her name register, no matter how hard I tried.

"Nothing familiar?" the judge asked.

I whispered something into my attorney's ear.

"No. We ask that the back payments be reduced," Mr. Smith said humbly.

"Absolutely not!" the judge stated vehemently. Suddenly, a shade of crimson seemed to wash over her face. "And until he pays all or a significant amount of the sum, he might as well get comfortable."

That's when my head starting spinning. What did she mean, I had to pay? I didn't do this. How could I be charged with nearly fifty thousand dollars in delinquent child support and not even know this woman who's accusing me? I felt myself getting angrier by the minute. But before long, the judge was banging her gavel and it was over, just like that.

"What happened?" I leaned over and asked Smith.

"Nothing, she's made her ruling; says you need to make a good faith payment before you can get out," he whispered as he grabbed his things and began to shuffle me back toward the door.

The judge was already calling the next name on her docket. At first, I was reluctant to move. I had expected so much more. Why hadn't he explained it better? When was I going home? What if we didn't have that kind of money? What if we couldn't come up with it?

"I'll be back there in a second," Smith said as he stopped to whisper something to the bailiff. I thought he was probably asking for more time until I noticed him slip the form back to the bailiff.

Now I was really frustrated and, for the first time, also scared. As I was moved back to the holding cell, I started giving serious thought to the women in my past.

ROXANNE

I gasped at the first sight of my husband in the courtroom. He stood wearing a dingy orange jumpsuit. It was clear to me that he hadn't been able to shower in days. His hair looked longer; I could tell he hadn't shaved because he had a visible five-o-clock shadow. The bags beneath his eyes proved he hadn't slept, or probably eaten much, in the last two days. My heart ached to see him standing there in handcuffs. To anyone who didn't know him, I was certain he looked far less than the upstanding citizen that I knew him to be. Parker's court appearance before the judge moved at lightning speed.

Everything moved so quickly I could hardly keep up. I was more disgusted than I was the moment he was arrested. There were only a few things that stuck out in my mind, like the judge's bitter words.

'Until he pays all or a significant amount of the sum he might as well get comfortable.'

Paying any large amount would surely wipe out our savings, not to mention if we had to pay even a portion. I shook my head, wondering how a mistake could go on for so long. And since this was a mistake, why was Parker so quick to agree to pay anything at all? It made no sense to me. I expected the attorney to prove to the judge that Parker would not, or could not, have done something like this.

Instead, before I could fully understand, we were being talked into some kind of deal and soon, Parker disappeared behind the door he had used to enter the courtroom. And as quickly as he had come into the courtroom, he was once again gone. My heart sank so low, I didn't realize such depths were possible.

James got up from his seat, so I figured it was time to go. The attorney raised a finger, stopped and talked to one of the court officers, and then rushed out of the same door Parker had used to leave the courtroom.

In the hall, I was very confused. "What happened in there?" I asked James.

"Smith'll be out soon; he'll explain everything," James replied.

I was seething. It was a rhetorical question; one I was trying to answer for myself. I had sat through a hearing and I was no closer to the truth than the moment when we had first walked in.

"Why didn't he convince the judge that she had the wrong person? How could Parker agree to pay this? I don't understand," I said, huffing.

James held his hands up, palms extended toward me. "Hold up a sec; we're on the same team. I saw exactly what you saw in there. I don't know anything about Smith's strategy. All I can tell you is, Smith will come and explain everything the moment he's done talking to Parker. He's the man to answer all of your questions."

James seemed a bit pissy, but I didn't really have time to get into his issues, considering I had my own. And although I realized that he was right, that still didn't change the mixed emotions pumping through my brain. I was anxious, angry and confused all at the same time and I wanted answers more than ever before.

The look on James's face told me to turn around. When I did, the attorney was walking in our direction.

"I think things went well in there," he offered with a smile. My eyebrows shot up, and then bunched together. Were we in the same courtroom? Did I miss something? He had to be kidding. "Your husband should be released by close of business today."

I shook my head; confusion had completely consumed me. "W-what happened in there?" I asked, pointing toward the courtroom door.

James sighed as if he wished I'd keep up, like my lack of comprehension was somehow frustrating to him. "Give him a chance to explain, Roxanne."

I sucked my teeth at his comment and stood with my hands on my hips.

"Okay, the only way your husband was getting out was if we agreed to pay at least twenty-five thousand dollars, and the rest would be paid in full by the end of the month. However, within that timeframe, your husband will take a DNA test, and we'll get to the bottom of this. If all goes well, hopefully we won't have to pay that remainder at all," he offered, as if he'd just solved the world's largest riddle.

Something still didn't feel right. I left James and Smith to talk about getting the money together and started wondering who in the hell would agree to pay thousands of dollars to support a child that wasn't theirs.

JAMES

A couple of days later, it was my turn to go through a series of emotional ups and downs. I was on the computer in my office when lightning struck. Well, it may as well have been lightning, considering that in all the years I was married to *Serena the Sicko*, I could count the number of times she had shown up at my office on one hand.

As usual, you always heard her loud ghetto ass long before you actually saw her.

"I don't need you to announce me!" she screamed, and soon after, she was bursting through my office door like she owned the place.

"What's your problem now? Is everything okay with Semaj?" I asked, becoming alarmed.

"Don't fucking worry about her. What's this about you not paying the mortgage?"

By now, she was leaning over my desk, her face inches from mine. I slid my chair back and pressed the button on my phone to summon my assistant. The last thing I wanted was for Serena's stupid ass to accuse me of laying hands on her yet again. This time I might not be so lucky and could actually go to jail.

My assistant stood at the opened door. "Mr. Carson, security is on the way up."

Serena spun around to face him. "You and security can kiss my natural black behind. This is none of your business!"

"Don't move, Roger," I said. Roger was nowhere close to being a protector. He was tall, thin, and very feminine, but I needed him as a witness. "Serena, this ain't the time and it's definitely not the place. My attorney tried to warn you about this day. You should've prepared for it."

"You disgusting bastard! What am I supposed to do to feed our children? If you had kept your fly zipped, none of this would've happened. Now you're trying to make me and your kids suffer?"

I didn't think this was the moment to point out that David wasn't really my biological son and that she received a support check from his father each month. I didn't want to set her off anymore than necessary, but I wasn't about to sit there and have her rip me a new one either.

I got up from my chair right as my phone rang. I was hoping it would be security, but, it was Pauline instead.

"Yes, Pauline?"

I was hoping this would be a clue to Serena that I didn't want to talk to her about something that her attorney should have pointed out. I noticed people were starting to take the long route so they could pass by my office, and gawk and what was going down.

"Is this a bad time?" Pauline asked. "I have some interesting news for you."

I sighed. "Yeah, I can't exactly talk right now."

"Okay, well, please come see me before you leave. This is urgent."

I put the phone down and turned my attention back to Serena the Sicko. I took a deep breath.

"You need to take your ignorant behind out of here before security comes." I tried to warn her.

But it seemed like she wasn't the least bit interested in what I was saying. Her nostrils were flaring and her eyes had narrowed so much, she might as well have been looking at me through slits.

I wondered how she could hate me so much that she had no respect for my job or anything else.

"You will fucking pay for this! Mark my words!" she swore. "Mark my fucking words!"

At that moment, I wondered exactly what she thought was going to happen. Did she think I'd keep paying the mortgage forever, while she refused to sell the house so we could split the proceeds? Because our salaries were nearly equal, I didn't have to worry about paying any kind of alimony. I was going to pay child support; I didn't want Semaj to ever go without, but this bitch must have been crazy if she thought she was about to be a kept woman on my tab. My mind flashed back to her and dude sexing each other up in our old bed and I almost wanted to spit on her.

I looked up as she turned to leave, just when security had finally arrived. The two guards crowded my doorway.

"Is everything okay in here, Mr. Carson?"

"I think so, guys," I said.

Serena looked at them both, then shoved her way between them when they didn't move fast enough. She was something else for sure. I couldn't believe she had come up to my job to complain about the mortgage after she had called the cops on me and tried to get me arrested. She had been pressing me to sign the damn papers, and I finally did. I wondered if she had even read the terms of the divorce, because that stipulation was bold and clear as day. I didn't feel a bit guilty about my decision. I wanted to be done with her as quickly as possible. I wondered if this meant she'd try to stop me from seeing my daughter the upcoming weekend. Knowing her ass, she would.

I was about to ease back into my seat when I remembered the call from Pauline. I didn't even get comfortable before picking up the phone and dialing her number.

"Yes, Pauline, sorry about earlier. I had some personal issues to deal with."

"No, I understand. I do need to see you right away though."

"This sounds serious." I tried to joke, but for once Pauline wasn't biting.

"Please come to my office?"

"I'll be right there," I said.

I noticed, but ignored the glances and whispers as I strolled the hall. It wasn't my fault that I had picked the most ignorant ghetto trick out of the bunch. I told myself that I'd stop by security to make sure they knew she needed to be on the 'special' watch list.

I knocked twice on Pauline's door, before she answered.

"James, is that you? Come in."

I was shocked to see the stone-faced expression on her face. She looked stoic; like she was about to rock my world. Standing there I couldn't think of a single more disturbing thing than the words that fell from her thin pink lips and what they meant.

"Did you hear me?" Pauline looked at me a bit cockeyed. "Maybe you should sit. This is quite shocking, but I thought you needed to know."

My legs suddenly felt like water. I stumbled a bit but I managed to flop down into one of the two chairs in front of her desk.

"How could I not be a carrier?" I asked aloud.

Pauline looked back at me with sorrowful eyes. I wanted to cry because I couldn't swallow the massive lump lodged in my throat. It was as if someone had used their bare hands to rip through my chest and squeeze my heart like a vice-grip.

"I'm so sorry to have to tell you this," she said softly.

It didn't take long for the information to settle into my brain. So if I wasn't a sickle cell carrier, that could only mean Semaj could not be my daughter.

I tried to shake the near impossible thoughts from my head.

LACHEZ

I was more than a bit disgusted with myself. When I opened the door and found Julius standing there, smiling like the cat that swallowed the rat, I tried to deny what I was feeling, but the throbbing between my thighs could not be ignored.

I returned his devilish grin and stepped aside so he could come in. That was yesterday evening. Now as I lay next to his sleeping body in my bed, I could just kick myself. I had no business letting him stay well past the time the kids finally conked out. I knew what he was hanging around for and I had stupidly played right into his ploy.

Now I had to figure out how to get his ass out the house before the kids got up and tried to get all in my business.

The only reason I answered the phone so quickly was because I didn't need the ringing to wake the kids. It was Darlene. I wanted to throw it out the window, but I couldn't.

"Not now, Darlene," I said the moment I plucked the phone from its stand and pulled it to my ear.

"I don't have time, I'll call you soon." I quickly hung up the phone and unplugged it.

Then, I used my elbow to nudge Julius real hard in the ribs. He stirred, but didn't quite wake up.

"Ah, Julius!" I bent down to scream in his ear.

He bolted upright, and started looking around the room, like he was trying to remember where he had laid his head the night before.

"Hey," he said, smacking his lips. I rolled my eyes. I had no idea what made me give in to him so easily.

"Look, you gotta go," I said in a no-nonsense tone that I hoped he wasn't gonna try and argue with.

"Damn, you a cold piece, Lachez. I mean, you get a brotha all worked up, suck up all his energy, and then turn him loose." He rubbed his eyes like a little boy, then yawned, sharing his god-awful morning breath. I thought for certain I'd keel over.

"You need to bounce, seriously. I don't want the kids to get up and find you up in here."

The crashing noise from the other side of the door confirmed the kids were already up. The noise was followed by screaming, and I rolled my eyes.

"Damn!"

"Guess it's too late to be worrying about the kids, huh?" he had the nerve to say, then used his fist to stab at the pillow a couple of times before laying his head back down, like he had a free pass to linger indefinitely.

"Look, they may be up, but you still gotta go!" I pulled myself up from bed, deciding that he was hanging around because I hadn't really made it clear that the party was over.

"You want me to go out there while the boys are up and around?" His eyebrows elevated, like he already knew the answer to his own question.

"Um, no, not quite, but I'm gonna need you to get dressed, 'cause I'm about to distract them, and you need to get to moving!"

"It ain't like they don't know I stayed."

"Like hell, they do." I shot back. "And whether you believe they know or not, we not about to give them proof. Oh, and don't forget to leave the money for Junie either." I didn't want him trying to duck out without handling the real business he was there to handle.

I walked out to the living room and found the boys in the kitchen fighting over cereal. One look at Junie's face and I already knew how I'd play this one.

"Everybody stop what the hell you doin' now!" I screamed, my hand placed firmly on my hips.

They literarily froze where they stood or sat. "I'll bet not a single one of you little scrubs brushed a tooth or even cleaned your faces! Get your narrow behinds into the bathroom and get busy!" I pointed toward the hall. "Nasty asses," I said as I watched the two youngest march behind Junie and make their way toward the hall.

"Oh, Ma, what's up with the money my daddy left?" Junie asked before they got out of my sight. I shot Junie the evil eye and got mad at the fact that he had the nerve to remember.

"We'll talk about that after some hygiene has taken place in here. Go do what the hell I told you to do."

The minute they rounded the corner, I rushed back to my room and tried to light a fire under Julius' ass.

"C'mon, c'mon, it's time to go, keep it moving." I used my arms to mimic sweeping motions. "Keep it moving!"

Julius gave me the look of death as he pulled up his jeans and zipped them. I walked into the room when I heard the water running down the hall.

"Oh, and let's not forget," I said, standing with my hand stretched out so he could comply.

Just as I suspected, he pulled a wad from his pocket and peeled off four crisp hundred dollar bills. Junie was trying to hold out on me. I'd deal with his ass later, but for now, I had to check Julius.

"Eh-hem…" He looked at me like he didn't know what was up. "This takes care of Junie, but what about me?" I asked, not hiding my building attitude.

"Shiiit, you not my woman," he had the nerve to say.

"Hmm, that's not what you was claiming last night, asking whose it was and all that."

Julius sucked his teeth and reluctantly peeled two more bills off his wad. Fortunately for him, he was out the door before I realized the additional bills were only fifties.

Just as I was about to tuck the money away, Junie appeared out of nowhere, his own hand stretched out.

He smiled. "Oh, that's right on time."

I rolled my eyes and started twisting my neck. "How much money you tell me you asked your daddy for?"

His mouth was frozen open. He realized that he was busted.

I nodded my head. "You wanna come again?" This time my hands flew to my hips, as I waited for his response.

"Ma!" he began, his begging hand falling to the side.

"You know what?" I plucked one of the fifties Julius had given me and shoved it toward him. Junie snatched the bill, but his smile quickly faded when his eyes registered the amount.

"This ain't no c-note." He pouted, his little face twisted into a frown.

"Yeah, and this ain't no damn partnership! When I tell you to call for money, you do what I tell you! I'm the boss in this house, you hear me?"

"But, Ma!" he whined.

"But, Ma, my ass, I know you not 'bout to start crying like some lil' bitch!"

He sniffled a few times and sucked it up, his little chest heaving up and down.

"You don't try to beat me outta what's mines? You understand?" I asked straightforwardly.

"Yeah." He sulked.

"Now remove yourself from my sight before I get in that ass for lying!"

As I watched him mope away, I made a mental note to check that lil' hustler's room; ain't no telling what the hell else he'd been hiding from me.

PARKER

How could a man be held in a cage like a fucking animal for something he didn't do? This was the question that stayed on my mind every waking moment. We would have to scrape up twenty-five grand to buy my freedom when I hadn't done anything wrong. And from what everyone was telling me, I probably wouldn't even be able to get any of that money back!

To say I was mad was a massive understatement. I wanted to know who this woman was, I wanted to see her face to face, and have *her* tell me, the court, and that fucked-up judge that I fathered her child and abandoned them. Smith's words haunted me hours after we last spoke.

"We've gotta do this the right way," he said. Why did the right way have to mean me still being behind bars, or better yet, having to pay to get the hell out?

"We don't need to piss the judge off in the process," he reminded me. I'd hate to see what would've happened if she wasn't already pissed. Did he not realize the judge was furious the moment she laid eyes on my folder? She hadn't even met me, or heard my side of the story, but I was already done as far as she was concerned. And he was still worried about pissing her off.

How come no one cared about pissing me off? When would I finally have my real day in court? Then, even though it had taken the back seat since this shit went down, my wife still had to have a D and C. Instead of being at her side, I was sitting here trying to figure out who was behind these bullshit charges against me.

I was trying not to get too anxious, but I had called Roxanne several times and there was no answer. My mind was fucking with me. I envisioned going home and the house being cleared out completely. Her questions told me she was struggling to believe my version of this story.

Then I thought about some chick from my past showing up in court, bouncing a baby on her hip while the other kids trailed behind her.

"Yes, Your Honor, that's him. That's the man who fathered my child, then vanished on us!"

A jury of my peers would be seated in stunned silence and the judge would literally throw the book at me, force me to pay more, and stay in jail longer!

That was the problem with jail; there was absolutely nothing to do but sit and think about what you had done or, in my case, what you hadn't done. Either way, you were stuck like Chuck and nobody gave a fuck!

"Say, Redman," one of the jailers called out to me. I turned my head but didn't move just yet.

"Whassup?" I asked. He was a thick brother, with a small afro. He'd been cool the moment I checked in. I remembered him being the officer who had asked if I was a threat.

"Nothing, man. I heard about your situation; that shit's wrong for real. A buddy of mine went through something similar. He lost his job after the AG's office garnished his check."

That made me ease up a bit. I frowned as I looked at him.

"What you mean, they garnished his check?" I didn't even want to entertain that idea, on top of what I was already going through.

The jailer stood next to the door. "Well, he wasn't in the hole as much as you are, but he owed, I wanna say something like ten grand. He didn't go to jail either; he said his H.R. director called to let him know that she received a letter saying his wages needed to be garnished."

"Just like that? No warning?"

"No warning. Actually, it was payday when she called to tell his what was up."

"Damn, that's fucked up! So how was he fired?"

"Dude's job had a morality clause. When they found out he wasn't paying child support, his ass was gone." He shrugged. "He worked in finance; boss said they lost confidence in his ability to handle other people's money if he couldn't handle his own."

"Daaaum!" I said. "He lost his job! See, that makes no sense. Now he's got no job so how's the bill gonna get paid?"

"That's what wrong with this shit, man. I don't know your situation but, hopefully, you have a cool job. But dig this, they lock you up for non-payment, and let's say you get fired behind being in jail. Then you have no job. How they expect you to pay then?"

He was making a good point, but I felt the need to clear something up. Unlike his friend who had stopped paying child support for whatever reason, I didn't have any damn kids, and hadn't stopped paying anything!

"That's foul, man. But, what I'm trying to tell everybody is, I don't have any kids! That's what's so fucked up about my situation. I don't even know this woman who's accusing me of this shit. I mean, I know it's the AG's office behind the bullshit! But I was trying to tell the judge this is a mistake."

The jailer shook his head. "Man, they don't care about all that!"

I let his words settle on my brain. I was getting myself all worked up and he wasn't doing shit but telling me about his friend's situation.

"So what happened with your friend?"

"Oh, he bounced back!" the jailer said. "He got current and got another job. But he went through the shit for something like a year." He shrugged his shoulders. "Man, it was wild. I tell him, he should never look at another female unless he's strapped."

"I feel you on that," I said, now wanting to end this conversation. I hated to hear what had happened with his buddy, but the truth was I wasn't his buddy and I hadn't done shit.

When his radio went off, I was glad.

"I'll holla later; gotta go," he said, walking down the hall and talking into the radio.

What struck me most from the conversation about the jailer's story was the fact that his friend's life was in turmoil for at least a year. *That* I was not prepared for! I thought about trying Roxanne again, then thought better of it. I wondered what the hell was taking so long with processing my release.

ROXANNE

I stood staring blankly at the bank employee after he uttered words I couldn't comprehend. Why was he making this so difficult?

"Mrs. Redman," he said, "you and your husband put these security measures in place yourselves. I'm just doing my job."

He gave me back the withdrawal form I had given him. His skin was flushed and his brown eyes seemed to pierce through me.

"Look, this is urgent, and I need this money, right now."

When his eyes went beyond me, I realized that he had mentally checked out and was ready to move on. I was frustrated, but he was already looking to the next person in line.

"You know what, let me see your manager." I couldn't believe the difficulty of the situation.

"Ah, she's away at a lunch meeting. I'm the one in charge right now," he said smugly.

I was seething. Was he trying to get under my skin? I knew that Parker and I had the stipulation on the account. At the time we never thought we would need to take more than five-thousand dollars out of an account for any given reason, but that was then, before there was a kid out there. I closed my eyes and took a deep breath.

Bryan's angry voice made me open my eyes.

"Ma'am, is there anything else I can help you with?" He offered a smile that was obviously forced.

"Um, yes, you can give me a cashier's check in the amount of twenty-thousand dollars," I said through gritted teeth. He was not the least bit amused or concerned about my building anger.

I had already had a horrible day and it was barely one o'clock. Parker's attorney made it clear that the judge would not authorize his release until we made a payment, so I had to run around scraping up cash. As it was, this withdrawal would clean us out. Sure, there was money in the checking account, but that had to be used to pay the damn lawyer.

"Ma'am, as I said before, per you and your husband's request, you both need to be present for such a large withdrawal. It's your rule; not the bank's and not mine. Now, if there's nothing else, I need to help the next customer in line."

There had been no more progress in my quest to find out more about the women in my husband's past either. After borrowing five thousand dollars from James, to make up the twenty-five-thousand-dollar good-faith payment which my husband agreed to pay for a child he said wasn't his, I was standing there fighting to clean out our own damn accounts.

Defeated and completely frustrated, I turned to leave. Outside, I used my cell to call Parker's attorney.

"Mr. Smith, please," I said to the receptionist who answered.

"He's in court. May I take a message?"

"In court?" My day was going downhill by the second. To make matters worse, the mid-June sun felt like its sole purpose was to make me hot during my time of sheer confusion and frustration. I stood outside the bank, my body drenching in sweat; nothing seemed to be going my way. I felt like a two-year-old, seconds away from a major tantrum.

"Yes, ma'am, is there a message?" she asked.

"When is he coming back?"

"I don't know his schedule, but I can take a message," she offered again cheerfully.

"Look, I ran into a problem at the bank. He's expecting me to meet him at the office in two hours with a check that I can't get. I need you to reach him right away."

"Are you a client?"

"Yes, I am."

"Oh, okay, well, I will send a message to his BlackBerry and let him know to call you. Which number should he use?"

I rattled off my cell number and she assured me that I'd hear something the moment he had a break. She wasn't sure when that would be, but at least I felt some, albeit very little, progress.

I suppose it was just as well because the damn bank manager was MIA.

There was really nothing else for me to do until I heard back from Parker's lawyer. I went to the car, climbed in, and decided to go get something to eat. I opted for an Olive Garden restaurant near the bank. I ordered my food, with a cold margarita, and took the seat near a window. Every time I saw a woman walk by, I wondered if she could be Parker's ex. Finally I picked up my cell and called Serena, hoping to get my mind off this mess.

"Hey, girl," Serena greeted. "How's everything going? Parker out yet?"

"Nah, still getting the money together."

"Hmm, you better than me." She snickered. "If I were you, I'd leave his ass sitting right there. All men are either dogs, or have dog-like potential."

I frowned a bit and started to respond, but decided not to. Serena was bitter; she'd been that way since that woman had appeared on her doorstep, talking about James. Instead of everything being about her for a change, unfortunately, I was stuck in the middle of my own misery.

"You know what, that's my other line," I said, reaching for the easiest lie.

"Well, make sure you call and let me know what happens."

I quickly hung up and went back to my sorrowful thoughts.

This was really driving me crazy. One minute I'm thinking our biggest challenge is trying to figure out how to deal with the loss of another pregnancy. Now I was faced with the possibility that there could be already be a child, one that belonged to my husband.

Before I could even control my emotions, tears began to run down my cheeks. I felt sick; I wanted this to be over and I wanted Parker and me to go back to our previous life.

But sadly, something told me, things with us, with our marriage, would never again be the same.

JAMES

Nothing in my life seemed to matter much anymore. I immediately took a few days off from work. Pauline understood and took the opportunity to tell me about the company's counseling services. I didn't think there was a shrink alive that could fix this one, but I thanked her for the information and sulked out of her office a shell of the man that I used to be.

I kept trying to understand how the test could've come out the way that it had. Didn't Semaj look like me? Didn't she have some of my features? We both liked pickles and popcorn. Is that learned behavior? I didn't want to understand this. Before going home, I made an appointment to visit the lab the next day. I'd get tested again. Maybe they had made a mistake, mixed my blood with another man's.

At the house, I pulled out every picture that I could find of my daughter and studied them like never before. She looked so much like Serena, it was hard to find my features in her face, but they had to be there; she was *my* little girl.

Late at night, when she woke, it was me that she called for comfort. When she and Serena came home from the hospital, I was so proud. My girls were home and I wanted to do everything in my power to keep them happy. I learned to burp her, change diapers, and sing lullabies.

I sat staring at the pictures that chronicled the first year of Semaj's life. The time really had gone by in a flash. I always heard people say that, but I'd lived it over the last six years.

"How do you convince yourself that you're not a father when you've spent years fathering your child?"

I remembered staying up into the wee hours of the morning when my baby woke and wanted to play or when she had a fever we couldn't break. I never uttered a single complaint to Serena. I felt it was the least I could do since she had suffered through morning sickness for months, swollen ankles, and a bunch of other ailments, including hours of labor to bring my daughter into this world. I was proud to be a father; that little girl had changed my life and made me want to be a better man each and every day. I didn't realize I was crying until I noticed tears falling onto the pictures.

When the phone rang, I rushed to look at the caller ID. It was my divorce attorney, Donald Reynolds. I quickly snatched it up and brought it to my ear.

"James, I got your message," he said, without even saying hello. "I'm so sorry this has happened to you."

"What do I do? How could this have happened?"

"Look, I need you to really think about this. Remember we've already finalized this divorce, and you agreed to pay thirteen hundred a month in child support."

The lump in my throat had returned. I did; I didn't mind, I wanted to make sure my daughter had the best and never wanted for a thing. I figured thirteen hundred was the least I could pay, regardless of the fact that there was no telling what Serena the Sicko would do with the money. I didn't want to shrink on my responsibility.

"What does that mean now?" I asked. I didn't quite know what to say or even what I should be concerned about.

"James, that is your daughter; you love that child. Biology doesn't make a father; it takes a bigger man to raise a child that's not his own," Reynolds said.

As he spoke, I could feel the wrath gaining momentum in my stomach and threatening to shoot up my throat.

My second line rang, and my heart dropped when I realized it was my old house number. Was it Serena? I hadn't even told her that I knew her secret. Donald was the first person that I had called, considering I couldn't get to Parker. It wasn't that my attorney was a friend, it's just that I had no idea what to do, or who to even talk to.

I didn't take the call. I was afraid it could be Semaj. I wasn't sure what to say to her yet. I still loved her, but the betrayal, the lie, the disgust. The hatred I felt for Serena had soared to a level that I never envisioned was possible.

"James?" Donald asked. "You still there?"

"Yeah. Sorry, my mind. What did you say?"

"I asked if you wanted to remain your daughter's father," he repeated easily, as if that's the kind of question you ask every day.

"What do you mean by that?"

"I know you're struggling with this right now and you probably will for some time to come, but there are some legal benchmarks you need to know about."

I was lost. "Benchmarks?"

"Yes, in cases like these, the law is very straightforward and clear. We need to first schedule a DNA test."

"A DNA test?"

"Yes, that's the only way the state of Texas recognizes a challenge to paternity."

I had a sick feeling in my stomach; me challenging the paternity of my daughter? This had to be some kind of nightmare.

"I want you to deal with the emotions, and let me handle the legal aspect of this. Take some time to yourself, think about how you want to handle this, but let's call for a DNA test. State law puts a limit on how much time you have to contest paternity. I believe it's three hundred days after the divorce is final, but I say we don't wait on this. Let's get the process started right away."

"Wow! This is so much; too much!"

"Again, take some time, but remember, the clock is ticking," he warned.

And it was, in more ways than one.

LACHEZ

I walked into Vanessa's Beauty Boutique and couldn't believe how bustling it was at five in the damn morning! I looked around in awe. Several females were in different stages of hairstyles, like it was two in the afternoon instead of five in the morning.

"I see you made it on time," Nessa said. She was walking out of a storage closet. It didn't matter the time of day or night, Nessa's hair was always tight. I'd always tell her she was her best advertisement. She was definitely representing in a big way.

I dropped my Coach duffle bag on the floor, and scratched the palm of my right hand, again. Nessa's expertly arched eyebrow went up as she looked at me.

"You wanna leave that there, or put it in the bottom drawer? We're going to the shampoo bowl."

She shook out a smock and gave it to me. I scratched my palm again before putting it on, then put my bag in her cabinet's bottom drawer.

She smiled. "You must be coming into some money."

I slipped into the chair and assumed the position. With my head eased back into the bowl, I closed my eyes and waited for Nessa to take my head into her hands. She tugged at my head, moving me closer to the center of the bowl.

"You know something I don't know?" I questioned.

"'Bout what?" Nessa asked.

"You said I'm coming into some money."

My mind wondered. Between what I got from Julius and Drew, I felt like I had already hit the numbers; nothing big but still enough to make sure I was turning heads when I stepped up in the place. And I'd still have some change left over.

"Oh, you know how old folks be saying when your right hand itches that means you got money coming." Nessa shrugged. "Just a stupid old saying, but seriously though, what's up with this party y'all going to?"

"Girl, I have no idea. I was told to keep it cute and get ready to turn it out," I bragged.

As she shampooed my hair, she told me that Toni was due in later and made sure I still wanted the more expensive fusion style weave. Since Toni was mixed and her short hair was more kinky than mine, Vanessa was able to hook her up proper. I liked my hair extra long; it seemed to drive the men crazy.

"Gurl, yes!" I declared as she wrapped my wet hair in a towel and motioned for me to follow her back to her station. "I wanna walk up out this mug looking like a vanilla-tinted Beyoncé," I joked.

"Hmmm…" Nessa chuckled. "Well, I have been known to work some magic, but that would be one helluva miracle," she said, with a hearty laugh to boot.

I sucked my teeth as I followed her back to her workstation.

"Puh-leeeease, Beyoncé wish she was shaped like me," I said, adding an extra twist in my stride.

Nearly four hours later, I got up from Nessa's chair and caught a glimpse of myself in the mirror. I looked like crisp, brand new money!

"Damn! You did your damn thang," I cheered, twisting and turning my head to get a better look at her work. She had hooked me up for real. Soft, golden curls framed my face and cascaded down and around my shoulders. Nobody could tell me this hair wasn't mine. Well, it was mine 'cause I bought it, but still, you couldn't tell it didn't come out of my roots.

I gave Nessa the money, along with a generous tip, and thanked her again before heading out.

When I walked back into the house after grabbing the mail, I was stunned that none of the kids were up yet. But as long as their asses stayed up last night, they should've stayed sleep until noon or one.

The phone rang and I jumped to catch it before it woke the dead. Unfortunately for me, I didn't check caller ID.

"Glad my life didn't depend on that call back," was the way Darlene greeted me.

"Whassup?" I instantly regretted answering the phone.

"I was thinking 'bout driving up. I'm just checking to see what you and the kids got going on today."

I couldn't believe she was acting like we were really cool like that.

"Oh, we're headed to Schlitterbahn and you know that's an all-day process," I lied.

There was silence.

Before she said anything else, I quickly said, "I need to run; we'll catch up later."

I hung up the phone. I started to toss the mail aside when something strange caught my eye. I had never received anything from the state Attorney General's Office. I noticed my county check, and smiled at Nessa's old wives' tale.

"I guess she was right about me coming into money," I said. But instead of opening that check, I was more interested in the letter from the Attorney General's Office. The small change I got for the kids wasn't hardly anything to smile about.

I ripped open the envelope from the AG's Office and plucked out the letter. With each word I read, my legs began to feel like wet noodles, and suddenly I could no longer stand on my own. I nearly collapsed when I realized what I was reading. I sat down and read the letter again.

"What the fuck?" My eyes took in the words, but it was my heart that was threatening to burst out of my chest. They had finally caught up with Renzo's daddy, and the sleazy bastard was finally about to make good on his back payments! I was stunned! My hands started shaking as I sat there reading the letter for the fourth time.

"How much money must that be?" I mumbled quietly. I felt myself wondering what all I'd have to do to actually get my hands on that money. Now the joke was on me. Sure Toni and I laughed about it all the time, but in the scenario we made up, the law had caught up with *her* ex, not mine. He owed far more money than my deadbeat.

"I'll be damned," I said. I kept reading.

"How many fucking thousand dollars?" I couldn't even fathom what I was reading. I didn't want to get too excited, but damn! The things I could do with that kind of money kept popping into my mind.

The party was about to be on for real tonight! I quickly picked up the phone book and started scanning through the rental car sections. By the time I was done, I had arranged for a stretch 300-limo to pick both Toni and me up. I looked at the letter and laughed out loud. This was really going to be a celebration.

The moment I gathered my composure, I looked up and saw Junie's nosey ass standing in the hallway.

"What you all happy about?" he asked, no "good morning" or "hey, Ma." The corners of my lips twisted in a frown, but then I remembered my new good fortune and smiled at my son.

"'Cause, we 'bout to be in the money!" I screamed.

"Whhhaat?" Junie asked, coming even closer. "We hit the numbers, Ma?"

"Nah, boy, get on over here. Matter of fact, go wake your brothers; it's time we had a family meeting."

I wasn't quite sure what all I'd have to do to get the cash, but I needed to make sure my lil' soldiers were all on the same page. I didn't need nobody asking them any questions and their little asses messing things up.

Later that night, Toni and I eased back in the limo sipping drinks like we were real big ballers. We were headed to club Hush. She was wearing a chili-red mini dress that hugged her curves. She looked good with her brushed gold accessories and a Python-patterned clutch bag that was hot to death!

The driver took I-10 west toward San Antonio past Highway 6. When he took the Park Ten Blvd exit and made a U-turn on to the feeder, I pulled out my compact to check my makeup.

"How my lips look?" Toni asked.

"You good to go."

When the limo eased up in front of the club, my heart nearly skipped a beat. It was like every envious eye in the thick snake-like line was stuck to me and Toni as the driver held the door for us. I felt like bona fide royalty.

We sashayed up to the velvet rope like paparazzi was on our hells, and before we could even get to the door a big bouncer plucked it open to allow us in.

I could feel the hate radiating from the little peons who stood in line watching with their mouths hung wide as we received the ultimate VIP treatment.

"Girl, this is the move right here." Toni giggled.

I loved club Hush with its neon lights and high energy music blasting through massive speakers. The multi-level dance floor was all the way live with out-of-this-world technology. But the ultimate was the massive sunken dance floor where they blasted a spectacular lightshow.

Everywhere you looked, there were tons of plasma and video screens.

The place wasn't packed yet, but later it'd be like a sweaty sardine can up in there.

"Now that's where we need to be," Toni said.

I followed her eyes up toward the skyboxes and saw some tall lean bodies mingling. Now it was my turn to drool at the mouth.

"Well, let's go," I said. I put my glass down and turned to make my way to those boxes.

"Wait, hold up," Toni said.

"What? Wassup? We here to kick it with the ballers, right?"

"Yeah, but we, I don't think we can go up there," Toni said, motioning up toward the boxes with her head.

"Girl, we VIP," I said.

"Yeah, but that's like the Skybox Black. I don't think we can get up there."

She had to be kidding me. After I spent all this doggone money, on my hair, new Gucci bag, the matching snow white Gucci shorts suit and stacked platform heels, and she acting like she scared?

"Toni, did we come all the way here to be on the outside looking in? We need to get up there no matter who we got to blow!"

Toni looked at me and frowned.

But I was serious. I had to at least feel like I had a shot at recouping what I'd spent and I wasn't about to do it hanging in VIP when the real money was up in that damn skybox.

"You coming or what?" I asked Toni. When I strolled toward the big bouncer guarding the entrance to the skybox area, Toni was hot on my heels. If he knew like I knew, he'd step aside and let nature take its course, 'cause I was not taking no for an answer.

PARKER

I didn't understand how processing out of jail could take as long as being booked but it did. I was ready to go but, once again, the wheels of justice were moving at a snail's pace for me. Yeah, I understood there was an issue with overcrowding, but I didn't understand how that meant me staying behind bars for weeks.

In the time I'd been waiting to be freed, I'd talked to both Smith and James on the phone several times. Smith told me that we still had so much to do and that I needed to set up a meeting with him right away.

Something about the urgent tone of his voice didn't sit well with me. I had a difficult battle ahead, but I didn't need a lawyer who didn't believe we could get this mess cleared up. But the most important part of our conversation came toward the end.

"Parker, we need to put in a request to have DNA testing done as quickly as we can get in."

"Okay, that's cool, but why is this taking so long?"

"Justice moves at its own pace," he said. "Don't forget to get in with me as soon as you can."

"No problem. I want to get a handle on a few things and make sure this mess is cleared up as soon as possible."

The conversation with James didn't go quite as smoothly. He was all messed up in the head and the heart. As of yet, he still hadn't let on to Serena that he knew what was up. I could tell the most difficult part was probably the fact that he was struggling to avoid his daughter's calls.

"I can't believe Serena did this to me, dawg," he'd said.

I didn't know what to say. I couldn't even imagine what I would've done if I had been in his shoes. It was so ironic how a week earlier, my world had been turned upside down, straight flipped; now here he was tripping out.

"How long are you gonna hold on to this. I mean, before saying something to her?"

"I'm trying to play this one real cool. I'm going by the books, doing exactly what Donald suggests. He says that I need to get my head on right, figure out how I'm gonna handle this before we make our move."

"But what about the divorce?"

"That's what makes this thing even more complicated. In that final divorce decree, I offered up thirteen a month for child support."

"Hey, man, I wouldn't expect anything less from you. You were manning up to yours; that's all that was. I don't know how you go about signing those checks now, knowing what you know," I said.

"Yeah, that's a part of the problem. It's not like I can tell Semaj, but not her Mama, and we all know she got about as much sense as a box of rocks," he said.

I didn't say anything but thought, that's why I never went dumpster diving when it came to finding a woman. I didn't believe in it. Most people would've probably considered me arrogant, but I figured there are enough thugs, gang bangers, and other losers for women like that. I only dealt with the crème de la crème.

When we hung up, I sighed, thinking about why both my boy and I were going through this kind of bullshit. If I didn't know any better, I would've thought this was part of a conspiracy.

I told myself that the moment I walked out of the Harris County Jail, I would vow that I'd never be back. Unfortunately for me, keeping that promise wouldn't be as easy as one would think.

"Shit, first I need to get out this mug." I wondered if Roxy was really doing her best to get me out.

Nearly two days after my court appearance, I was about to lose my damn mind! I didn't understand why I was still in jail. I needed to be home, I needed to be trying to track this woman down. I needed to clear this shit up!

Whenever I tried to call Roxanne, she wasn't answering. I had spoken with James and he left me wondering what the hell the world was coming to.

I didn't like Serena but she had stooped as low as possible, to have a man thinking he had fathered a child when she knew he hadn't? Man, I needed to be home. I kept hoping he wouldn't haul off and do anything stupid, like ring her fucking neck! I tell you, just when you think your problems are the worst, someone's always got you beat.

He was in real bad shape when I called, and I understood why too. I hoped he would do the right thing.

"Man, whatever you do," I told him, "make sure you stay away from Serena until you figure this shit out!"

"I know, dawg, I know," he said, but he didn't sound too good.

"No, I'm serious. I don't think it's wise for you to even see her ass right now. There's no telling what you might do, man, and trust me, you don't want to wind up in here."

I could tell he was in a zone all his own, and I couldn't say that I blamed him either. I wanted to call Serena myself and get in that ass for what she had done, but that wouldn't help. Besides, I needed to get my own shit straight.

I was so ready to get out that I thought I'd lose my mind. I didn't even have the heart to ask him about the status of my bail situation, if you could call it bail. It was more like ransom, if you asked me. Either way, his news was far too unbelievable to swallow.

For once, since I'd been locked up, my problems didn't take center stage. I felt sick for my boy.

His news was enough to make mine seem a bit smaller. I eased back on the bunk and started thinking about women, just women in general. I thought about Roxanne and how quick she was to start doubting me, doubting what we had, and it made me sick.

Then I started thinking about the women who didn't make the cut with me and why they didn't. I was picky when it came to women; there was no doubt about that. For a long time I thought I'd wind up alone because I didn't think many friends could even measure up to my standards, but I refused to lower them.

There was Jeanine; she had wanted to get married so badly that she had accepted anything I had thrown her way. Sometimes, I'd do shit to see if she'd complain, and she never did. I suspected it was because she was holding out for that ring and my last name.

Andy was another one who thought she had found her Mr. Right in me, but she had too many damn issues. I liked a woman that was strong-willed, but damn, know when to let a man be a man. She was so hell bent on proving to me that she had balls, she had lost sight of the fact that no straight man wanted another set when he had his own.

Then I started thinking about some others whose names I couldn't remember, but either their faces or bodies or skills between the sheets made them memorable.

Suddenly I bolted upright.

"What if?" I mumbled.

I sat, thinking for a bit longer. I never believed in messing with women beneath my level. I wasn't about to rescue anybody, and

I wasn't looking for a ready-made family. I wasn't moving any-body out of the hood, and the projects were nowhere on my radar. Those were the kinds of women who had illegitimate kids, and then tried to sue you for child support, I decided.

The women I dated had to be educated, upwardly mobile and, more importantly, they had to have something other than a deep desire to get a man going for themselves. Yes, I was very selective and had been very careful, so I didn't understand how something like this could be happening to me. I felt it deep down in my bones; this was nothing more than a big mix-up.

I was thinking about some of the women I'd had, when I heard a sound that I never thought I'd hear.

"Redman, you're being processed!" a jailer yelled.

Again I eased up, but this time I was more excited than ever before. I was finally getting out!

ROXANNE

Things were strained at best since Parker had been home. I greeted him with mixed emotions. I was glad he was out of jail, but I still didn't understand how he could agree to pay for a kid he claimed wasn't his.

At the front door, we shared a passionate kiss, and a long warm embrace, but James was right behind Parker so that didn't last long.

"Look, there'll be enough time for that later," James joked, disrupting the impromptu welcome home celebration. "We got business to discuss."

I giggled and moved away from Parker, using the tips of my fingers to wipe my lips.

"Man, damn that business for now. I gots to put some soap to water and wash my ass. You can hang out and wait, but first things first, my brotha!"

I watched as they exchanged fist pounds and James nodded in agreement.

"You know, while you do that, why don't I go pick up some Bar-B-Que. I mean, ain't not telling how long we gon' be up trynta sort this mess out."

"Now that sounds like a plan," Parker agreed.

I didn't want to hassle him. I wanted him to ease back into being home but, at some point, I hoped he was gonna address this huge issue looming over us.

Nearly an hour after James had left for food, he was back banging on the front door.

He was a welcomed sight with bags and containers of food, and a heavenly aroma. That's when I realized how hungry I was. My stomach grumbled as if to prove it wasn't simply my imagination.

"So look," James was saying as I walked back into the room.

"We've gotta see if Smith can get around the notices."

"Yeah, but it's not looking good," Parker said.

A frown made its way to my face.

"What do you mean, it's not looking good? You said you didn't father this child!"

When both sets of eyes were staring at me with surprised focus, I realized what I must've sounded like. I took a deep breath and tried to adjust my tone.

"Um, what I mean is, I think James is right. Let's see what Smith can do about the notices. Then, after that, we can go back before the judge and prove this kid isn't yours. That sounds simple enough to me," I said.

Parker didn't take his eyes off me. "You don't understand," he said, as he slipped a piece of brisket into his mouth.

"Then make me understand. All I know is, our savings are wiped out, we're in debt to James here, and we're still on the hook for twenty-five-thousand more dollars. And let's not forget, we face even more legal bills, all over a child you *say* isn't yours! It's a no-brainer; we need to put this foolishness behind us!"

"What he's trying to say," James started. "It's not always as cut and dry as that."

"Yeah, you should know," Parker said, like he and James shared some kind of inside joke, but they didn't elaborate and I wasn't in the mood to hear about James's drama. We had enough of our own.

"Anyway, dawg." James dismissed Parker, and then turned to me. "The problem is the notices that were ignored," James stressed.

"What does that mean? We've already determined they were sent to the wrong address," I reminded them.

"Yeah, but usually when mail is sent to the wrong address, it's returned. None of the many notices were ever returned undeliverable, so according to Smith, it makes it look like Parker was ignoring his responsibility."

"And unfortunately for me, one of those notices was informing me of my rights to contest paternity. Since I never got it before the deadline, it was like I never contested," Parker said.

I heard what they were saying, I understood, but I was convinced there had to be another way.

"Okay, and what does that mean?"

I didn't want to believe all of this had been going on and we were completely clueless about it. It sounded too unrealistic to me. Of course I had heard of women who went off on their own to have children when the men didn't want them or the kids. But, at some point, these women usually came around or at least made some kind of contact, even if it was done years later. This situation simply didn't make any sense.

"That's what we need to find out. Maybe if he can prove he didn't live at those addresses, or that he didn't know about the notices, that will clear this shit up," James offered.

My mouth hung wide, but my eyes were probably even wider.

"That's it! That's the great strategy? I refuse to believe that you are going to have to pay for a kid that's not even yours!" I said passionately.

Both James and Parker turned their gaze to me. Serena's words started ringing into my mind.

All men were dogs or have dog potential... I shook the traitorous words from my head. Sure, when we dated, I knew he was seeing another woman, but I was okay with that. He was upfront about it, saying he and Adriane weren't serious.

Adriane was a flight attendant who loved to travel and couldn't see herself settling down. I'd seen pictures of her, she was pretty enough, but Parker told me there was no future for them. At the time, I thought it was so refreshing to have a man who was upfront and not trying to play the field. I'll never forget the day he broke it off with Adriane for good.

"I think we should take our relationship to the next level," he had said that night over dinner. Excitement flushed through my veins.

"This is the best news ever," I replied.

From that moment on, it was like we were kicking off a fairy-tale romance. Parker would surprise me with little gifts, dinners at expensive restaurants, weekend trips and more. Nine months after that announcement, he asked me to marry him and I'd never been happier.

Parker was a planner. Our wedding date was set six months after the engagement. Six months after that, we bought a new house, a bigger house in Sugar Land, and the day he carried me over the threshold, he vowed that we'd fill the empty rooms with kids.

Like most marriages, ours wasn't perfect, but I didn't think we had any secrets. This thing had done so much more than left me questioning the man that I loved.

"Roxanne!"

I snapped back to reality, only to discover them both staring at me blankly.

"You know, I think I need to go to bed. I'm tired of all of this."

I left the guys to decipher this mystery all on their own.

JAMES

"Dawg, when your ass landed in jail for not paying child support, I thought for sure this was the wildest drama we'd face this year," I said to Parker. "Now, my shit's all twisted, too."

"Look, we better not talk about this now." Parker looked toward the hall. He was right. Serena didn't know, and Roxanne knowing would guarantee Serena would find out.

"Yeah, you're right, but talk about strange. How could we be damn near in the same boat?" I asked.

Parker looked at me and said, "Man, my shit is jacked up, no doubt, but I wouldn't trade with you for a second. Besides, what's going on with Semaj? Have you decided what you're gonna do about her?"

I cringed at the mere mention of her name; it was enough to get me all choked up. How could I face, or not face, my daughter anymore? I thought about looking in her eyes, eyes I once swore were exactly like mine, and saying, "Uh, there's been a mistake?"

"I don't know what to do," I admitted, answering Parker's question, and I didn't. I didn't know how to even begin to approach this situation. I didn't know how to break this kind of news to a six-year-old.

"Man, don't forget what your lawyer said," Parker reminded me. "This is a lot to swallow but, man, you don't want to end up paying for a kid that's not yours any more than you have to. I know what I'm talking about."

He leaned in a bit closer, and then glanced toward the hall. I guess he was trying to make sure Roxanne wasn't lurking around anywhere.

"I'm thinking, I may have to borrow against my 401K to pay off the rest of this shit!" he whispered.

My eyes got wide. "What?"

Parker looked somber. At that time, I was wondering like his wife was. How could he be considering paying for a kid that wasn't his?

"But isn't Smith gonna try and clear this up?" I asked, my voice crackling a bit.

"Before I got out, one of the jailers told me about his friend. He said it took a year before his boy was able to reclaim his life and fix his mess."

"A year?"

"Yup."

"That's a long time to be tied to some shit you didn't even do," I said.

"Yeah, it is, man. It is," Parker said as he put a beer bottle to his lips and took a long swallow.

My eyes lit up when I thought about something that hadn't crossed my mind before. I waited for Parker to take another swig of his beer, and then it was my turn to lean in.

"You think I could press charges against Serena for this?"

Parker frowned. But then it looked like he was giving serious thought to what I was saying. "Press charges?"

"Yeah, you know; either that or sue her ass. I mean, isn't that fraud or something? People sue for all kinds of shit now-a-days. Remember dude who sued the cleaners for fifty-four million dollars over a pair of pants?"

Parker was looking at me, but he hadn't said anything else.

"Well, I'm just saying, shouldn't I be able to sue that bitch for lying and saying I fathered Semaj when she knew damn well she'd been fucking someone else all along?"

"Man, that's deep," Parker said. But I didn't know if he understood, I was as serious as cardiac arrest. "Yeah, it is, but I want to know if it's possible."

LACHEZ

"Did I tell you that I could help you out if you just trusted me or what?" Kelly Johnson asked.

I sat across from my counselor, a medium-sized woman who always dressed up in velour sweat suits with matching girly tennis shoes, and rolled my eyes. She was sweating profusely, and all we were doing was sitting down talking.

All of her grandstanding was working my last nerves, but I told myself this was a small price to pay if I could get my hands on that paper. When I sighed, she leaned over the table and glanced around.

"What's wrong?"

"Nothing," I told her.

She looked at me, squinting her slanted eyes like she didn't believe me, but I didn't really care. "So tell me more about the letter. Did you bring it with you?"

"Oh, yeah." That reminded me of the *real* reason I had called and asked her to meet me. Usually, I didn't like dealing with counselors, doctors, and psychiatrists unless I had to, but I did have to admit, after her friend hooked us up, Kelly had given me the inside track.

She coached me on how to work the system, and so far everything she'd said had been right on the money. And you know, I like anybody who can help fill my pockets.

I dug into my bag and pulled the letter out. It wasn't that I didn't understand it, but I wanted to make sure there were no strings attached. I wanted to be sure I'd be able to get some money out of this. Otherwise, what was the use?

I sat back as she read the letter. My cell rang. It was Darlene who I was sure was calling me every name but a Child of God because I wouldn't talk about her visiting the kids. I wanted her to be one of those distant grannies; send cards, gifts, and money but stay her ass away! I hit IGNORE and watched her number disappear from my phone screen.

"How do you feel about finally being able to confront the deadbeat who fathered your son and left you to handle the responsibility all alone?" Kelly asked, breaking my train of thought.

I looked at her sideways. I frowned and glanced around the restaurant. Did she forget where we were? I was simply asking for some advice; I wasn't expecting a damn impromptu counseling session.

"Look, I'll help you with this and everything should be fine."

She folded the letter up and slid it back to me. I didn't want to jump through hoops to get money that was owed to me. I was hoping it would be as simple as showing up and getting a check. I had already called and was given a date to show up at Family Court. As we waited for food to come, I thought back to the look on Toni's face when the big bouncer stepped aside and allowed us to go mingle with the real ballers.

But she was stuck on stunned all night long, from the moment the limo had pulled up in front of her place. I got out to go knock on her door and when she walked out and her eyes feasted on that limo, she looked like she was about to pass out. When she realized it was there for us, her entire demeanor changed instantly, and I could tell. There was more twist in her step and, if I'm not mistaken, her posture even changed a bit. I could hardly describe how it made me feel, having Toni acknowledge that I made this happen for us.

"Damn, I know you musta hit the numbers this time for real." Toni squealed as we climbed into the limo.

"Girl, it gets even better. I'm buying all the damn drinks tonight!"

"Whhhaaaat!"

She slid in and looked around.

"Damn, this is crunk for real! A moon roof, too? Ooh, and a full bar!"

I poured her a drink and eased back in the seat, like this was all the norm for me.

"So seriously, how? I mean, what gives?" She shrugged, pulling the glass to her lips.

"Not only did I get my check but, girl, Drew and Julius came through." I shook my new lustrous honey-blonde locks.

"What? Damn! Nessa told me you were in there throwing money around like it was going out of style," Toni said, her face twisted into a frown.

I took a sip of my own. "I know you ain't hatin'."

"Nah, girl. I don't believe in that haterade. I wish I could work my jelly like you." She looked around the limo again. "Shoot, I ain't hatin' 'cause when you do good, obviously I do good, so it's all good!"

We touched our glasses together and turned them up.

"Besides, I got a call from the Attorney General's Office. They left me a message, but I'ma call them back and I pray they're gonna tell me when and where to pick up my damn money!" Toni said.

"Ooooh girl, I sure hope so," I said, reaching my palm up for a high-five.

When the waiter came balancing food on his tray, my mind

instantly switched back to the issue at hand. That and the fact that I was starving.

"You got results from the doctor on Lorenzo?" I took the opportunity to ask.

She nodded, chewing the food in her mouth.

"Yeah, I meant to talk to you about that. It looks like it's all good, and like I told you, when it runs in the fam, that makes it even more legit," she said, talking about my son's ADHD diagnosis.

"Cool," I said. I didn't feel like hanging around too long, 'cause I had things to do. "So when do I need to come in and see you to make it all official?"

"I'll call and let you know, for sure. For now, lay low and let's concentrate on that court appearance.

My eyebrows inched up. "What do you mean, court appearance? You didn't say nothing about me actually having to go to court." I was a bit startled.

"Look, it may only be a meeting with the judge. The AG's Office usually handles everything, and since there is no one to contest, I'll double check that for you and let you know before the date."

"Okay, but I ain't trynta go to nobody's court," I said. We ate in silence for a few minutes more, before I looked up at her.

"You know, your girl must really hate these people," I said.

She frowned. But just as she was about to say something, her cell phone rang. Kelly checked her caller ID, held a finger up to silence me, pulled the phone to her ear, and then started talking. I took another bite of my sandwich, swallowed a gulp of tea and took that as the perfect opportunity to get up and bounce up outta there.

"I'll talk to you in a couple of days," I tossed over my shoulder as I dashed out of the restaurant before she could end her call and try to get me to stay.

PARKER

I sat alone, drinking and thinking long after Roxy had gone to bed. She'd been tripping lately, acting like she still didn't trust me or didn't think I was telling the truth about this situation. It didn't help that I hadn't met with Smith yet because I had some urgent business to tend to at work.

I wondered if the judge would toss me back in jail if I didn't come up with the rest of the money. I wondered what the hell James was going to do about his situation, how long he was going to hold on without telling Serena's evil ass about his secret, or her secret, that is. I couldn't believe she actually thought he was still gonna pay the mortgage after the divorce. Serena was a trip, for real.

My thoughts were interrupted when I looked up and saw Roxanne standing there. She yawned; I wasn't sure how long she'd been there, but I didn't feel like fighting with her.

"Are you ever gonna come to bed?" she asked, her voice still sounding kind of groggy.

"Oh, yeah, I am, I'm just—"

"Just what?" she asked, cutting me off. Her tone indicated that she was quickly losing patience with me. "You can't bring yourself to come to bed while I'm awake? You feel better stumbling to bed after you've spent hours late at night drinking alone?"

"Roxanne? Why you trippin'?" I tried to ask, but she was really going off on me.

Her hands flew to her hips and all traces of sleepiness had suddenly disappeared.

"Let you tell it, I'm always trippin'. First, I was trippin' when I asked about where this mess may have come from, then I was trippin' again when I suggested that maybe someone from your past, or someone you're not thinking of, is behind this. All logical questions to me, but a sign that I'm trippin' to you." She shrugged, and threw her hands up in defense. "I don't know what you want from me, but under the circumstances, I've been more than accommodating."

"Wait; hold up a sec," I tried to interrupt.

"No, *you* hold up a sec! What I'm saying to you is, I've endured so much, I can't think of too many women who'd still be by your side. We're broke, and this shit is still not over! Then, to hear you talking about not even wanting to go back to court?" She looked at me with evil eyes. "I have every right to be not just upset, but pissed off!"

At that moment, I decided not to say another word. Nothing I said was going to make things better between us. She was pissed and she needed to let me have it.

I sat there as my wife was going smooth off, arms waving and head twisting. For a second, I had a flashback of stupid-ass Serena. I wondered then if my wife had been getting advice from her friend about what to do or even how to handle me.

Serena was nothing but a bitter, man-hating-ass bitch, and I had hoped Roxy would be smart enough to know that no married woman should take advice from someone either single or close to being single.

But as I listened to her go on and on about how foul it was for me to say half the things I'd said, my suspicions were confirmed.

James didn't want to deal with her, but I told myself that I needed to tell Serena's nosey ass to tend to her own problems and stay the hell out of mine. Wasn't it obvious she had enough issues of her own?

ROXANNE

I woke one morning to find the space next to me in bed empty. I slid my hand over the sheet and it was cold. I wondered how long he'd been gone. I closed my eyes and considered not even looking for him. The constant bickering and fighting were starting to take their toll. I smelled the aroma of coffee floating into the room and tickling my nostrils, so I eased myself up out of bed. I swung my feet to the floor, stretched, yawned, then pulled myself up.

After a trip to the bathroom, I went to the kitchen and found Parker at the table, looking through mail.

"Morning," he mumbled, like he really didn't even want to talk to me.

"You okay?" I asked, picking up on his lackluster tone and hoping that would encourage him to fix it.

He slammed a letter down on the table. "This shit is really starting to get out of control."

"What now?" I almost didn't want to ask. I walked to the cabinet to get a coffee mug.

"Okay, this is a letter notifying me that I need to pay fourteen hundred and five dollars a month in child support," he answered hopelessly.

I was infuriated. "You have got to be kidding me. This is in addition to what we paid to get you out? Let's not forget, we still got another twenty-five thousand left on that bill!"

I waited for his response, but nothing came. I looked up to see him staring off into space. Every so often, he'd zone out to his own world and it made me so angry.

"Smith and I are going back to court and, before we go, I plan to talk to him about asking for a DNA test," he said.

That was the best news I'd heard since this mess went down. But I didn't want to overreact, so I pulled out a chair and sat quietly, sipping my coffee.

"So you still don't know who this woman is?" I asked a few minutes later.

"Nah," he said, half-shrugging a shoulder. I was sick with this foolishness. I had to admit, this was the kind of stuff that set me off. How could he still not know the woman? She'd claimed he fathered her child, he'd been arrested, and we'd cleaned out our savings and he didn't know who the hell was accusing him? Why wouldn't he have been eating, breathing, sleeping and dreaming this woman's name until he came face to face with her?

I sighed. I was not looking forward to going to work, but we needed the time apart. Parker had taken some time off from work, supposedly to straighten the entire thing out. Yet, simple things, like not even knowing who was behind the situation, made me wonder exactly how aggressive he was being. Then, the next words from his mouth almost left me stunned.

"What's the point of going back before this judge? It's obvious she's already made up her mind. God Himself could come and testify on my behalf and I'd still be stuck with this bill."

Here we go again!

"You've gotta be kidding me!" I was so angry I could have gouged his eyes out with my fingernails. "There's no way you can *not* go! What happened to the claims of mistaken identity? What happened to being the wrong person? You don't wanna go? Isn't that what got us in this mess in the first place? If you would've responded to that first letter, maybe we could've headed this thing off before it came to this."

"Damn, Roxy!"

The last thing I wanted right now was to get into an argument with him, but when he hauled off and said stupid things that didn't make sense, I couldn't help myself.

I was looking into my husband's distant eyes. Everything about his expression read fury. But I couldn't help but wonder, was it me that he should be mad with? I hardly thought so, and I started to tell him as much, but decided against it; this situation was hopeless.

"Look, I need to get ready for work." I took a final sip from the coffee mug and got up to go get dressed. He didn't say anything, so I walked out of the kitchen.

JAMES

Things weren't getting any better and I needed to do something. I could hardly sleep for thinking about what Serena the Sicko had done to me. I was sick because the more I researched and looked into cases similar to mine, the more I realized nothing ever happened to women like Serena. I couldn't even sue her ass, or at least if I did, some judge would throw it out.

I was reading this post a man put on this website: maddaddies. com. Dude was going off, not only on the woman who had fooled him for years, but on the AG's Office, state lawmakers and anyone else he could think of.

I also read about another case in Florida where a man divorced his wife after fifteen years, and then learned that none of their four kids were his! How the hell was something like that possible? Then I considered myself somewhat lucky. If after fifteen years I found out a kid wasn't mine, there'd be one less person on this earth.

This was what I thought about all the time. I constantly wondered how a judge could put a man like Parker in jail, force him to pay thousands of dollars for a kid that wasn't his, and not do a single thing to a lying vicious, lowdown female dog like Serena. It defied all common sense.

My cell rang, and it was Parker. "Whassup, dawg?" I answered.

"Checkin' up on you," he said. He sounded a bit better, considering what was going on in his world.

"Oh, you caught me minutes from meeting with my lawyer, dawg. After this, get ready for Serena's wrath. I'm sure she ain't gonna be happy, 'cause it's about to go down."

I heard the surprise in his voice. "What? You letting her know you know what's really up?"

"Gots to, dawg; gots to. I've been avoiding my baby's calls for weeks. Serena even showed up at the job, acting an ass when she realized I wasn't paying the mortgage anymore. I can imagine how she's gonna flip out when she learns about losing more than a grand a month in child support."

"Ww-what? So you cool with not paying for your…um, I mean, for Semaj?"

I appreciated him catching himself, but I'd accepted the fact that Semaj was not my biological child. Despite the fact that her ghetto-ass mama had the audacity to name her after me—her name was James spelled backward—the bitch probably knew all along that the baby wasn't mine.

"Look, dawg, it's like this. I ain't rich, I still have mad love for that little girl, I probably always will, but what happens when I meet another woman and start having real kids of my own? Do I introduce Semaj as my child when I know she's not? And not only that, why should I be paying when some other fool is out there running around spending his money freely and shunning his responsibilities?"

"Oh, I feel you; you know I do," Parker cosigned.

"So, I'ma 'bout to handle this now. I told you, I have smething like three hundred days after the divorce is final. But I'm ready to cut all ties with Serena and anything remotely attached to her. Unfortunately, I can't do it without hurting Semaj, but that's something her ignorant mama should've thought about when she was out creepin'," I said.

"I can't believe she didn't think you'd ever find out," Parker added.

"C'mon, man, this is Serena we're talking about here. You know how she is. She does what she wants, when and how she wants, and doesn't expect any consequences whatsoever. Ain't no telling who she was laying up with, but I know one thing, I ain't footing the bill anymore," I said, getting all hyped thinking about it more and more.

"Well, good for you, man, good for you. Handle your business," Parker said.

"Cool, I'll holla at you when I'm done here. Oh, I'll swing by the house if you'll be there," I said.

"Yeah, hit me on the hip to make sure, but I should be either at the crib or close to it."

I pulled into my lawyer's parking lot. "Later, dawg." I liked Donald's style. He was ready for me. Donald was a slick white boy who knew his shit. Always dressed to the nines, he was real aggressive and believed in a no holds-barred type of action at all times. When Pauline had first referred me to him, she'd described him as a shark, and she was right.

"James, let's get started right away. I've drafted the papers for you to sign, questioning paternity. Because we're within the time-line, I'm adding this document as an amendment to the original decree."

He was moving so fast, I felt a little like I was being rushed. I thought we'd talk about a few things first but, as always, Donald was on point and wasn't trying to waste my time, or his.

"So, what's gonna happen to her?" I asked.

"Who? Your, um, the child?"

"Nah, not her; her mother, Serena, my ex."

"Oh…" Donald leaned back in his chair. "Well, when you say what's gonna happen to her, what exactly do you mean?"

"Can I put her ass in jail? Can I make her pay me back for all the money I've spent on Semaj? Ain't no way in the world I would've agreed to the kind of child support I voluntarily paid when I moved out had I known the truth."

Donald pulled himself closer to the desk. "The problem really is what you just said yourself; you voluntarily paid the support. Unfortunately, that's money lost. What you need to do now is look toward the future. The fact remains, we found out in time for you to get this reversed and, well, you're getting an opportunity most men never get."

It was a cold hard pill to swallow. I wanted to hear that Serena's ass would go to jail, or at least be fined for her deceit.

"So nothing happens to her?" I asked again.

Donald shook his head.

"Do we need a DNA test?"

"Not in this case, although the judge, or even Serena herself, may ask for one. The test we're sending in from your job is sufficient." He shrugged. "It clearly shows that you don't carry the trait for the genetic disease that your daughter could only have if you both were carriers."

I didn't correct him when he referred to her as my daughter, but each time I thought about it, there was a bit of a tug on my heart. I could only imagine how confused Semaj would be. But Donald told me this was the best way to handle it. She was too young for me to offer up any kind of explanation anyway. I only hoped that if her mother had even an ounce of common sense, she would sit the kid down and tell her the truth.

"So, you ready to do this?" Donald asked.

"Yeah, I am. Where do I sign?" I asked, looking at the document he had placed in front of me.

"Your signature is required wherever you see red arrows, and your initials wherever you see green."

I felt odd as I flipped through the pages. Not about taking action, but about what this would mean for, or to, Semaj. But like I'd told myself before, I needed to start looking out for me, because when it was all said and done, I was the one getting screwed for years and years.

LACHEZ

I was still floating on cloud nine when I thought about the possibility of getting my hands on some real serious paper. But until that happened, I had to try and get someone to replace the sponsor I had lost. There was no doubt that I missed Drew's money more than I missed him. So that meant I had to get out there and work my jelly.

I met Rodney Gold at that NBA party Toni and I went to a few weeks ago. He was brown-skinned with a fade and a body that said he should've been suiting up for somebody's team. I was expecting big things from him. At first, I pissed when I learned he wasn't no damn athlete, well, at least not one who was paid. But he did have potential. I'd gone out with his lil' pretty ass a couple of times, but now it was about to go down. I needed some cash something terrible.

When I got to his place, I already knew what was up. Like I said, I had things to do and needed some cash. He had soft music playing. There was nothing special about his place, dark and drab, leather furniture, his money had obviously gone into his entertainment system and that was cool with me. It only proved that he had a good amount of disposable income and I planned to help him spend it.

"What's up, boo?" he asked, flashing a sexy smile.

"You; it's all about you tonight," I said, smiling back and stepping out of my clothes before he could say another word.

Rodney's eyes rolled up and down my body, and then he grabbed his crotch.

"Damn? Like that?" he asked, damn near licking his lips.

"Yup, just like this," I said.

It didn't take long for us to set it off. Not even twenty minutes later, Rodney was doing the damn thing; he was hitting my spot with a vengeance and I was enjoying it.

"Sssss, damn, take it, baby," I cooed, clutching him tightly.

"Whose is this?" he asked as he thrust his hips. "Whose…is… this…"

I wrapped my legs around him even tighter, dug my fingernails into his back, and tried to keep up.

"It's all yours, baby! All yours!"

"You damn right it is."

I was loving everything he was doing and saying. As he was working it out, I was busy trying to work on a way to turn this pleasure party into some cash.

"Yes, Rodney, yes. Oh, yes!"

His eyes widened, and I stared deep into his pupils. I could see myself working with him for quite a while.

"Right there, baby," I encouraged.

We'd been going strong for quite some time, and that had given me the time I needed to come up with a plan.

"Oh damn, girl! Damn!" he cried.

"Yeah, baby, don't hold out on me. Go deep." I taunted him sweetly.

"Oh, I am," Rodney huffed as he worked his hips even harder.

When it was all said and done, I turned my body so we could spoon. Basking in the afterglow of satisfaction, Rodney kissed my ear. I snuggled closer to him and inhaled the smell of sex in the air.

I didn't want to go to sleep, and I damn sure didn't want him falling asleep on me. Even though I felt like that might give me an advantage. If he said no, I'd have to put him to sleep, and then ramble through his place to see what I could find to pawn.

I eased my body into an upright position, until he was nearly lying on my chest.

"Damn, that was nice," I cooed.

"Shiiiit, *nice* ain't even the word," he commented.

I chuckled. How does one go from sex to "I could use a little cash to hold me over."

He pulled his head back to look up at me. "Whassup?"

"Oh, it's nothing." I sighed, deciding to go with the flow and abandon my original plan if need be.

"Something's wrong. Now c'mon, lemme fix it," he urged sincerely.

"Well, it's…nah…" I shook my head. "I don't even wanna trouble you."

He repositioned himself to see me better. "Look, are we kicking it or what?"

At first, I didn't respond. I wanted to let the silence linger for a minute.

"Of course, baby, after all that work you just put in, I ain't going nowhere," I testified excitedly.

"Okay, then, so tell me what's going on. I wanna help."

"It's a money thing, and well, you know, I don't want you to think I can't handle mines, but my kids daddy was supposed to help me out, and—" I shrugged.

"You know what, I can't stand when cats don't step up."

He pulled himself up from the bed and walked over to the closet. He disappeared behind the door and I heard what sounded like him working a safe. I started getting happy. If he had a safe, that meant he had big dollars!

Cha-ching! I had really hit the jackpot this time. Unfortunately, my happiness didn't last too long.

Rodney came back to the bed and smiled at me. "Here you go, baby, and next time you need something, don't hesitate to ask."

He dropped five crisp one hundred-dollar bills on me like he was blessing me with five grand. I couldn't help the frown that made its way to my face. I told myself to handle this delicately, but he needed to know.

"Um, this is five hundred," I said, hoping he'd made a mistake.

"Yeah, you can thank me in a few." He smiled, sticking his chest outward.

My head was spinning. Was he for real? Did he think he was doing something big? I could spend five hundred dollars before I made it from his place to mine. I thought he was doing big things. If you got a safe, you gotta be balling outta' control, don't you?

"Um, thank you," I snarled.

That's when he musta got a clue, because worry lines suddenly creased his forehead.

"What? You said you needed money," he balked, pulling himself away again.

I took that opportunity to swing my legs onto the floor and search for my clothes. They weren't much, but I clutched the measly five bills and started getting dressed.

"Baby, whassup?" he asked, like he really didn't know.

Once dressed, I turned to him. "I don't believe, after I invited you to the paradise between my thighs, you insulted me with five hundred measly dollars." I was disgusted.

He stood looking at me like he was trying to understand what I had said.

"So you trynta say my five hundred ain't enough?"

"Baby, that's not even how I roll; five hundred dollars?" I snickered.

"Bitch, please!"

Oh but no he didn't! I thought, until he continued without skipping a beat.

"I don't know what you think this is, but Bank of America ain't stamped across my forehead. And if I knew this was gonna be a business transaction, I woulda gave your ass what it was worth, and trust me, you'd have at least four hundred ninety-nine dollars less than what you got now," he had the audacity to say.

I knew then, I needed to pull Drew back in, lean on my current crew a little harder. Trynta recruit wasn't what it used to be.

PARKER

I sat at my kitchen table, staring at the letter. I had a meeting with Smith later and I planned to ask how these people expected me to give some woman hundreds of dollars every month, after paying nearly fifty grand. The shit kept getting better and better. I released a frustrated laugh.

I wasn't expecting James so early and when the doorbell rang, I put the letter down to answer the door.

"Registered mail delivery for…" The guy looked down at his clipboard. "Um, R. Redman?"

"Yeah, I'll take that," I said.

He looked at me and said, "And you are?"

"Mister Redman," I said.

"Good enough; sign here." He pushed the clipboard toward me.

"Thanks." I accepted the thick envelope and quickly closed the door.

Normally, I wouldn't even think about opening my wife's mail. But with so much shit going on, I wanted to be on top of anything else that might pop up.

I ripped the envelope open, only to feel like I had taken a massive blow to the gut. I actually had to find a seat. The more I read, the more my blood boiled.

"So my fuckin' wife is doing background checks on my ass now?" I started reading more of what Findout.com apparently discovered about me. I didn't get to read too much more because the doorbell rang again.

I picked up the papers and rushed to the door and pulled it open.

"Damn, James, man; good to see you, real good to see you." I gave my boy a brothaman hug and let him into the house.

"What's up?" he asked.

"Ssshit!" I shook my head and led him into the kitchen. "Man, this shit gets crazier by the minute."

"When you hooking up with Smith?"

"Ah, later this afternoon. He needs another payment. And, man, good looking out on the loan. I never told you that but you know I 'preciate you!" I said, referring to the five grand he loaned us.

"Man, it ain't nothing. You'd do the same for me. Besides, I'm hoping this shit gets straight soon, 'cause I don't know how much longer your ol' lady's gonna be able to hang in there," he said.

He was joking, but serious at the same time. And I knew where he was coming from, 'cause shit had gotten real icy since I'd been home. Roxy wasn't the same, nor was she trying to be.

"You ain't said nothing but a word. Look at all this shit," I said, passing him a few of the pages.

I watched his eyes grow wide as he took in the words.

"What the fuck is this?" James asked, finally pulling his eyes up from what he was reading.

I was still reading myself. "Seems like wifey is doing some investigating of her own."

"Hey, dawg, you ain't never lived in Atlanta," James yelled, pointing at one of the many errors on the pages.

"Yeah, I know. Never went by the name Preston either," I added.

"Well, according to this." James shook the page, and chuckled. "That's one of your aliases."

I wasn't sure what pissed me off more; the fact that Roxanne was digging into my past like she didn't trust me, or all the lies these people had compiled about me.

"It should be illegal for these companies to do this kind of shit." I was really frustrated. "This shit isn't even about me; they've got all kinds of bullshit in here."

"Yeah, I feel you, but looks to me like you got a bigger problem on your hands," James said. "And I ain't talking about whoever this is claiming you're her baby's daddy either."

Later that afternoon, I was sitting in Smith's office across from his desk, waiting for him to wrap up a phone call. My mind was still spinning from the fact that my own damn wife was trying to dig into my past like I had lied to her or something.

This shit was really starting to mess me up. I was hoping Smith had some good news 'cause I needed it more than ever.

"Okay, well, thanks for that information. My client's here, so I need to run," Smith said, finally wrapping up his call.

I watched as he put the phone back onto its cradle.

"Sorry about that." His expression made me think the good news I was expecting probably wasn't gonna come my way.

I took a deep breath and said, "I'm trynta make it."

Smith sighed and leaned back in his large leather chair. His office was neat and clean, with cherrywood furniture and soft jazz playing in the background.

"I wanted to talk to you before we go back to court. There's some information you need to know," he began.

"Okay?"

"First, let me tell you a bit of history that may clear a few things up. There've been so many changes since welfare reform in 1996. Now, when the government accuses you of fathering a child, no matter how flimsy the evidence, in most states, you are only about one month away from having your life wrecked."

His bushy eyebrows went up. He must've been reacting to the look of confusion on my face. I wanted to ask what that had to do with me, but he started back up again before I could.

"Unfortunately, what this means is federal law gives a man thirty days to file a written challenge questioning paternity. If he doesn't, he is presumed guilty." He shrugged. "And once that steamroller of justice starts rolling, dozens of statutory lubricants help to make it extremely difficult, and very expensive to stop. In most cases, even if there's conclusive DNA proof that the man is not the child's father."

My heart started beating faster and I felt myself getting all worked up. Quite surely, he wasn't saying what I thought I was hearing.

"Are you trying to tell me that this DNA test won't mean shit?" I asked.

We had already talked about requesting the damn DNA test. I wanted to get the mess over with quickly and I thought, for certain, a DNA test was the best option. Since those tests were used to free convicted rapists and murders, quite surely a judge would free me from paying for a kid that wasn't mine.

Smith used his massive hands to gesture the need for calm. I was trying to maintain my composure, but the truth was, I had already given him a two-thousand dollar retainer, we'd wiped out our savings, and had borrowed to come up with half of the fifty thousand dollars that I didn't owe any damn body to get me out of jail! And now he was trying to tell me the one thing I had hung my hopes on could amount to absolutely nothing? I was stunned.

"I simply want to keep you informed all the way. I don't want any surprises. This thing could get real messy and it could go on for a while," he explained.

And I thought it would be as simple as taking a test and proving the kid wasn't mine. He was the expert, or at least he knew more than me about the law, but my gut feeling was telling me that no judge in his or her right mind would force me to pay for a kid if DNA proved the kid wasn't mine. I could appreciate him wanting to keep it real with me, so to speak, but I was ready to move forward.

"So what do we need to do? Does what you're saying change any of our plans?" I needed to know.

Smith said, "No, no, nothing changes; we'll still proceed the same way. As a matter of fact, I wanted to see when you wanted to get this test done."

"As soon as possible, so let's set it up. Then I want you to tell me more about how this automatic daddy bullshit works."

Smith flipped a folder open and started to explain the Federal law. "Here's how it works. When an accused 'obligor' fails, for whatever reason, to send his response on time, the court automatically issues a 'default judgment,' declaring him the legal father. It doesn't matter if he was on vacation, was confused or, as often happens, didn't even receive the summons, or if he simply treated the complaint's deadlines with the same lack of urgency people routinely exhibit toward jury duty summonses. He's now the dad; no ifs, ands, or buts about it."

"But what about the DNA test?" I asked, still trying to cling to a little hope. "I mean, this woman, she'll have to take the test and then we'll both go before the judge and she'll say I'm not the father and this thing will be cleared up, right?"

"I'm trying to prepare you for the possibilities, and anything is possible; that's all I'm saying," Smith countered.

I leaned forward in my chair. "Okay, and I appreciate that, I really do, but let's get this thing set up and, get the ball rolling."

ROXANNE

I wasn't in any particular hurry to rush home. My work day had come to an end, but I had a few things I needed to do at the office. On the top of my to-do list was contacting that lame-ass Internet company that had charged my credit card but never sent the information I'd paid for. It had already been nearly a month. I dialed the number and waited for someone to answer.

"Yes, my name is Roxanne Redman. I'm calling because I ordered a background check and you guys charged my credit card, but I have yet to receive the information," I hissed.

"Ah, ma'am, we can check that for you. Let's see here. Can I get your account number?"

"I don't have an account number."

"Hmmm, okay, well, what about the credit card you used? If I can get that number, I should be able to find out what happened," he said.

I rattled off my credit card number and listened as he tapped away on a keyboard. A few seconds later, he said, "Oh, okay yes, I see here Mrs. Redman, actually, that delivery was made five days later. We have a signature and everything."

Now I was confused. I didn't receive the package, so who the hell could've signed for it? I felt my cheeks getting flushed.

"Can you tell me who signed for the package?" I asked.

"Yes, ma'am, well, hold a sec," he said. Again, I could hear him tapping on the keys. "Yes. It says here a one, R. Redman, signed. Would the delivery time help by any chance?"

My heart was racing now. What if Parker...? Actually that's the only person it could've been.

"Let me check my notes here. The driver said your husband signed for the package. He noted you weren't home and he signed as the homeowner. From what I can see here, ma'am, we didn't have any instructions to ask for ID or stating that you were the only person who could sign for this."

I swallowed hard. Privacy had never been an issue with Parker and me. I'd never had to say don't open my mail. I'd never opened his so this added to the growing list of things that was starting to piss me off about Parker.

"Ma'am?" the guy called out to me.

"Oh, yes," I answered.

"Is there anything else I can help you with? Perhaps I can look up another account?"

"No, that's it. Thanks for your help." I quickly hung up. I sat at my desk, thinking about the best way I could approach this situation. Yes, Parker had violated my privacy. He had no business opening my mail. We've never been this way; never had a reason to be suspicious of each other.

What would I look like preaching about privacy when I was violating his in probably the worst way possible. On one hand, I had a right to know about his past, considering what we were going through. I had every right to know what he had done in the past, before me. But, on the other hand, I should've asked.

"Like hell," I said aloud. The reality was, ever since this shit struck our home, he'd been acting like I had no right to question him. Besides, what the hell was he hiding? I didn't really have time to ponder that thought before my cell rang.

It was Serena. I rolled my eyes and considered allowing voice-mail to get it, but then thought better of it. Another person's perspective might actually help.

"Hey, girl," I greeted her, hoping she wouldn't immediately go into her tirade about James, and how he was trying to fuck up her life. I wished she would figure out that everything didn't always have to be about her.

"Roxanne, you left work yet? Wanna meet for a drink? Where are you?"

"Actually, I'm still at work," I said. "But I could use a drink or two before going home to my problems."

"Let's meet at Pappadeaux, the one off 59, near the fountains."

"I can be there in thirty."

"The first round is on me," she said. And she actually sounded better than she had in a long time, cheerful almost.

"Then I'll be there in twenty," I joked.

I dashed through traffic like a madwoman. I was wired; I needed to hear someone who wouldn't tell me that I was being paranoid or looking for trouble where none existed. Something deep in my gut told me that Parker was hiding something; he wasn't divulging everything about this child support crap. I knew my husband. There was no way in the world he'd pay unless he had done something he didn't want me to know about.

Serena was holding court at the bar when I arrived, and that made me wonder if she had called me from the restaurant. As usual, the place was packed with a bustling after-work crowd. At least four men had Serena damn near surrounded. And I could see why. Serena was wearing a tight-fitting royal blue wrap shirt and a black skirt, with a pair of stilettos that were dangerously high. The shirt had all her goodies spilling out from the top and the black pencil skirt looked like it was dark denim.

"Okay, fellas, my girl is here," she said the moment she saw me walk up. I was hoping they'd get the message and leave. I didn't know the men and I didn't want them all in my business. She looked like she enjoyed being the center of attention.

I felt a little awkward sliding onto the barstool next to hers, I was dressed in a modest-looking gray pants suit with a tank under the jacket.

But by round two, I was in rare form. The liquor was kicking in and I didn't even try to fight it.

"Okay, so I go calling these people like a fool, with a bone to pick, only to be told he'd intercepted the doggone mail," I said.

Serena looked awestruck.

"Gurl, I thought I had problems with that loser ex of mine, but shit, this makes no damn sense at all!"

"I know, I know, and the sad part is, he never said shit about it. He never said, 'Hey, I got some mail and opened it by accident. I didn't realize it was yours.'"

Suddenly, Serena's finger was wagging. "*No*, of course he didn't say that shit. He understood exactly what he was doing. He was going behind your back. So here's what that tells me."

"What?"

"That his ass is probably lying about all this baby mama drama shit, too," Serena said with elevated eyebrows, like her simply *saying*, made it so.

I sighed and brought the glass up to my lips. I couldn't deny it. Serena had a damn good point. If he wasn't hiding anything, why wouldn't he mention anything about intercepting my letter?

"Think about it. He spent all the money you guys had, and wiped out your savings, paying for some damn kid he basically hid from you. It doesn't make sense. There's not an innocent man alive who wouldn't be fighting these charges like crazy." She sipped her drink again, and then stared me dead in my eyes. "Now ask yourself, why isn't *your* man fighting to hang on to his money? Hell, *your* money? Because he knows damn well who this woman is, and he knows damn well the kid is his. You realize what that means, right?"

I listened as she said everything that had been dominating my mind for weeks now.

"That means you'll have to help pay for *his* fucking mistake, a mistake you had nothing to do with. And get this, the state is just charging him now. Wait until whoever this heifer is finds out about your salary. Girl, then her ass will be dipping into your hard-earned money, too."

"Oh hell no!"

Serena smacked her lips. "You realize I'm well versed in this kind of foolishness, right?"

The horrific thought left me speechless. Serena had a point. That was something I never even considered. Of course this woman was out for money. And of course, when she figured out she could get more, I'd be working my ass off to pay for her little bastard child!

"What'er you gonna do?" Serena asked, eyeing me closely.

"I, ah, I don't know what to do," I admitted.

"Girl, you betta than me; that's for damn sure. I told you from day one, I woulda left his ass rotting right there in jail. Now, we all but know his ass is hiding something. Shit, I'd teach his ass a lesson," she said.

"I'm not about to be helping his ass pay for *his* damn mistake!"

I sipped my drink. "Especially since his ass hid it from me in the first place," I added.

"Well, girl, do what you gotta do then."

That's when I realized exactly what I had to do.

JAMES

"You've gotta be kidding me, dawg," I said, hardly believing what Parker was saying.

"She's gone; just like that!" he announced like it was the first time he was breaking the news. Roxanne had up and left him. I had told his ass she wasn't taking the shit all that well. I warned him that while he was trying to figure out what was going down with the baby mama drama shit, things at home seemed to be on shaky ground. But I had to admit, I didn't think it would go so far so fast.

"Damn, dawg, what happened?"

"We got into it, she started in on me about the damn letter from the website, one thing led to another, and then she started screaming and hollering about how she wasn't gonna pay for another woman's child. Next thing you know she was packing her shit!"

"Damn! Like that?"

"She also started talking about how no innocent man would pay for something he didn't do."

I could hear the frustration in his voice. But the next sound I heard made me drop the phone and rush into the front room.

"What the hell!"

Glass was everywhere. I stood in the doorway, stunned and unsure of what to do. I looked around, and that's when I noticed it; a brick had been thrown through my window.

"Serena's stupid ass," I mumbled. I rushed back to the room and picked up the phone.

"Damn! What happened?" Parker asked.

"You won't believe this shit!" I tried to remain calm. "Look, I need to call the cops. A brick flew through my window."

"Oh, Serena must've gotten the letter, huh?" he joked.

"She makes a brotha wanna…" I stopped short. "Lemme' get back at you later."

I dialed 9-1-1.

"Nine-one-one emergency. How may I help you?" the operator asked.

"Someone threw a brick through my front window," I said. I was only calling this shit in because I was determined to see Serena pay for something. I'd heard what Donald was saying, I even understood the law, but still, if I knew her crazy ass, this was bound to be only the beginning.

A few minutes after the call, officers were knocking at my door.

I spent a few minutes showing the officers around and answering their questions.

"Is there anyone who would want to hurt you?" one officer asked.

"I believe my ex-wife either did this or had someone do it."

I realized that after I'd signed those papers and they were sent off, the shit would hit the fan. I had told myself to get ready but, as usual, Serena was in rare form. As the officers and I stood outside, guess who pulled up, tires screeching and all. She damn near pulled onto my lawn and left the door wide open as she jumped out of the car. I believe it was still running.

"You fucking bastard!" she screamed, waving a piece of paper like the lunatic she was.

I jumped back, hoping the officers would witness an assault in the making.

"First, you try to stop paying for a place for us to live! Now you try and pull this shit!" she screamed.

"Ma'am?" One of the officers tried to intervene.

"NO, you don't understand!" She turned and pointed at the

officer. "This bastard is trying to disown his own fucking daughter so he can save a buck!"

"Serena, you need to calm down," I said.

"You son of a bitch! You want me to calm down? How about you stop being a fucking bitch and be the man you always talked about. I can understand you wanting me to pay, but this shit!" She waved the paper again. "This shit is low, even for scum like you!"

"Mrs. Carson, did you throw a brick through your ex-husband's window?" the other officer asked.

Serena's face contorted into a frown. "A brick?" she balked. "I wouldn't waste my time with a brick; that's small time," she admitted. "But if you think that's bad, just wait."

"Ma'am, we're gonna have to ask you..."

Serena turned on the officer and asked, "Have you ever been married?"

"Ma'am that's not the point," the officer said.

"All I'm saying is, this man is trying to ruin my life. First, he went after me, breaking into my house to watch me with another man, and then he stopped paying the fucking mortgage. Now the bastard won't pay child support! He's got to be stopped!"

"But this isn't the way to do it," the officer said. "You need to go before a judge. Otherwise he can press charges against you."

"You will not get away with this. S-E-M-A-J! That's your fucking name, my daughter, your daughter, she's named after you! You fucking bastard! You will not get away with this!" she screamed as she stormed off to her car.

"Wow!" an officer said after Serena peeled away in her car.

"You should really consider a restraining order," the other officer suggested.

"Yeah, I call her Serena the Sicko!"

Hours after the officers had left, I was giving Parker a play-by-play of what had gone down.

It felt good to hear my friend laughing again, and it didn't take long before he was back to clownin'.

Parker chuckled. "She did not tell the officers how her ghetto ass made up a name."

"It was deep, but listen. I needed someone else to witness the shit I go through with her. The sad part is, I'm actually scared of what the bitch is gonna do next."

"She burned rubber up outta there, man?"

"Tires screeching!"

"She ain't even wrapped a little tight," Parker joked.

I started laughing, too, until I heard tires screeching yet again.

"Oh shit, dawg! I think she's back."

"You better call for back up; tell 'em to send in SWAT! Seriously, don't fuck with her. She knows how to work the system. Your ass'll be six feet under, fucking with her, man."

I heard what Parker was saying, but I was curious about why she was back. The guys had just finished the window and I prayed she wasn't there to throw something else through it.

"I'll get back with you later," I said. This felt like déjà vu, but I dialed 9-1-1 and reported a crime in progress.

"You need to get officers back here. My ex-wife is back, and I don't want anybody to get hurt," I said as the pounding sound boomed throughout the place.

"What, Serena?" I yelled. "I've called the cops!"

She knocked again. This time, when I pulled the door open, Semaj was looking up at me with two suitcases at her feet. Before I could even react, Serena's stupid ass was back behind the wheel and once again peeling down the street and out of my neighborhood.

"I dunno why you don't love me anymore, Daddy, but Mommy said I had to come," Semaj said, sobbing.

LACHEZ

"Gina, I ain't got time for this shit! I don' already told your ass, I ain't giving you no more credit. Your shit been adding up. Now, I need to go. I got other things to do," I screamed through gritted teeth.

"Can I just...I mean, lemme hold a few, at least till I get my check," she begged.

I rolled my eyes, mad that I even had to deal with that kind of small-time change. Gina had been at my door for nearly thirty minutes, begging for credit so she could get a few smokes. I couldn't even think straight; I had the kids working the phones and this trick was working my nerves.

"Ma, my daddy said he ain't got no money right now," Junie came and told me while I was still arguing with whiny-ass Gina at the door.

I instantly slammed the door shut and spun around to face him. "Have you lost your gotdamn mind? Don't you see me talking to somebody at the front door? And you runnin' your mouth, puttin' our business all out in the fucking streets like you ain't got no damn home training?"

He jumped back a bit. I'm not sure what the hell he was thinking, but he must've lost his damn mind.

"Get your ass back there and see if Renzo came up on anything," I yelled.

He knew not to even try me. He turned and sulked down the hall.

I opened the door and threw two wrinkled cigarettes at Gina. "Don't bring your ass back here until you have my twenty."

She fell to the ground, scrambling to pick up the cigarettes before I could even close the door good.

I didn't know who was leading the pack when it came to working my nerves. Gina, Darlene, the kids, or these lame-ass men I was dealing with.

The moment Junie went into the back room, I snatched the phone and dialed Julius' cell number.

"Hello?" I said.

"Lachez, that you?"

I pulled the phone away from my ear and looked at it real good. I could hear Darlene's voice.

"What are you doing on my phone? I tried to call someone and it wasn't you."

"Well, I figured I'd call you; got tired of waiting on you to call me back. I wish you would let the kids come spend some time with me. It's summer, for God's sake, Lachez."

"Gon' with that ol' bullshit, Darlene. I'm not in the mood right now. 'Sides, I need to run."

"But wait—"

"But my ass! I got business to handle," I said.

"Lachez, I'm gonna set a date, and if you don't bring those babies to me, I'm coming to get 'em if I gotta walk myself."

"Like hell you will," I said.

Then, I hung up on her. It was easier that way; I wasn't in the mood to fight with Darlene. Once I made sure she was gone, I dialed Julius' number again.

When he answered, I lit into him. "What's this you telling Junie about not having any fucking money?"

"Well, hello to you, too, Lachez," he commented sarcastically.

"Look, I ain't got time for your damn games. You need to tell me when you bringing the money by," I said. I waited with one leg tapping. After a few awkward moments, he finally spoke.

"Lachez, I need a little more time," he insisted, like I was some kind of debt collector.

"You had time, huh?"

"Why you trippin'?" he asked, sucking his teeth.

"You want to see *trippin'?* How 'bout I go down to the attorney general's office and we can set this thing up the right way, Julius! How would you like that, huh?"

"See, there you go," he mumbled. "You act like I don't do right by you. I'm just saying, every time you put Junie up to calling, don't I come through? Now you threatening to get *the man* all up in our business and shit?" he hissed. "You ain't even right."

"You must think I'm stupid," I said, serving up much attitude.

"Nah, it ain't even like that, but check it, you think I'ma keep listening to your threats when I know damn well you ain't exactly walking on the right side of the law yourself? I ain't even saying I ain't paying. Check it, I'm saying, I need to get my money straight. Shit, I got other responsibilities, too."

I softened a bit, catching his drift. "Well, you need to bring something by."

"Now, Lachez, you know damn well if I drop by there to give you anything less than what you want, you'll start going off and shit! That's how you do!"

He had a point there, but he needed to understand exactly how broke I was. I didn't have time for what he thought woulda' happened; I needed some cash. And at this point, I figured anything was better than nothing at all. I was still no closer to collecting on the fifteen G's.

"Look, I understand things are tight, but if they tight for you, imagine how it is for me with these damn kids always needing and wanting shit."

"Damn! What you want me to do, Lachez?"

"How 'bout you bring some damn money up in this bitch! That's what I want you to do!"

"Give me a couple of hours," he muttered, after a few seconds of silence.

I hung up. I needed some air; this shit was starting to get the best of me and I was getting fed up.

As I walked to the mailbox, I started daydreaming about opening it up and finding that check for thousands of dollars. "Dayum, that would really solve all my problems," I grumbled as I grabbed the key and emptied the mailbox.

My heart nearly stopped when I saw a letter from the AG's Office. I closed my eyes and took a deep breath. Could my dream be coming true? Would they just send a check like that? In that amount? I was so damn excited, I couldn't wait to get back to the apartment to open the envelope.

As I strolled back, I ripped the envelope open, only to have my jaw drop to the ground. I stopped walking and started reading.

"A fucking DNA test! Oh, but hell no!" I screamed. This shit was getting way out of hand. I had no idea why I had to go through all this just to get the fucking money. She didn't say nothing about no damn DNA test! I was furious!

I rushed inside, dug up my counselor's card, and flipped it over to get her cell number. I didn't even give the bitch a chance to answer good.

"I just got a letter about a fucking DNA test! You didn't say shit about all that!"

"Look, calm down, okay!" Kelly yelled back at me. It was obvious she was in a bad mood, but what she didn't know was where hers may have been bad, mine was *real* fucked up.

"Calm down, my ass. You never said nothing about a damn DNA test!"

"Look, you're making far too much out of this. Just ignore it. What can they do?" she suggested easily.

She had a point there. If anyone knew the system, she damn sure did. Didn't she? Or maybe she needed to call her friend; one of them needed to fix this shit, that much I knew for sure.

"But what about the money?" I wanted to know, needing that more than ever.

"Just do what I tell you and you'll get the damn money," she snapped. I had to pull the phone away from my ear and inspect it. She musta' been losing her mind for sure. It had to be something in the water!

When I pulled the phone back to my ear, I was listening to the dial tone. That's when I started wondering if Kelly or that friend of hers even really knew what the hell they were doing. I decided to call the one person I knew would have answers.

"Toni girl, whassup?"

"Girl, some ol' shit, different day. What about you?"

"You know what, I'm trying to figure something out here. They catch up with your baby daddy yet?" I asked.

"Yeah girl, but now the bastard's trying to say the kid isn't his," she said.

"What?"

"Yeah girl, just another headache to add to my growing list." She sighed, then her other line rang, and she clicked over after telling me to hold on.

"I can't just ignore an order to have a DNA test, can I?" I asked myself aloud while I held the line for Toni to return.

That was the million dollar question, or in my case, at least the one that would make me thousands richer.

PARKER

Going home took on an entirely new meaning, knowing that I was going home to an empty house. It had been a few days and Roxanne still refused to talk to me. I wanted to give her an update on the mess of a case, but when she left, that in itself said she didn't really give a damn anymore.

It only took a few minutes to take my blood for the test. And I tried to wait for this mystery woman to show her face, but after six hours and she still didn't show, I had to rush to my office to talk to my H.R. director. I was pissed that I had to talk about borrowing against my 401-K, but I had to do what I had to do. I also took that opportunity to talk with her about the garnishment they had placed on my check.

"Diane, how does this work? You guys can take money out of my check without warning me?"

Diane was a pretty Hispanic lady who took her time to explain anything you needed. And this time was no exception.

"We have to follow federal law, which dictates that we must garnish wages when instructed to do so from any government agency. Unfortunately, that law doesn't allow us to give you the opportunity to challenge the order."

"But this is all a mistake," I said.

"Your case may very well be, but there are so many others, too many actually, where it's not a mistake. There are men who run from their responsibilities; women, too," she quickly added, as if I cared about political correctness.

I decided this was the wrong place to try and fight my case.

"You bring me a notice from a judge or the attorney general's office and, again by law, I'm required to remove the garnishment," she said. She turned to face me completely; her hazel eyes were sympathetic. "I have no reason to believe you are like so many other parents I've dealt with before. Usually a person who's guilty of this oftentimes has a financial life that's in complete shambles. Some men even quit and move on to other jobs when their orders catch up with them. Like I said, I don't want to get in your business, but keep in mind, I'm only doing my job."

"I understand."

We went on to discuss the real reason that I was in her office. She told me that she would try to expedite my request, but she wasn't sure about the additional penalty I'd have to pay. I told her it didn't matter, I needed the money as quickly as she could get it to me, and left.

Now, walking into the house, I wondered what had been going through Roxy's mind when she'd decided to pack up and leave me over some bullshit. As my mind went over the many things I would've said to get her to stay, the phone rang. I was hoping it would be James, but it was Smith instead.

My heart thudded. Why the hell was he calling?

"What's going on?"

"Well, I was notified that the young lady didn't show up for the DNA test," he said, a defeated sound taking over his voice.

I was worried about missing her after staying for six hours, but this news wasn't a huge surprise to me. But I didn't understand how she could skip the test, but they're taking money out of my damn check? This shit was enough to make me wanna take a gun to somebody's damn head.

"So what does this mean?" I asked, hoping he'd perk up a bit.

"Well, several things actually. First and foremost, we go back to court and ask the judge to see this as a clear and transparent attempt to strong arm you. Hopefully, she'll agree with what we're seeing and we can have this order removed and get this thing thrown out," Smith said. But even with that he sounded flat, completely unbelievable.

On the other hand, I had to look at the bright side. Could this thing really and truly be close to being over? What about all that stuff about missing the deadline?

"Well, I hope you're right. I won't get my hopes up, but how soon do you think we can get in front of the judge again?"

"With this woman failing to show up for the test, I'm hoping expeditiously. I'm also hoping the judge will call her to the carpet the same way she's done you."

"This is great news, after all," I said, hoping he'd follow suit.

He sighed as if he was carrying a heavy load. "Yes, well, let me get to work. I will contact the judge's clerk and make them aware of what's going on and try to push our agenda forward, which is to get in there as quickly as possible. I'll contact you as soon as I have a date set up."

"Thanks, I really appreciate all of your hard work on this," I said.

"Don't thank me just yet; we still have quite a hill to climb."

Even that gave me hope. Weeks earlier, I'd faced what seemed like Mt. Everest, with no clear cut way of getting over it, much less up it.

I felt myself rushing to hang up so I could tell Roxanne the wonderful news, and let her know that finally, an end was finally in sight. But just as quickly as I got excited, depression began to creep in. Roxy was gone. She had left because she had no faith, didn't believe in what I was telling her. But it was obvious now that I was right all along. This woman had to know we were hot on her trail, and she had something to hide. Otherwise, she would've been there with her kid to take the test.

I plucked a beer from the six-pack in the fridge and started off to find sports on the TV in the family room. I considered calling James to share my good news, but then I remembered all that he was dealing with, and figured maybe calling Serena instead and telling her about herself would help in some small way.

I eased back on the sofa and tried to relax. That's when my mind strayed to that fateful mistake I had made. I told myself there was no way in hell I could let it come out, not even now. I didn't want to, but thinking about it meant there was more than one dreaded phone call I needed to make.

ROXANNE

I nearly passed out when I noticed my home number pop up on the caller ID. Shit! How did his lying ass find out where I was? I was hoping he'd think I was at a hotel or something. I'd been doing well avoiding Parker's calls on my cell, but he'd figured out where I was. I sat, staring at the number. Serena had gone to the store, and I was glad she was gone. She'd swear I was being weak by even thinking about talking to him.

When the phone suddenly stopped ringing, I released a huge sigh. He needed to wonder about me, wonder about what I was up to, even though he had obviously discovered where I was hiding out.

My heart nearly left my chest when the phone rang again, startling me. I glanced over and confirmed it was Parker again.

I picked up the phone, took a deep breath, and as cheerfully as I could said, "Hello?"

There was silence at first. I wondered why he was hesitating. He had tracked me down, but I'd be dammed if I would make any concessions. This was his mess, one he had created, and I was not about to extend the olive branch.

"Hello?" I said again, getting ready to hang up.

"Uh, Roxy?" he asked, more than greeted, as if he was somewhat surprised to hear my voice. I wanted to ask who the hell was he expecting, after he'd obviously gone through the trouble of tracking me down, but I played it cool. I'd at least hear him out.

"Yes, it's me," I answered, struggling to remove the edge from my voice. My absence from home told him exactly where I stood. I told him I'd rather sleep at Motel 6 than next to his lying ass when I left.

"Oh, ah, how are you?" he asked, his voice sounding quite shaky.

I instantly started wondering if he was finally ready to come clean. He had to be tired of the bullshit and charade. I certainly was. I figured this was the call where he comes begging me back home.

"I've been better, but can't complain, I guess," I said.

"I've missed you," he told me using a voice just above a whisper. It was the tone that at one time used to make me so weak. Now, it had little, if any, effect at all.

"So, what's going on with your case?" I asked, cutting straight to the point. I didn't have time for any of his foolishness. I didn't need to be sweet-talked and I didn't need to be talking to him unless he had made some substantial kind of change.

"Oh, well, it finally looks like things are starting to make sense," he told me.

I wondered why he stopped talking. Quite surely, that statement deserved some explanation, but if he thought I was going to ask, he had another thing coming. My silence must've been a clue because he quickly started talking.

"This woman, the one who's accusing me of this, she never showed up for a DNA test," he said excitedly, as if that was sure to turn things around.

Again, my silence must've prompted him to continue. After another pause, he quickly asked, "You know what that means, right?"

"How would I? I've never been through anything like this before," I said.

"Well, what it means is that this may all be over real soon!" he exclaimed. Then he actually had the nerve to wait for my response or reaction. I wondered who had draped him with a judge's robe and authority in the short time I had been away from the house.

"So she didn't show up for a test, and this somehow means that you aren't the father? What did the judge have to say about all of this?" I asked in a tone that told him I wasn't the least bit impressed.

He sighed like he was exasperated.

"Look, Roxy, I'm trying here. I realize this isn't moving fast enough for you. Hell, it ain't moving fast enough for me, but you're taking this thing way too far; moving out and shit."

I felt myself getting heated, but I wanted to stay calm; I really didn't want to go off on him. To me, he was still no better off than he was the day he got arrested. Yeah, he was out of jail, but he still owed a crap load of money, and he was still fighting to prove that the kid wasn't his. It was almost like he'd gotten that news, rushed to call me, and wanted some kind of reward for his trouble. Well, his so-called good news didn't prove a damn thing to me.

"And it looks to me like I'm gonna stay out until you decide to come clean! I'm sick and tired of being the understanding wife who stands by her man!" I yelled, no longer able to contain my building frustration.

"You know, that's why I wasn't even gonna tell you anything," he said. His voice was laced with anger. "I was gonna wait until I had this shit all worked out. I kinda knew nothing would be enough for you. You act like I'm sitting here purposely trying to deceive you, like I'm in cahoots with another woman or something. I keep telling you that I have never met this woman before; I have no idea who she is. I ain't been with her, or anybody else who could claim I'm their baby's daddy, but you don't wanna hear that shit! You wanna keep beating a brother down. So if that's how you wanna do this, then cool with me. Like I said, I wasn't 'bout to say shit to you in the first place."

"Then why did you call? Sounds to me like you couldn't wait to hop on the horn and share your so-called *good news* with me."

"Did you ever stop to think maybe I wasn't calling for you?"

Fury began to creep up my veins. What the hell was that supposed to mean? If he wasn't calling Serena's house for me, then why the hell was he calling? It was no secret that there was no love lost between the two of them. Ever since James had filed for divorce, Parker had taken every opportunity he could to put her down, and talk about how she was worse than the scum on the bottom of his shoe.

The thought crossed my mind, but I figured his call had something to do with whatever the hell was going on with Serena and James.

"Well, if you weren't calling for me, who where you calling for?"

"You know what? I think I need to go 'cause you 'bout to make me haul off and say something I'm bound to regret," he said.

I sucked my teeth, but before I could even respond, the dial tone was singing in my ear.

"Oh no he didn't," I said, but it was obvious he did.

JAMES

It had been three days since Serena's stupid ass had dropped *her* child off at my front door without so much as a 'hi dog' to me. And surprisingly, shortly after that, her voicemail picked up as soon as I dialed her number. I was so tired of her, but more importantly, I had to figure out what to do about Semaj.

I called my attorney twice for advice but I was still waiting for him to get back with me. I looked into Semaj's face for the hundredth time, trying to figure out why no resemblance to me had never bothered me before. She didn't have my eyes, my nose, my mouth, or even my complexion. It all seemed to make sense now, but back then it had never even crossed my mind, much less bothered me.

"So, are we having pizza or hot wings?" She stood in front of me, waiting for an answer. For the first time, I noticed her mother's characteristics in her, and it scared me until the unbelievable truth slapped me in the face yet again. She was not my child, not my biological daughter, so when those characteristics developed into the real replica of her evil mother, I'd be long gone.

"Daddy!" she exclaimed, this time with a twist of her neck. It was slight, but after dealing with her crazy mother, I recognized the signs very well, even in infancy.

"Semaj, we need to talk, baby," I said softly.

She rolled her eyes and smacked her lips.

"Yeah, I know, but first we gotta get some food. We having pizza?"

Because I knew her so well, I understood she really wanted pizza and couldn't care less about the chicken wings, which was alright by me. I wish that I didn't have to tell a six-year-old that I wasn't her daddy.

"Okay, so you want pizza, don't you, Daddy?" She shrugged, waiting for me to answer, but something was preventing me from talking, from answering her simple question.

"Daaadeee," she stressed, throwing her hands on her tiny hips. "What's wrong with you?"

I didn't realize my eyes were wet with unshed tears until she said something about it.

"Why are you crying? You hurt yourself?" she asked. She'd dropped the bossy, grown lady act and looked genuinely concerned. Semaj walked toward me, and then said softly, "We could have the wings if you want to, Daddy."

I cracked a smile and looked at her. "Why don't we have both? We could get pizza and wings, together."

She looked at me skeptically, and then slowly shook her head like she wasn't sure if the offer was acceptable.

"Then you'll stop crying?" she asked sincerely.

I nodded.

"'Kay, then I want pepperoni, pineapple, and bacon, um, with extra cheese," she added excitedly.

"Okay, that sounds cool," I said, clearing my throat.

Unfortunately for me, after we ate, and watched a movie, I was in no mood to talk, certainly not in any mood to tell her she was not my child. I wondered if she'd even understand. I sat for a while, watching her sleep. Her eyes looked nothing like mine. I told myself that her mocha-colored skin came from her mother. Now I questioned everything from her heart-shaped face to her coarse grade of hair.

I swallowed a lump that had lodged in my throat and wondered why I had to be going through this bullshit. After sitting there for what seemed like forever, I decided to take my ass to bed. I'd have to deal with Semaj tomorrow. Once I got out of the shower, I was good and tired and ready to crash, but I figured I'd try Serena's ass one more time. So I did. I nearly lost my voice and courage, when on the second ring, I heard her answer.

"Hello?" she repeated, with enough attitude to let me know not to expect anything close to a pleasant conversation.

"Ah, Serena," I started as calm as possible. "Why did you drop your daughter off here?" I was still so mad I didn't know exactly what to say to her.

"Oh, so now she's just *my* daughter!" Serena snapped nastily.

"Serena, I know," I said.

"You know *what*? Shit! You ain't nothing but a lousy deadbeat-ass bastard. That now, all of a sudden you've decided you don't want to help support *your* daughter?"

It was obvious she wasn't about to make this easy, just like she did with everything else. There was no easy way to say this, but I needed to knock her ass down a notch. She was trippin' hard, like a woman who hadn't done a damn thing wrong.

"Look, I tried to take the high road here, but your ghetto ass—"

"My ghetto ass!" she screamed, cutting me off. "You got a whole helluva lot of nerve! If I'm ghetto, what the fuck are you, reneging on a promise to support your child?" She was breathing fire. The way she was yelling and carrying on, one would've thought she really had a leg to stand on.

"Serena!" I hollered, trying my best to shut her ass up. I looked toward my bedroom door. Then I lowered my voice and said, "Look, I don't want to tell her, but I will if you don't bring your ass back here tomorrow and pick her up."

"You threatening to tell our daughter something about me?" She chuckled. But I could tell she was really nervous.

"Serena, give it up," I said, really starting to get frustrated.

"Give it up? Give what up?"

"Serena, I know your secret. Semaj is not my biological child."

It felt strange saying it aloud again, and saying it to her. There was silence on the other end. I could hear the TV still playing in the background, so she hadn't hung up, but had I done the impossible? Had I rendered her speechless?

I waited a few seconds for her to say something, to deny what I knew, what the blood work had proven was true.

"Serena?"

She was there; I heard her breathing. Then, without any warning, she did something I would've never thought in a million years she'd do.

LACHEZ

In the days following the AG's letter notifying me about my need to have my baby tested, I had become a paranoid fool. Every little sound around the house made me jump. I felt like I was scared of my own damn shadow. I was checking the caller ID more than normal and I had held two family meetings with the kids, trying to make sure they weren't talking our business outside the damn house.

But the craziest of all things happened one day when I was walking to the mailbox. This couple was walking and they kept looking up at me like they were talking about me. It wasn't like I was dressed all wild or anything, but they kept staring at me, or at least I thought they were. After a few minutes, I went about my business, shrugging it off as my growing paranoia.

"Girl, you really 'bout losing your mind, huh?" I told myself as I snatched my mail, flipped through it, and rushed back to the apartment. Would the attorney general's office really send someone to spy on me? That didn't even make no damn sense. I shook it off and went to check on the kids. Money was still tight, even though Julius had brought a hundred dollars by the house a few days earlier. That little bit of change didn't even last long.

I always told myself going backward was a waste of time, but I didn't have the time or patience to slowly massage a new target. So against my better judgment, I decided to hook back up with Drew. Surprisingly, he was still cool, and it was still all good.

"Junie!" I screamed the moment I opened the door. They had shit all over my living room. The place looked like a typhoon had rushed through the place.

The three of them came marching out from the bedroom where I was certain they'd been playing that damn PlayStation. Nobody uttered a word. I stared them down for a few minutes, hoping they felt fear.

"Y'all think y'all got some kinda maid service around here?" My hands flew to my hips.

Junie rolled his eyes and I literally had to stop myself from smacking him upside his damn head. But I knew enough to recognize I was just pissed that none of my hustles were working out. Still, I wasn't quite ready to hit Drew up yet, so it was extra dry and the pressure was messing me up. I checked myself about taking it out on the kids.

"Get to work!" I screamed before heading to my bedroom. I needed to come up with something real quick like. I hated being broke more than anything else in the whole world. When I didn't have money, it was like the sun wasn't shining. It didn't matter if I was spending it or not; just having it, or knowing I had it, was enough to make me feel good. When I didn't have it, it was as if I was hitting rock bottom. I was a fiend for money like an addict craving for his next hit and to make matters worse, I had no idea when or where I'd be hitting the jackpot again. The shit was downright depressing.

Behind my bedroom door, I wondered what would happen if I didn't get my hands on some cash soon. The kids needed new tennis shoes; they were always growing like outta' control weeds. And my weave could stand to be tightened up, but shit, I at least needed some pocket change. For a while, I was pacing back and forth, wearing a serious trail in my carpet as I tossed ideas around in my head. I couldn't take that damn test, but there had to be another way for me to get that money.

"That kind of money would fix all my problems," I muttered. I didn't even know what so much in cash would look like. I'd never had anything close to that kind of money. Would it fit in a duffle bag? I could go someplace real fly and nice with that kind of money, and then come back and still have more to spend.

"Damn, I need that money," I hissed, rubbing my hands together. At this point, I was willing my right hand to itch. I couldn't believe we weren't even close to the end of the month and I had already blown through all my checks and couldn't get a lick to save my life. I really didn't want to mess things up with Drew this time around, so I wasn't even about to go there. Suddenly, I started thinking like a desperate woman.

"What's the worst that could happen with me not showing up for that DNA test?" I questioned aloud. "Shit, they'd throw my ass in jail," I answered myself.

Then suddenly something dawned on me. What would happen to the boys if I went to jail? Not like where would they be taken, but like, if I went to jail, who would bail me out? My eyes lit up and that all-elusive smile returned to my face. I'd finally come up with a plan that I was certain would work.

PARKER

I was fired up! I stood next to Smith, listening to this judge rattle off a bunch of bullshit and I swear, if I hadn't been hearing that shit with my own two ears, I would've accused the person telling me of lying.

"So, Mr. Smith, you're requesting that the wage garnishment be removed and your client be released from his obligations," the judge said snidely. "All because of what?" she questioned, using her hands to emphasize her words.

"Your Honor, the young lady didn't show up for the test," Smith said with some authority in his voice. "We'd like to submit this, her 'no show,' as evidence that this is nothing more than an attempt to extort money from Mr. Redman."

As he spoke, I looked into the judge's face and tried to see any signs that she might be willing to at least hear us out, but there were none there.

"I will send another order for DNA testing, but that's not the point," the judge said.

I was dumbfounded. And although I tried, I couldn't help myself. "Another order? What makes you think that's gonna do any good?"

"Mr. Smith, I suggest you control your client, before I hold him in contempt of court," she snarled, giving me the evil eye.

"Contempt of court? She gets to avoid a court order to take a DNA test and I'm being threatened with even more jail time?

Why don't you send someone out after her? They're taking money out my check, making me pay thousands of dollars, and I'm trying to tell you I didn't father her child and you won't even hear me out—" I was so pissed, my ears were burning.

Her gavel sounded and I started to say something else, but Smith touched my arm and started speaking.

"Your Honor, we're simply asking for the court's understanding here," he said softly, as if he was trying to reason with her.

I was beyond disgusted and my patience was getting the best of me. Here I thought this shit would surely be over once we saw the judge and now she was sitting there trying to do everything but the right thing. I dry rubbed my face and shook my head; this was fucking unbelievable.

"I will deal with her; you make sure you do what you're supposed to do." She looked at me with cold steel-like eyes.

"But, Your Honor," Smith whined.

My head started to spin as I tried once again to remember whether I even knew anyone by the name of my accuser. I didn't! Who was this woman? And how, and why did she zero in on me? I quickly zoned out of the court proceedings, which seemed to be heating up when the judge leaned forward to address my attorney.

There had been a few women, but I'd never slept with anyone whose name I didn't know. As picky as I was, I needed to know who to blame, when and if something went wrong. I wasn't the type to hit it and quit it. Even when women were throwing it at me, I'd had to dodge quite a few, but I'd never fucked simply to be fucking.

"Do I make myself clear?" I heard her cold voice ask Smith.

"Yes, Your Honor," he said.

"What is she talking about?" I whispered to Smith.

He all but ignored me. "When will your honor rule on the request to throw out the charges? We submit to you that my client is not the man you're looking for."

"Oh really?" the judge asked sarcastically. She leaned back in her chair. "Well, until he pays his outstanding debt, the court will not render a decision on anything remotely related to this case."

"But it's not me! I didn't do this! I don't even know this woman!" I yelled.

"One more time!" the judge warned. "One more word out of you and you're being remanded!"

I closed my eyes and shook my head. The rest of the hearing went on without me saying another word. What was the point? She had found a man to blame for walking out on her kid and she was determined that I pay. It didn't matter that the kid wasn't mine; it didn't matter that I didn't know this woman. I was responsible and she was nailing my black ass to the wall.

As Smith and I walked out of the court building and onto the busy downtown streets, I felt like a man beaten and defeated.

"What now?" I asked before he could speak. "You thought her not showing up would help our case, but it hasn't. Now what?"

The lost expression on his face made me feel even worse. He shook his head, and then looked me in the eyes. "So, you've never seen this woman before; her name doesn't even ring a bell?" he asked, almost as if he too found the thought unbelievable.

"No, doesn't ring a bell at all."

As we strolled to a nearby parking lot, I kept wracking my brain. Then suddenly it hit me. I didn't know this woman, but maybe that should change. Maybe it was about time that I hired someone to find this woman. I didn't understand why her personal information was blotted out on the paperwork, but it was. There had to be a way around that. I'd get someone to find her so that I could confront her my damn self. Then I'd ask her to her face, why she was under the impression that I had fathered her child.

I started to share my idea with Smith but thought better of it. I looked at Smith and forced a smile to my face.

"Well, I guess you'll contact me when you figure out what our next move should be."

I recognized the confusion on his face, but it didn't matter to me. "Yeah, that's what I'll do. You keep your head up. We'll get to the bottom of this. Okay?"

"Sure," I said, as I turned and walked away. All I could think about was what would happen the moment I came face to face with my so-called baby's mama.

ROXANNE

I didn't know quite what to do. Shit! I had my own problems. I was trying to deal with the issues with Parker but, instead, I was playing counselor to Serena. We were in her living room as she boo-hooed into her glass of wine.

"It's gonna be okay," I said. But it was kind of hard because she wouldn't come clean about exactly what was going on. It had been three days since I'd walked in to find the phone off the hook and Serena curled up in a fetal position crying her eyes out. I figured it had to have something to do with James, but she wasn't saying. Today, she was sitting on the couch but still crying just as hard.

"What happened?" I asked softly. It's not that I was trying to get all up in her business, but this was starting to work my nerves. I didn't leave my house of drama to come and deal with hers.

"It's James," she finally mumbled as if she wasn't sure she wanted to have this conversation with me. Serena kept crying and shaking her head. It was obvious she didn't want to tell me what was going on. I found this quite odd, since I didn't have to ask for *her* two cents when it came to Parker and all our drama. Her opinion was always readily available, regardless of whether I wanted it.

"James, is he okay? What's going on?" I asked.

Serena looked up at me, with an expression on her face that seemed like she thought she'd already said too much. She was trying to blink back tears. Her lips were trembling, but she wasn't saying anything. I wondered if this had something to do with why Semaj was gone. I figured maybe she'd lost custody or something; maybe that's why she had been all emotional over the last few days.

"Serena, I asked if James is okay. What's going on?" I repeated as sweetly as I could.

She looked like she was about to talk, and then suddenly she choked up and started crying again.

"You wouldn't even understand," she said in between sobs.

"Try me," I said.

Serena looked at me again, and then she said, "With your next to perfect life, I don't even see how you could possibly relate."

I frowned as she got up and walked to the back. I was awe-struck. If my life was so damn close to perfect, what the hell did she think I was doing there with her? All of my belongings were crammed into one of her guest bedrooms and she thought my life was near perfect? Did she not realize that Parker and I could hardly have a civil conversation? I started to go after her, and make her tell me exactly what the hell she'd meant by that comment, but after taking a few gulps of my own wine, I decided not to. If she wanted to stay holed up in her room crying and feeling sorry for herself, then who was I to judge? But from where I was sitting, Serena didn't have a damn thing to be crying about. Neither of her children were home, probably both with their fathers, and James had given her a more than fair settlement, plus child support after the divorce. I didn't understand the problem.

When I was alone, my thoughts still wandered to Parker and what was going on with his case. I wondered if he was ready to come clean and tell me what was really going on with this damn woman. I looked around the living room. Serena's place was still full of expensive furniture, pictures of the kids at the beach, Disneyland and Sea World. After a divorce, many women are left destitute, but she was still living lovely.

"She doesn't have a damn thing to cry about," I mumbled aloud.

There was a knock at the front door; that made me jump a bit. I looked toward the hall, wondering if Serena had even heard it.

When the knock came again, I got up, drained my glass, and walked to the door. I pulled it opened to find James and Semaj standing there.

"Roxanne?" he asked, looking like he'd seen a ghost.

"Hi," I said, ignoring his reaction to my presence. I figured it must've been him who told Parker I was there. Now he was trying to play it off, so for him to try and act like he didn't know was lame.

Semaj seemed just as upset as her mother.

"Is my mom home?" she asked as she rushed into the house.

"Yeah, she's in the room." I pointed toward the hall. James walked in and dropped Semaj's suitcase near the hallway. Then he turned to me and said, "So, I guess Serena told you that I'm not Semaj's biological father?" he threw out casually, as he walked past me.

The stunned look on my face must've answered his question.

"Oh, shit! I thought you knew. I, I actually thought that's why you were here. You know, to try and talk to her," he stammered.

While his news was shocking, I couldn't believe James was trying to play me. I shifted my weight to one side and looked at him real good.

"You thought I was here for Serena?" I asked.

"Why else would you be here?"

Suddenly, something dawned on me. If James didn't know I was staying with Serena, then maybe he didn't tell Parker, and Parker didn't know I was staying here. So why in the world was he calling Serena?

JAMES

Ever since I'd dropped Semaj off at her mama's, I'd felt like shit. I tried to call Serena to explain why I'd dropped her off, but Serena's stubborn ass wasn't talking. Once she hung up a few days ago, she hadn't been taking my calls either. I'd been back at work for several days now and I felt like everyone around the office was all up in my business. What kind of sucker is married to a woman and doesn't know she's fucking around? Then, as if that wasn't enough, she'd passed a kid off as mine when she knew damn well she was screwing someone else.

It didn't matter what I was doing, or where I was, the moment I stopped moving, I started thinking about Semaj and her stupid ass mama. Lord help that girl, with Serena as her mother. I also kept thinking back to the reason I took her home in the first place.

When my lawyer finally called back, he told me to take her back home right away. He had told me that everything was being worked out through the courts, and I needed to behave as if my obligations as Semaj's father no longer existed.

"She could haul off and accuse you of kidnapping her child! Take her home right now!" he had said.

I didn't think I'd be able to; I didn't think I'd have the heart to look Semaj in her eyes and tell her that I was not her father. But the minute I told her to pack her things, and she started to cry, I followed her into the room and dropped the bomb.

"Semaj, honey, there's something you need to know."

She stopped stuffing her clothes into the suitcase, and then turned to me. "What? That you don't love me anymore, Daddy?" When I didn't respond, she turned away and continued to toss her things back into the suitcase. "Mama told me you didn't want me anymore."

"Semaj, sometimes adults don't always tell the truth. They try, and most of the time they probably mean to, but sometimes they don't."

"But that's lying, and you and Mommy said lying isn't good," she said.

"Yes, I know, because lying hurts. It causes hurt and even a little white lie often causes more trouble than you can imagine."

"But I didn't lie about anything," she said, her eyes wide as she stared at me.

"No, it's not you; it's your mother. She told me that I was your father, and I'm not," I said softly. I could feel my eyes watering.

At first Semaj didn't say anything; she stared at me with those wide eyes and her tongue slightly pressing down on her bottom lip. That's what she did when something perplexed her. Her tiny eyebrows gathered into one and she tilted her head ever so slightly.

"Why are you lying, Daddy?" she asked with such seriousness that all I could think was, from the mouths of babes.

"I wish that it was a lie, but it's true. Honey, I took a test and it showed that I'm not your father, even though your mommy said I was." I didn't know what else to say. "So I have to take you back home and—" My voice cracked before it finally trailed off.

Semaj never uttered another word to me. Tears ran down her cheeks as she stuffed the rest of her clothes into the suitcase and walked to the front door, where she stood with her arms crossed at her chest. Even during the ride over to her mother's house, she never said anything to me. The next time she spoke was when Roxanne, of all people, answered her mother's front door.

That reminded me to do what I had started to do, before I started thinking about how things went down with Semaj and me. I picked up the phone and called Parker.

"Where you at?" he answered, sounding like he was out of breath.

"At the house. Why, where you at?"

"Oh, my bad. Your name just pops up; not your number. Look, I got some serious shit going on. I need to hook up with you. What you doing?"

"Nothing, dawg; dropped Semaj back at the house. Hey, why didn't you tell me Roxanne was staying with Serena?" I asked, still shocked by that.

"Man, I thought you knew. You didn't know?"

"Nah, I mean, when you said she moved out, you didn't tell me she was going over there."

"I thought she was going up the street to a hotel or something. But look, check this; that ain't even on my mind right now. You know, I went back to court, right?"

"Yeah, that's what's up. I was calling to see what that judge said 'bout ol' girl not showing up," I said.

"Man, that bitch is a ball buster. She didn't even care; didn't give a damn!" Parker said. I couldn't believe what he was saying. I felt bad for my boy, considering I could've been in a similar situation. The only difference between us was that he'd missed a deadline and I didn't.

"So where are you, dawg, and what's up? What ya'll gonna do next?"

"Well, I've got some pictures of my so called baby's mama, and I need you to see 'em, 'cause I know damn well I don't know this bitch. She ain't even my type."

"Whoa! Damn, dawg; you move fast."

"Yeah, I had to take matters into my own hands. It's time to try and figure out why this hood rat would point the finger at me when she knows damn well I ain't never touched her ass. I'm close to your side of town. Can I roll through?"

"Yeah, dawg, c'mon. I wanna see this broad."

"I'll be there in a few," he said.

LACHEZ

"My mama. The cops, they took her," Junie cried. He shrugged his shoulders, and started talking again. "The cops got her and we need money to get her back…" he cried, "…for bail."

I watched my son as he did exactly what we'd practiced. Mickey had already made two calls, and if all went well, this little performance should net us a few grand. I felt myself getting excited.

"If you bring the money, Auntie's gonna go and get her out," Junie said. His crying had let up a bit and that told me Julius' cheap ass was asking too many damn questions. I shook my head and sucked my teeth as I listened to the one-sided conversation.

"Nine hundred," Junie said, as clear as day.

I squinted my eyes at him. I told his ass to ask for seven. This boy of mine; I didn't know what to say about him.

"Yeah, uh-huh." He nodded his head, like Julius could actually see him. "You want me to tell her to call you?" he asked. He played with the cord, and then switched ears. "Um, okay, I'll tell her to call you."

It was taking everything in me not to snatch the phone and tell Julius about his cheap behind. But if I did that, he'd obviously know my ass wasn't in jail, and that would cause a serious problem.

"Okay, Pops," Junie said. He looked like he was about to hang up, and then hesitated to answer another question. "Yeah, we cool," Junie said. "We straight. They in the back; I'm trying not to let them know what's going on."

Junie's eyes looked up at me for the first time since he'd fallen into the zone. I knew he'd be able to handle Julius, but I had to be honest, I wasn't expecting it to be this difficult.

Within seconds, Junie was off the phone and jumping into his explanation. He was talking a mile a minute, which let me know he was probably making shit up as he went along.

"I know you told me to ask for seven, but I figured if he'd agree to seven, we could get nine," he quickly said. "I know he's got a grip, 'cause he told me he was expecting some money."

I pursed my lips and glared at him. His ass was always second guessing me, and I was getting tired of it. If I didn't need to know what all Julius had said, I woulda smacked his hardheaded behind.

"What he say?" I snapped, cutting straight to the chase.

"Um, he wants me to call Auntie Toni. He wants her to call him. He said it didn't make sense to drop off that kind of money to some kids," Junie said.

Ain't no way in the world I wanted Toni in on this. Her ass would be trying to hit me up for a fee. And it was obvious Junie was already expecting his own damn cut, asking for nine when I said seven. I wasn't about to split my money up like a cake everyone should have.

I didn't like this shit with Julius. Everyone else offered to drop off some cash; no questions asked. When we got to Julius, he had three million questions. I sucked my teeth.

"What to do, Ma?" Junie asked, breaking my train of thought.

I spun on him and said, "Next time, your lil' narrow-ass behind better do what the hell I tell you. I told you to ask for seven. I didn't say take it upon yourself to up the ante," I said firmly.

His eyes grew big as he stood, staring up at me. I couldn't stand when he altered the damn plan. If he'd stuck to the plan, Julius might have agreed to give up seven, but knowing his cheap ass, nine was too close to a grand for him. I knew how Julius' warped mind worked.

"Sorry, Ma," Junie finally said softly. He cast his stare downward and lowered his head.

Careful thought and planning had gone into this; now his little ass may have blown it. I couldn't stand how my son was always looking out for himself when I was trying to bring money into our house.

I had intentionally crafted each dollar amount to the person we were targeting. Both of Mickey's daddies were hit up for five hundred each. Neither tripped when the call was made; they agreed to drop the cash off the very next day. In addition to Julius, I had Junie call Kevin; my newest. His nose was wide open, so he didn't hesitate to offer up a whole grand. He was dropping his money off tomorrow evening. I didn't want to lean on Drew, because we were still trying to patch things back up after the whole abortion situation.

I paced the living room, wondering if I could afford to go without Julius' contribution. Sometimes I told myself he wasn't even worth the hassle.

"Remove yourself from my sight," I said to Junie, who was standing there shaking like a damp leaf. He took off toward the room to join his brothers. "And don't think you getting that two hundred if Julius does come through!" I yelled.

He didn't even break stride. He was just glad to be out of striking range.

I needed some air. I figured a walk to the mailbox might help me clear my thoughts, and I could decide what to do about Julius. I wasn't about to bring Toni in on it; no way I was paying her shit.

When I rounded the corner, I noticed a white van parked across the street. At first, I didn't pay it no mind; it was just another vehicle on the street. But when I glanced up at it, I thought I saw someone duck back behind the door panel, as if they'd been caught. I played it off by looking away to open the mailbox.

I pulled the mail out and didn't even bother getting excited about the letter I noticed from the courts.

What now? I wondered. I was no longer naive enough to think they were sending me a check, but what I read in the letter was enough to make me run back to the apartment, and quickly call up my counselor. Now this shit had really gotten out of hand. I got her voicemail.

When the phone rang so quickly after I hung up, I thought it was my counselor calling back, but, of course it was Darlene. She always picked the absolute worst possible time to call and fuck with me.

"Hey, I was hoping I'd catch you," she said, the moment I picked up the phone.

Before I started in on why I couldn't talk, she began.

"I don't know what you don' got yourself into this time, but somebody's looking for you," she said.

I didn't know whether to trust what she was saying. Knowing Darlene, she was simply trying to keep me on the phone.

I rolled my eyes but took the bait.

"How would you know someone was looking for me, and what do you mean you don't know what I don' got into?"

"Some man came by here asking all these questions about you and the kids. I'm not sure what's going on, but Lachez, whatever you're doing, you better stop!"

"Look, Darlene, don't you think it's a little too late for this mother role you tryna play? I mean seriously, I can handle mines. And why would someone come looking for me way out there? That don't make any sense."

This was exactly why I didn't like talking to Darlene. She was so dramatic, so negative, and of course, never passed on a chance to try and bring me down.

"You should let my grandbabies come here for a couple a weeks, at least until you work this thing out."

"Work what out? What are you even talking about, Darlene? What man is looking for me? You're talking in riddles and I really ain't got time," I said.

"Lachez, I'm trying to tell you, you need to get your life together. If you don't care nothing about yourself, at least care about your kids."

"Blah, blah, blah, Darlene, you know what, the next time some man comes looking for me at *your* place, tell his sucka' ass I said unless he got some money for me, he need to go *look* for some other chick, 'cause I ain't got nothing for him!"

She sighed, like it was all she could do to make me understand what she was saying. But before she could make another plea, I hung up and unplugged the phone.

PARKER

A few days later, we sat across from each other, brews on the table, and pictures of this woman scattered across the table.

"She a white chick, dawg?" James asked.

He was just making it over since we last talked about the pictures. He and Serena had gotten into it that night he was supposed to be on his way.

"Yup, but that's besides the point, man. You know I don't go for the ghetto fabulous type at all; I don't care if she was purple, she ain't my type."

James examined a few of the pictures closely. There were some where her hair was long and flowing and she was dressed up. Other pictures showed her with short hair. She wasn't bad looking, not by a long shot; she just wasn't my type. The flashy jewelry, the extra long fingernails, and the 'round-the-way-girl type of outfits.

"I wouldn't be caught dead with a chick like this," I said, looking at one of the many pictures. "I wonder why, or how, she even chose me. I've never seen her a day in my life."

James looked like he was meditating on the damn picture. I was hoping it would've jogged his memory, that maybe he could tell me if he'd seen her before or maybe after seeing her face could connect it to her name.

"Tall, thin, but she curvy for a white girl," James said, almost like he was getting off or something.

James shrugged his shoulders. He picked up another picture and glanced at it like he was lusting.

"How many kids she got?" he asked, an eyebrow lifted.

"What you asking me for?" I shot back at him. I reached over and tried to see the picture he was looking at. "I've seen pictures of her with three kids, but they could be a neighbor's kid, she could be baby sitting, or who knows; maybe all of hers aren't even in these pictures."

"She may not be your type, but I'd fuck her."

"Man, who *wouldn't* you fuck?" I joked.

He picked up another picture. He turned it a few times and examined it from various angles. "Yeah, I'd fuck her real good," James added.

"Well, maybe *you're* her baby's daddy, 'cause I sure in hell am not!"

James shook his head. "Nah, you don't forget a piece of ass like this. I mean, look at her; I bet she's a screamer, too. You think she likes back door action?"

I frowned at him.

"Man, I don't care if she takes it up the ass or not, I just wanna know why the hell she's lying on me."

"All women lie," James said as he tossed the pictures onto the table and kicked up his legs, crossing them at the ankles on top of one of the nearby chairs. "You believe that bitch Serena won't even face me? She won't even try to defend what she did," he said, taking another swig from his brew.

"How in the hell could she defend what she did? Think about it, what explanation under the sun would you be willing to accept? Oh, James, honey, I knew we were married, but the dude who was hitting it before you wouldn't stop so I just, we just kept doing it. And when I got knocked up, I had no idea who the daddy was, so I stuck it on you?" I looked at him. "Would that have done the trick?"

"Nah, dawg, *that* woulda caught me a case. Seriously, I don't believe in laying hands on women, you know this, but I woulda probably lost it, listening to some bullshit like that. If that cat was hitting it all along, why did she even agree to marry me?" James shrugged.

"Who knows why they do the shit they do?"

We drank and eased back for a while. I wondered what Roxy was up to. I still hadn't gotten over the fact that she was sitting up with Serena, of all people. I didn't even want my mind to venture there.

"People have died over less," James suddenly said, leaving me a bit confused. "I mean, think about what the hell she did. People have killed for far less," he continued.

I wasn't sure if he was talking about my situation or his own. Certainly, both cases were ripe for a crime of passion or temporary insanity plea.

"You talking about me, or you?" I asked for clarification.

James tilted his head, as if he was pondering the weight of my question. "You know what, dawg, both them bitches, both of 'em, could be dead for what they've done to us! I mean, for real. Serena's stupid ass, and this chick right here." He picked up a picture for good measure. "Yeah, both those broads could be six feet under for fucking with a man's life like that."

"I feel you," I agreed. Although murder was a bit drastic for my case, I could definitely see why James would want to strangle Serena's ass.

"It's a good thing you found out when you did though," I said. "You could be like me. Just because I missed a damn deadline, these fools are trying to say I'm the daddy just *because*; like daddy by default!"

"In America, too, dawg," James added.

"You know, I wouldn't kill her, not right away anyhow, but I damn sure would like to know why she chose me."

"How'd you find her?" James asked.

"Oh, I hired someone to find her ass."

His eyes got wide. "You hired? Like a private investigator?" he asked like he couldn't believe it.

"Yeah, man. I'm like, this judge needs to be *shown*, she ain't taking nothing less. So I hired his ass and it only took him a few days to get the information I needed." I slapped my palms together. "Just like that!"

"So, you know where she lives?"

"Yeah, not only do I know, but shit, I've already been there. You see the pictures, don't you?"

"What?" James frowned. "Where she stay?"

"Bitch lives on the North Side, Guns Point," I said, referring to one of Houston's most notorious neighborhoods. The Greens Point area was once riddled with high crime and constant shoot-outs, hence its nickname: Guns Point.

James leaned in and looked me dead in the eyes. "Well, why did you roll out there alone?"

I'll admit, it probably wasn't the smartest thing to do but I just wanted to catch her off guard. I'd been over there enough times hoping to catch her, but so far I'd been missing her. A couple of times I thought I heard her kids, but they didn't answer the door.

"I'm going over there again, but I really am scared of what I might do when I finally come face to face with her. I wanna ask her what the hell she was thinking when she reported me as the father of her child."

"Sometimes you gotta take shit into your own hands. Dawg, the courts don't give a damn about us!"

"You know what," I said. "I'm so mad at this broad, ain't no telling what I might do!"

"Okay, dawg, I need to come with you 'cause I'm not sure whose life I'll be saving, yours or hers, but you'd better believe I'll be packing when we venture over there to Guns Point," James joked.

ROXANNE

I was nowhere near prepared for yet another move, but that's exactly what I found myself doing. This time, I was checking into my new home at the Marriott off Highway 59 near Sugar Land. I walked into the butterscotch-colored room and dropped my bags near the bed.

"Well, looks like this is gonna be home for a while," I said aloud as I kicked off my shoes and looked around the room. The setting seemed serene and I was so tired, I wanted nothing less than a steaming hot shower and a good night's sleep.

Between the drama at home and the drama at Serena's, I was about on the edge. I pulled silk pajamas out of my bag and made my way into the large bathroom with my toiletries bag.

I pushed thoughts of my estranged husband from my mind and tried to convince myself that I could wash my problems away beneath a strong and powerful showerhead. Even though I realized it wasn't that easy, the thought brought a slight smile to my face.

"And what the hell'd I ever do to Serena's bitter, evil ass?" I asked my reflection in the mirror as I stripped down for my shower.

"Nothing, that's what. I've never done a thing to her; except try to be a friend." I turned on the shower.

Steam began to invade the space in the bathroom, and when I stepped in, my mind instantly went to the strange argument that had landed me in a hotel.

Semaj had knocked on her mother's bedroom door until I thought her knuckles would bleed. I felt sorry for the child, so I finally went there to try and pull her away. But she fell to her knees and cried until Serena finally opened the door.

Serena looked at me, and then down at her daughter. Surprisingly to me, she stepped over Semaj and strutted to the living room.

"Will you cut the theatrics," she tossed over her shoulder. I stood there unsure of what to say or do. I didn't want to be all up in the girl's business, because Serena had made it clear she didn't want to share.

I walked out to the living room, where Serena was puffing away on a cigarette. I tried not to balk because this was, after all, her house, but smoking?

"Serena, you wanna tell me what's going on?"

Serena took another drag, or three, from her cigarette before she even acknowledged that I had said something, much less to her. She sat there blowing smoke circles damn near in my face.

"What do you mean, do I wanna tell you what's going on? What are you now, my mother?" she asked nastily, after a long and uncomfortable silence.

I was taken aback. Serena sucked in more nicotine, and I felt my cheeks getting warm. This wasn't even about me; I wanted to tell her that her ex had already dished the dirt. And what a dirty mess it was.

Semaj came stumbling into the living room; she found a corner of the sofa and curled herself up in it.

"Um, Serena, I was just asking, thinking maybe you needed someone to talk to. James, when he brought Semaj back, he assumed that you had already told me, well, you know about." I turned toward Semaj. I couldn't bring myself to repeat what James had said.

"So now you're judging me?" She frowned. "Oh, I see, your perfect little life is so far above reproach that you're now looking down your high and mighty nose at me?"

She smoked that first cigarette completely to the butt, and then she lit up another one, much to my horror.

My hands flew to my hips and I frowned, still eyeballing her.

"What the hell is that supposed to mean?" I asked, throwing back some of the attitude I was getting from her.

"You know, you and Parker both, you think you're better than me? Y'all sitting up there with your little perfect lives, looking down at James and me; especially Parker's wannabe WASP ass. He doesn't talk to certain kinds of women, he's so holier than thou, but he ain't shit, just like the rest of them sorry-ass clowns who go out there, get an education and a good paying job, and then they wanna act like they mamas ain't never had their lights cut off or stood in line for free cheese," she snarled.

"Where the hell is all of this coming from?" I asked. I couldn't believe her, or how this had suddenly turned into an attack against Parker and me. She couldn't be serious.

"So your ex tells me some shocking news, and somehow I am standing in judgment of you because I wondered if you needed someone to talk to? I wanna get this straight," I said.

Smoke from her mouth danced upward toward her head. She sat there giving me the most evil of all evil stares.

"And if you felt this way about me, about us, why did you open your home to me? Why did you act like you cared?"

Serena leaned forward. "Look, I deal with people like you and their problems every damn day. I have to admit, I needed to see firsthand that your shit ain't all you make it out to be. You act like that damn Parker is so perfect, but looks to me like he's like all the rest of 'em—" she began before I cut her off.

"So all along you've been sitting here gawking at me and Parker and all this stuff we've been going through?"

She dismissed me with the wave of a hand, and shook her head, like I was the one who was pathetic.

"You're so fucking clueless," she snapped.

I was floored! I needed to get away from her, and get away quick.

"How else was I supposed to stay on top of what was going on inside your fairytale world, princess?" she asked sarcastically.

I started to slap that cigarette from between her lips, but remembered her daughter was in the room. I headed toward the back, packed my shit and rushed up out of there.

"You don't know me! Judge me all you want! You don't know shit about me!" I heard her screaming as I made my way out to the driveway. She sounded like a madwoman who had finally lost it. I had no idea why she had suddenly turned on me.

As I drove away from her house, I thought about exactly what she'd said. Serena was right. I didn't know her; didn't know her at all.

And little did I know then, I'd learn exactly how much of a stranger she really was to me.

JAMES

From time to time, I would dream about Serena, think about what would've happened if she was a civil person, and how she'd try to explain away what the blood work had proven. I still couldn't believe she had no plans of even addressing what she had done.

Most men would be thrilled that they didn't have to make that payment every month, but it was kind of like mixed emotions for me. Even though the tests proved Semaj was not my biological daughter, I still wanted the best for her; I still wanted her to be taken care of. Day in and day out my mind would stray to mistakes I'd made during our marriage. It's funny when I was married and trying to play by the rules, I was like a chick magnet. Parker and I would go out and we were like rock stars. It didn't even matter when we flashed our wedding bands; they seemed to attract women even more.

Looking around my empty place now, I felt so alone. It never really bothered me before, but the shit was starting to get to me. I thought about calling Parker, but that wasn't the kind of company I wanted. With no beer in the house, I decided to make a quick run, and then I'd figure out what to do with myself. It was a week night, but could've been a weekend; I felt like doing more than sitting around talking about our women and the problems in our lives. I quickly nixed thoughts of calling Parker. I'd been spending lots of time on maddaddies.com, too, and it wasn't doing anything but fucking with my head. The stories were more and more unbelievable.

I needed a change of pace or this thing with Serena was about to swallow me whole.

The moment I turned the ignition in my SUV, I heard a commercial for gentleman's club on the North Side.

"Shiiit, those were the days," I reminisced with a massive grin. I remembered when Parker and I would hit 'em all up, having a good time. Well it used to be a good time, until Parker started ragging on the sistahs so hard, he took the fun out of tits and ass, if that's possible.

"You know what, I'll swing by and see what's jumping at one of those spots. Shit, why not?"

I jumped on 45 and headed north. The DJ was talking about a special going on at Harlem Knights 2000.

"I think that's out there on Jensen Road," I mumbled as I headed toward the club. I figured that's just what I needed. "Miami Tuesdays, huh?" I repeated as I pulled into the parking lot.

When I stepped into the lobby, I turned to the right and there was an ATM machine. I pulled out my wallet and grabbed five twenties from the machine. The music was pumping the moment I strolled down the long hall. When I turned into the main room, I looked around, with lights and a blue décor, a girl was working the stage, but nothing to really get me excited. I looked around; the place even had a gift shop, pool tables, and of course, a V-I-P section.

When the dancer came to the edge of the stage, I looked at her and nodded slightly. A waitress stopped at my table.

"Table dances are only five dollars tonight," she said. "What can I get you to drink?"

"Crown and Coke," I said.

She smiled and left, her hips swinging as she walked away. It didn't take long for the place to get crowded. I glanced up in the mirror to see the dancer leaned back on her elbows; she was balancing herself on her behind as she spread her thighs, and gyrated her hips to the music. A dude wearing a cheap-looking business suit and glasses rushed to the edge of the stage and started showering her with money. On the other end of the stage another woman was working the crowd. A line had formed. I figured they were there trying to see her up close. The dancer bent over and spread her cheeks for a thugged-out-looking brother who stuffed her g-string with cash. I eased back into my seat, with drink in hand, and enjoyed the show until a cinnamon-colored beauty strolled by my table.

"You want a table dance?" she asked sweetly. Her face looked innocent, but her body was lethal.

"Sure, why not," I said. By this time, I was on drink number three, and feeling real nice.

"What's your name?"

"Honey." She smiled.

For the rest of the night, Honey was more like my private dancer, and when it was closing time, at five in the morning, she looked at me and cooed, "I could go home with you if you'd like."

I considered her offer and figured what the hell. I felt like I'd been holed up inside that club for days, instead of hours, when I walked out into daylight. I needed to call in to work, to let them know that I wouldn't be in.

As I waited for Honey, I made the call and tried to figure out where we should go for breakfast.

Over breakfast, Honey told me she'd been dancing for five years and was getting tired of it. She was attractive, with short, curly hair, almond-shaped eyes and heart-shaped lips.

I purposely withheld information about myself, not sure if this was gonna be a one-night stand or what. She, on the other hand, couldn't stop talking about herself, which was fine with me.

Around nine, I paid our bill and took Honey back to my place. Things moved at lightning speed once I closed the front door.

"Where's your bathroom?" she asked.

Seconds later, when she walked out of the bathroom, she was completely naked. She strutted over to the sofa and sat across from me. Honey wasn't shy about showing off everything she had. I looked at her longingly for a while and then motioned for her to come and sit next to me. I ran my hand across her breasts. Honey squeezed her eyes shut and looked like she was preparing herself for more. I took her breasts, touched them, held them, squeezed them, and ravished them with force.

I slid my tongue slowly around her beautiful dark circles, coming close but not quite touching her nipples. As if her reflexes had taken over, Honey's legs spread. She moaned her approval, then reached out and slowly began to massage my hardening length with one hand.

She continued to stroke my erection. I stopped, pulled back a bit to look at her face. Inches from it, Honey appeared even more beautiful than she had at any point since we'd met.

I wondered if Honey could be the change of pace I needed.

LACHEZ

When I heard the knock at the front door, I got excited. Everyone had dropped off their loot except Julius' cheap behind. But finally, I thought, he had come around. It took a little creative thinking, but I was able to keep Toni's ass out of my business and Julius still agreed to bring the cash. I jumped up, and rushed to the back to call Junie.

"There's a knock at the door. C'mon, your daddy's here to drop off the money," I whispered. I was excited and scared at the same time; I wanted everything to go well.

Junie's eyes grew wide, and a grin stretched across his face. I pulled him by his T-shirt before he could rush back up front.

"I'ma go into my bedroom. Remember what we discussed. You tell him your Auntie Toni went to the store and she'll be back; hopefully he won't want to stay and wait for her. Get the money and come back here and give it to me before you let him leave," I ordered. "You understand me?" I needed to check the cash, along with Junie and Julius if necessary.

He nodded, but still I was worried. Junie had a habit of changing up the plan at the last minute.

"Junie, don't fuck with me, and don't fuck up my money. Do exactly what I tell you, you understand?" I warned with a pointed finger.

"Yeah, Ma!" he yelled, and then rushed up front.

I stepped into my room and listened with the door slightly open.

The knock came again.

"Okay, here I come!" Junie yelled as he rushed to the door. When he opened it, I expected to hear Julius' voice, but I didn't. I couldn't go out there, but I stood in a fog, wondering what the hell was going on.

"Um, she ain't here," I heard Junie say, but then there was silence.

I felt myself boiling. I'd told the boy exactly what to say and what to do. Why hadn't he invited Julius in? He was supposed to get him in the house, get the money, and then bring it to me. Instead, he was telling him that Toni wasn't there. I'd distinctly told the boy to tell Julius that Toni had gone to the store.

I couldn't go outside, but all kinds of thoughts were racing through my mind.

"My mama ain't here and I'm old enough to be here with them," I heard Junie cry. "I don't even know you, man!" he said, and that's what made me rush up out of the room.

I was so glad I came out when I did. What I saw was enough to throw me off the deep end. Some dude was standing in my living room; Junie and his brothers were looking up at him like they'd literally seen their lives flash before their eyes.

"What the hell is going on here? And who the fuck are you?"

Dude was over six feet tall, with a muscular build and he looked way too polished to be standing in my damn house. I didn't date no man who thought he was prettier than me. This one had his nails painted, and his hair and face perfectly lined up.

"Who the fuck are you and what are you doing in my house, harassing my kids?" I asked again.

"Mama, he said he was looking for you," Junie said, his voice still shaking with fear.

I reached out to Junie and motioned for him to step behind me.

I turned back to the stranger in my house. "Now who the hell did you say you were?" I asked, really running out of patience with him. I had taught my kids how to swing a bat so I wasn't worried about anything going down. If it came down to it, the two oldest would get his kneecaps, I'd dig his eyes out, and my baby would bite him to the bone.

"You don't know me?" he asked, pointing at his fucking chest like that was supposed to help ring a bell.

My face was all twisted when I answered.

"No, I don't know who the fuck you are, and why you up in here trynta' bully my kids is beyond me!"

That fool was holding a folder and when I told him that I had no idea who he was, he pulled a picture from it.

"This is you, right?" He stood, waving the picture in my face.

I looked at it but didn't answer right away.

"Yeah, this is you, isn't it?" he asked again.

"So what if it is."

"And you're saying you don't know me, right?" he asked again.

"Look, I don't care what you pull out of that damn folder of yours! I don't know you, ain't never laid eyes on you, and if you don't get up outta here, I'm calling the law!"

"Oh, call 'em. That's what I want you to do. Call the fucking law and tell them I'm here and I refuse to leave until you tell me why the hell you would report me as being one of your babies' daddies!"

My mouth hit the floor.

"OHMYGOD!" I said, before I could control myself. I started backing up. Then I remembered the boys were still standing here. I turned to Junie.

"Take your brothers to the room," I ordered. He stood frozen for a second. I squinted my eyes and looked at him. "I said, take your brothers to the back!" This time, he scrambled to get out of my way.

"Okay, now wait a minute here," I said to the stranger, who was fuming mad. I didn't like the fire I saw burning in his eyes.

"No, *you* wait a fucking moment here!" he yelled and moved closer to me.

My heart was racing. I felt warm with an unusual kind of fear. What the fuck to do?

"You need to chill," I said, backing up.

"No, your ass need to chill, because if you don't call the law, you need to call somebody! You've ruined my fucking life, lady, and I want to know why!" he hollered.

Just when I didn't think things could get any worse, another voice startled me nearly to death.

"What the fuck is going on here?" Both the stranger and I turned to Julius, who was standing in the doorway, a scowl on his face and his fists clenched at his sides.

PARKER

The shit just gets stranger and stranger. I was at home now, unable to fathom what was going on in my life. No one was answering the phone, not Smith, not Roxanne, not even Serena so I could ask her where Roxanne was. I needed to talk and outside of James who had to run off, I couldn't find anyone to listen.

I finally gave up, grabbed a glass, a fifth of Henny, and eased back to have a drink. This could not be my fucking life. When James quickly dropped me off, I tried to go by Serena's but neither she nor Roxy answered the door. It was as if everyone had vanished! I had been calling Smith all along and that bastard wasn't answering either.

After my first drink, I thought back to the chaos that had almost broken out at that chick's apartment, especially when that dude showed up.

"What the fuck is going on here?" his voice boomed behind me. I turned to see dude mad-mugging me.

"Um, Julius, ah, I can explain," Lachez suddenly stammered. She rushed toward the doorway, trying to calm the brother down.

His beady eyes shifted from her to me. He nodded slightly in my direction. "Who's this chump?"

My beef wasn't with him, and I was prepared to let that be known, but I wasn't about to be too many more of his *chumps*.

"Ah, he was just leaving," Lachez said nervously, touching dude on his chest.

I didn't know what was going on with the two of them, but I wasn't about to leave until I had stated my case. "This your woman?" I asked dude.

"Who wants to know?" he asked suspiciously, as he stepped closer to me.

"Look, my beef ain't with you and—"

"I asked who wants to know," he repeated, cutting me off.

"Julius, don't be starting no shit up in here. You know Junie good for calling the law; I don't want no problems. I told you; he was about to leave," she said, and then turned to me like I was supposed to jump because she had spoken.

"I'm her baby's daddy," I said, staring straight in her eyes.

The horror on her face told me that I had said something she really didn't expect. Dude's face twisted into a frown, I braced myself for whatever he was about to deliver, but instead his rage suddenly turned to her.

That's when James walked up.

"What's going on, dawg?" he asked. James looked at dude, then back at me as if he was just waiting on the word to make a move. But I wasn't there for that kind of drama.

I motioned toward dude and Lachez.

"What? Your baby's daddy?" the man asked Lachez.

Now it was Lachez's turn to experience fear. She stumbled back, holding her hands up in surrender. "I swear, just listen, I swear, I can explain," she offered.

"Who's this fool? This another Johnny situation?" Dude asked.

Her head started shaking, "Now, why you gotta go there? I'm trying to explain but you need to calm down," she said to him.

I seized the moment and started talking directly to dude, man to man.

"Look, man, I'm not sure what's up with y'all, but your girl here is tripping for real. She's basically extorting money out of my ass and I wanna know why?"

He looked at me, then back at Lachez.

"I thought you said this wasn't another Johnny situation," he said through gritted teeth.

James stood by watching it all go down.

Her green eyes grew wide and she started shaking her head. Her lips were trembling and, for the first time since I'd laid eyes on her, she seemed scared. The tough girl act was a thing of the past.

"I swear it's not. Just hear me out?" she begged.

"I'm tired of your lies and shit, Lachez. How are you hitting him up for money?" he asked.

That's when I spoke up.

"Man, I was arrested one day, told I owe something like fifty grand in back child support, thrown in jail, and now they want to take money out my paychecks. The only problem is, I don't have any damn kids. Then the judge tells this one…" I motioned toward Lachez. "…to show up for a DNA test and she's a no-show, so I started looking into this shit myself."

"Whoa! Hold up a sec," Dude said. He looked at Lachez. "You trynta tell me she hitting you up for child support, too?"

Now he had me interested.

"Did I tell you they want to garnish my paycheck?" I tossed in.

"That's fucked up, Lachez; that's real foul. So you got ol' boy here thinking he your kid's father, me thinking the same, and you trynta tell me this ain't the same ol' Johnny bullshit?" he yelled.

Dude looked like he was about to try and kill her with his bare hands. I stepped in. "Okay, man, look, she ain't worth it. What's the story with this Johnny guy?"

Dude looked at me. "This bitch had some clown, Johnny, thinking he fathered her kids, milking that man dry; only problem was she had me and two other suckas thinking the same damn thing. Johnny beat her ass so good, she was in the hospital for a week!"

I turned to Lachez; I was certain my eyebrows were touching my hairline. "Wwwhat?"

"Yeah, that's her hustle, man. That's how she gets down, it's how she makes her money; just like she put the kids up to calling me for money, talking 'bout her ass was in jail and needed bail."

Just when I thought I had heard it all.

✪ ✪ ✪

The vibration in my pocket brought me back from the nightmare at Lachez's apartment. My cell was ringing. I wondered who was calling at this time of night, but then I remembered I had been trying to track down a bunch of folks. I fell asleep after zoning out on that new website James had turned me on to. I wasn't brave enough to put my story on maddaddies.com yet, but at least I knew I wasn't alone, going through this kind of madness.

"This is Parker," I answered.

"May I speak to Brian?" a female voice asked.

"Brian? I think you have the wrong number," I said.

"Oh, I'm sorry," she said and hung up.

I yawned, got up and went to my bed. The next morning, I was up and working the phones. I told Smith what I had learned the day before and, for the first time, he sounded excited. The next words out of his mouth were music to my ears.

"I'm gonna try and get an emergency hearing with the judge. In light of this, she has to do something."

I sat there, thinking, *I sure in the hell hope he's right.* I called in to work, took care of a few files from home, and sat near the phone waiting for Smith's call.

ROXANNE

When I unlocked the front door, I was shocked to see Parker sitting at the kitchen table. He turned when the alarm sounded.

"Oh, I wasn't expecting you to be here in the middle of a work day," I said, trying to strip my voice of the accusation.

He got up and walked toward me.

"Yeah, I'm working from home today," he said easily.

"Well, I just came to get some of my things," I said. I wanted to comment on his appearance. He didn't look bad, but different. I wondered how things were going for him. Some of the things Serena had said were still playing out in my mind. I wondered if he had any idea what Serena thought of us.

"Look, I know you don't want to hear about this anymore, but so much has happened since the last time we talked, Roxy."

The pleading in his voice made my heart soft. I was still upset with him, but after all the shit Serena had tossed my way, I wondered if maybe I was being too hard on him.

Parker shook his head, as if he didn't even want to waste his time trying to explain. The hopeless look on his face made me feel kind of bad.

"What happened?" I asked quietly. I was genuinely interested.

His eyes lit up. Parker looked at me and then he rushed to the kitchen. "It's all in here," he offered, beckoning me to follow him.

When I made it to the kitchen and looked at all of the pictures and papers scattered across the table, I was speechless.

"What the hell is all of this?" I asked, pulling my eyes away from the display on the table.

"That's what I've been trying to tell you. It's all a scam, this whole thing, it's a scam. This woman…" He picked up the picture, and extended it toward me. "She's a lowlife hustler. Roxy, I told you I didn't have any kids. I swore to you that I was telling the truth and I was. This is the proof right here. I showed up at her place and one of her boyfriends told me that's her thing, that's what she does, it's how she makes money."

I couldn't believe what I was hearing. What woman, what mother would do some shit like that? I started looking at the pictures, and flipping through the notes. Soon, I could feel my eyes getting all misty. I swallowed a huge lump in my throat.

"Oh my God…" I started to speak.

Parker moved in closer to me. "I was trying to tell you all along. I didn't lie, see, she just picked me. I still don't know exactly what all is going on, but I've got Smith on it now and he's trying to get the judge to see us in a hurry."

I was speechless. I felt like shit. I had no faith in him; I was so busy thinking he was just what Serena said all men were. I had unfairly lumped him into the same sad and pathetic category she had placed all men in, despite what I knew to be true. I couldn't even look him in the eyes. I felt so ashamed.

"You mean to tell me this woman just picked you and decided to hit you up for child support?"

He shrugged. "Yeah, basically."

"Wow!"

I was wondering what must've been going through his mind at that very moment. I didn't know how he even could stand to look at me. I was so disgusted with myself that I wanted to cry.

I sat at the table, dumbfounded by what Parker had told me.

He chronicled the entire sordid story from the day he hired the private investigator to the day he had shown up at this woman's front door.

"Weren't you scared? Anything could've happened," I said.

"I had nothing else to lose," Parker admitted, shrugging his shoulders. "Nothing at all. You had left me, we were nearly broke, and the judge didn't seem to give a damn."

My heart sank when he said he had nothing else to lose. I had foolishly walked out on him. I had allowed Serena to give me advice when her situation was even more messed up than mine. And I like a fool, had listened to her, actually taken her lame advice, and had walked out on my husband.

I looked up at Parker. This time, I didn't even attempt to stop the tears that were threatening to run down my cheeks.

"I am so sorry," I cried. "I should've listened to you. Instead, I immediately thought the worst," I admitted.

"It's okay; I understand. Look, we were already going through a lot when this shit came up. Think about it, we'd miscarried for the third time, I was in jail, and you didn't know *what* to believe. I understand," Parker said. He opened his arms; I got up and walked over to him.

"I'm so sorry." I sobbed. "I really am."

Parker took me into his arms, held me tightly and rubbed my back.

"I've missed you so much, Roxy," he whispered in my ear. After a long and passionate kiss, I pulled back from him.

"Did she say why she picked you? I mean, I know she does this for a living, but why you specifically?"

"She said it was all her counselor and the counselor's friend."

Parker looked at me and I looked at him. I didn't know if he could read my mind, but he wouldn't have to.

"Her counselor?"

"Yeah." Parker nodded. "Strange, I know."

"I didn't get the chance to tell you about the fight I had with Serena. The reason I left her place," I told him, sitting on his lap.

Frown lines quickly covered his forehead.

"You know Serena used to be a counselor; too bad we can't see if she knows this woman's counselor," I said. "What's the counselor's name?"

"Kelly Johnson," he said.

"Well, no point in wasting time and energy with Serena; you know there's no way in hell she'd be willing to help me out!"

"Oh, Parker, OHMYGOD! You're probably right, you would not believe, how she's been jealous of us all along," I said. He looked shocked. "I know, think how I felt when she finally confronted me. We should find out more about who this *counselor* is that this woman's been working with, even if Serena won't lift a finger to help."

JAMES

Honey had just left when the phone rang. We promised to hook back up again and I put her in a taxicab. Parker had been trying to reach me, but I was busy. I was sure he'd understand once I shared all the details with him.

"Hey, dawg, what's going on?" I greeted when I finally returned his call.

"Man, I've been trying to find your ass close to forever," Parker said.

"Dude, I know, I know, but I hooked up with this chick from Harlem Knights—"

"What?" Parker yelled. "Look, we can talk about that later, but for now, Roxy and I need to see you. We need to discuss some important shit. We can come to you or you can come to us."

"I'll be there in about twenty," I said. "Damn, this sounds serious. You talk to that girl again?"

"Yeah, man, and you won't believe what she and Roxy just told me. C'mon through; we'll talk when you get here."

My mind was racing when I jumped into my ride and rushed over to Parker's. He and Roxanne were back together again? And what could that chick have possibly told him that had something to do with Roxanne? The shit was strange to me. I had been floating on cloud nine until he called with his news. I couldn't get over there fast enough.

When I walked through Parker's door, Roxanne was in the kitchen looking at pictures I assumed were of the Baker woman.

"Man," Parker greeted me. "What's up?"

"Shit, you tell me."

"Hey, James," Roxanne said, looking up from the table.

"Wasn't Serena a counselor at one time?" Parker asked.

"Um, some kind of family crisis something or another. I don't know what her exact title was, but I know she used to work in an office where they helped women get money, child support, disability checks, if their kids got that ADHD, you know stuff like that," I said. "But that was years ago."

Roxanne and Parker were looking at each other like they were sharing a secret.

"If she used to work in one of those offices, she might know what we could do. We need some kind of inside help. Think about it; you said yourself there was no other connection between you and this woman," Roxanne said to Parker.

"What's going on?" I asked, tired of being in the dark.

When Parker told me his story, and then Roxanne told me about the fight she'd had with Serena, I didn't want to burst their bubble and tell them I didn't think Serena would be willing to help, but I knew they had already figured as much.

"What you think?" Parker wanted to know.

I shook my head and looked at my friend. I felt bad for him, felt bad about what had gone down with Serena and Roxanne. Especially after all the misery they'd been experiencing over the last couple of months.

"So ya'll are serious about trying to go to *her* for help? Especially after what happened with the two of you?" I asked Roxanne.

She shrugged. "We know it's a long shot, but we're desperate. We can't find any connection between Parker and this woman and since Serena used to be a counselor, or worked in that setting, I don't know. What do you think?"

"Hmmm, I don't know. But she said you and Parker thought you were better than her?" I asked, still trying to swallow all they'd said.

"Yup." Roxanne nodded.

"Man, I realized that she had issues, but I would've never thought she would've told you how she really felt. Damn, this is deep," I admitted. "It never dawned on me that she was jealous. But it all makes sense now, there were times when she wanted to know where you two were going on vacation, what you bought Roxanne for birthdays and anniversary gifts, and shit like that, but I chalked that up to you women being gossipy."

"Well, apparently it was a whole lot more than that," Roxanne tossed in.

I felt bad for Parker and Roxanne. It was one thing to have Serena pull the kind of shit she'd done on me, but to confront our friends like that? I couldn't believe it. I also knew deep down inside if she couldn't stand them, and hated me, hell would have to freeze over twice before she tried to offer up any kind of helpful advice or information.

I looked at Parker. "Well, let's try to get to the bottom of this shit with North Side girl first. I'm not sure about going to see Serena for help, especially after what Roxanne said. Man, life is getting crazier by the minute."

I wanted to help Parker clear his name.

"Maybe we could try to appeal to Serena, just ask if she has any connections that could help us clear this mess up," Roxanne suggested. "She has to still know a counselor or two."

"You think that evil bitch is gonna do anything to help anybody?" Parker asked.

"Well, if you're asking me, after that tongue lashing I took from her unstable behind, I'd have to say no," Roxanne said. "But what do we have to lose?"

As if answering her own question, Roxanne shook her head, then said, "What am I thinking? Going to Serena will be like wasting precious time."

I didn't think she was the answer either.

"I say we head to the North Side," I said.

"Well, fine, let's lean on Lachez, I'm about ready for this madness to be over. I'm tired of being treated like I'm some deadbeat ass father or the stereotypical black man."

"I feel you," I said. "And I agree with Roxanne. Trying to get help from Serena would be a waste of time."

Parker's phone rang.

"Yeah," he said.

"Right now?" He looked at Roxanne, his eyebrows shot upward. "Nah, that's cool, that's cool. I can be there by three-thirty." When he hung up the phone, he looked at me and his wife, and then said, "That was Smith. He got us an emergency hearing. We're gonna see the judge today, at three-thirty."

LACHEZ

Ididn't feel good about going to court, but I didn't really
have a choice. The last thing I wanted to do was go before
some fucking judge and be hassled about who my babies'
daddies were.

But that asshole made it very clear he'd be back with the law if
I didn't show. Now Julius was demanding a DNA test, talking
about he ain't dropping another dime until he had proof Junie
came from his seed. I wished people would learn to mind their own
damn business. My shit was going good until muthafuckas started
poking their noses in my business. My head was still spinning
from the drama when my phone rang. Needless to say, I was sure
it wouldn't be my so-called counselor; I'd left her a message, telling
her ol' boy had shown up at my front door and she hadn't called
back yet.

"Hello?"

"Lachez, this is Parker Redman. My lawyer called and said we've
got an emergency meeting with the judge. Do you need a ride?"

I rolled my eyes at his arrogant ass. He thought because I lived
in the hood, I didn't have a fucking vehicle? I was current on
my payments, and ain't had to hide my ride in a while. Where he
get off, judging me? Just like Darlene's simple ass always under-
estimating me.

"Just tell me where to be and what time," I snapped at him. He
had his fucking nerves. I tried to tell his ass, it wasn't like I had

received a red dime of his money. I didn't take well to men, much less some man I didn't know trying to control me. This Parker Redman needed to ask somebody. He just showed up outta' nowhere, throwing salt all in my shit?

"Look, Lachez, I don't want no crap out of you, you hear me? Not only will I have your ass thrown in jail, but I'll slap your with such a massive civil lawsuit, you'll be making payments to me until your youngest is grown," he hissed.

"Damn, I said I'd be there; now all that other shit is totally uncalled for. You ain't gotta be threatening no damn body!" I screamed.

"I'm not threatening you; I'm just letting you know how crucial it is that you show up. That's all I'm saying," he claimed. He had obviously checked himself, because his voice softened up a bit. But still, I wasn't the one to fuck with and he needed to know.

"I said, I'd be there; you need to tell me where to go and when to show up," I said.

He was working my last damn nerve. He had already fucked up my hustle. I hated to see that money walk out the door, but Julius had made himself clear and he wasn't playing.

Later that afternoon, I stood in front of a judge who, to my surprise, was reaming Parker and not me. He had the nerve to show up with his big-time attorney, both of 'em looking down their noses at me. I started feeling a whole helluva lot better after listening to this judge going off.

"I have told both you and your client, Mr. Smith, the court does not have time to entertain every little thought or idea you come up with. I don't see why this couldn't wait until our scheduled court date."

I turned to look at Parker and his lawyer. I guessed the woman sitting behind him must've been his wife, with her Plain Jane looking behind.

"Your Honor, if it would please the court, we'd like to get to this right away. We found and brought Ms. Lachez Baker, who is prepared to testify that Parker is not the father of any of her three children or responsible for their welfare. She will also testify to the fact that she was approached by her counselor and specifically asked to implicate my client in this scheme to extort money. That's all this is," Smith said.

The judge leaned forward. "I told you both last time, the court's concern lies with the children. This case is not about who slept with whom; it's about the fact that your client ignored several notices indicating that he had a deadline to respond or resume financial responsibility for the child or children in question."

Parker's lawyer shook his head. "Your Honor, are you telling me that despite the fact that this woman is prepared to confirm that he didn't father her child, you are still holding my client responsible?"

"This isn't about who is being coerced into admitting or saying anything. This is about the fact that your client neglected the multiple notices that were sent to him, giving him the opportunity to challenge or deny paternity; he did not." She picked up her gavel and banged it twice, and then looked up and said, "Now that's the ruling of this court. Mr. Redman is to pay fourteen hundred and five dollars a month in child support. Is that clear?"

My eyes got wide. Who was he gonna pay that kind of money to? This shit was far more interesting than I'd expected. Finally, I was glad I showed up after all.

"What?" Parker screamed.

"Mr. Smith, your client, you'd better get him under control. There will be no outbursts in this courtroom," the judge warned.

Parker was no longer the calm, cool, and collected man who had shown up at my front door. Now he was standing there, a vein throbbing at his temples and sweat forming on his forehead. His clothes were all drenched and it didn't seem like things were going his way. From the way the judge was reading him and his lawyer the riot act, I could tell I had no business even showing up, but I did have to admit the drama was irresistible.

But soon she turned on me. I wasn't prepared for her line of questioning.

"Young lady, do you know who fathered your child?"

"Um, no, ma'am, I don't," I answered truthfully. The woman sitting close to Parker gasped. I didn't really give a damn what she or any of these people thought of me.

The judge looked back at the lawyer and Parker. "So Mr. Redman could very well be her child's father," she said, and then shook her head. "But that's all beside the point. The point is, he blatantly ignored all summons from this court, and only came forward to challenge them when he was forced to pay." She looked at me and then back at them. "My order stands."

"What kind of shit is this? Is this America?" I heard Parker scream.

"You're trying me, Mr. Redman," she warned easily at first.

But it was Parker's attorney who kept things going.

"That to me is modern feminism. Women are completely disconnected from any responsibility for their actions, immersed in feelings of victimhood, and empowered to use the power of the state to exact financial and emotional ruin on men, men they don't even know. Your honor, I object!" he yelled.

The judge gave a warning glance, and then calmly said, "Mr. Smith, you are very close to upsetting this court. I'm warning you; you are on the very edge."

"You're warning me? After you all but just gave this woman a free pass to unlimited cash, you think I'm the one who needs to be warned here," Smith continued. "There is no way these types of laws are constitutional. Our government is not allowed to steal money from people without due process."

"Your client blew off his due process just like so many other arrogant men. Now if I have to tell you again, my order stands, I will hold you in contempt of court!" she yelled back.

Parker then shouted, "I never received any notice! I told you that, but you didn't want to listen. What happens if she sent it to the wrong address? What if I never even lived at that address? You mean to tell me, she and other hustlers like her can just grab a name out of the sky, plaster an address, and boom! The sorry bastard is required to pay? The notice doesn't even have to reach me? They just have to send it to the last known address, or any address, for that fact?"

"Bailiff, please take both Mr. Smith and his client into custody. Gentlemen, you are both in contempt of court!"

The lady broke down crying. I watched with my mouth hung wide as both Parker and his lawyer were arrested and escorted off to jail. I didn't wait around for the judge to say another word to me. I scrambled up outta there as quickly as I could, hoping I'd be able to escape before she turned on me.

PARKER

Two days after the courtroom melee, for the second time, I walked up out of jail. I was really beginning to feel like a criminal. This time when I was released, I still felt like a defeated man. I believe the judge had purposely arranged for Smith and me to be released at different times. He was gone by the time I left.

Roxanne was waiting the moment I walked out. I was so mad, I hardly wanted to speak. My anger wasn't geared toward her, but she was there, both she and James, so I figured she understood what I was going through.

"I wouldn't have believed this if you were telling me what happened in court the other day," she began without as much as a greeting.

"I can't believe it myself and I'm the one going through this shit!"

She eased the car onto the road. "What are we going to do?"

I was at least relieved that she was once again including herself in matters related to me and this mess. But the sad truth was, I didn't have an answer for her. Shit, I didn't know myself. I just knew for certain that the judge would side with us once she saw Lachez, but it was as if she wasn't moved at all.

"Why did that woman say she didn't know who her kid's father was?"

I shrugged. I'd been replaying this mess in my mind over and over again all the while I was locked up. None of it made sense. Why did the judge agree to the emergency hearing if she had no intention of changing her mind? What if Lachez had said for sure that I wasn't the kid's father? Would that have really made a difference?

As if she was reading my mind, Roxy softly said, "It seems to me nothing would have changed that judge's mind. It's almost like they found someone who can pay and that's all that matters. She said this is about missing a deadline, so she doesn't even care about the facts of the case. And then for her to say a child shouldn't have to suffer because of the mistakes adults make?" Roxy balked. She shook her head. "I don't understand."

"I tried to tell you all along what I was up against. I tried to tell you that these people, these courts, they're not interested in the truth. They just want someone to pay!"

"Man, that's so obviously clear to me now." She slowed for a light, and then turned to me when she stopped. Roxy reached for my hand and said, "I'm so sorry; I didn't mean to add to the problems you're having. I couldn't see beyond my own selfish thoughts. I am really, really sorry."

For the first time in weeks, I actually felt better. I smiled at her. "Hey, I understand; I really do."

We drove home in silence for the rest of the ride, again, my mind racing with thoughts of how I could undo this mess. When we pulled up to our house, James was in the driveway. When he saw me, he jumped out of his truck.

"You alright, dawg?" he asked.

"As well as can be expected, man," I said.

We all went inside where Roxy poured the three of us a drink.

For a while, it seemed like everyone was lost in their own thoughts. James looked up and said, "We've gotta take this to her job, dawg.

It's the only way. After what I witnessed in that courtroom, I can't think of any other way for you to get out of this bullshit."

I looked at him with hopeful eyes. At that point, I was willing to try anything. I had become a desperate man, one who was clean out of options.

"So we go to her job and say what?" I asked.

"We threaten them to fix this. First, I think we need to confront this counselor, and make sure she's the one working with this girl. Then we get her to admit what she's done," he offered.

"Do you really think it's gonna be that easy?"

"That's why we need to talk to her. Maybe we should go drop in on your friend Lachez first. If we get her to give up the counselor, then we confront her with proof, evidence we'll take to her job if she doesn't do the right thing," James said.

"It might just work," Roxy chimed in. "What other options do we have at this point? That judge..." She shook her head. "It'll take a whole lot to get her to even consider something other than forcing you to pay."

I placed my glass on the coffee table. It was time to take some action. Sitting there hoping for the best, or hoping Lachez would do the right thing on her own, were not options.

"Okay, so first we go to Lachez. She's simple enough to pressure. I get the feeling she's got quite a few hustles working and, if need be, we'll threaten to turn her in to police or the government. I'm sure they'd be interested in knowing about her side incomes," I said.

"Yeah, then once we get her on tape, we go to the counselor and confront her," James added.

I nodded. This had to work. I was getting tired and I was afraid of what might happen once I got tired of being tired.

ROXANNE

I didn't know what to expect when we decided to go over to that woman's apartment. For Parker's sake, I hoped that she'd do the right thing but, I had to admit, I wasn't the least bit optimistic. She could've done more in court, but once she realized she would be getting some money, she no longer gave a damn about doing the right thing.

As the three of us pulled into an OfficeMax parking lot, I thought about what had happened after court. James and I had spotted her trying to run up out of there, but I stopped her. She was as disgraceful as she looked. I'm not saying there was a proper attire to wear to court, especially when you're not the one involved in the hearing, but this woman had the gall to show up in a skintight cat suit. She was wearing a pair of knee-high boots with an extra large knock-off Gucci bag. She was a sight to behold.

"Lachez!" I yelled. She was at the elevators, pressing the button like she was trying to escape. She turned and saw James and me headed for her, and she started slapping the button even harder.

"Why didn't you say more in there?" I asked.

She frowned, looked at me, and then James. "Say more? What the hell for? I ain't trynta get all caught up in a bunch of drama."

"You're already caught up," I said. "The day you decided to single out my husband for your little get-rich scheme."

She sucked her teeth at me. "Get rich? Bitch, I ain't received a dime from your buster-ass husband. If you don't like what the judge said, go take that up with her, not me!" She twisted her head to emphasize her words and smacked the button again.

"But you know he's not the father of your children," I said, attempting to reason with her. "Why didn't you tell the judge he wasn't?"

"Look, you were in there just like me, I know you ain't stupid; that judge ain't trynta hear shit. Besides, is it my fault your man and his lawyer couldn't keep their mouths shut?" She shrugged one shoulder. "If the state of Texas wants to give me free money each and every month, who am I to say no?" Her seductively arched eyebrows went up.

"So you don't care about what impact this has on his family?"

"Again…" She smacked her lips and rolled her eyes. "Why the fuck are you out here blaming me? Looks to me like you need to go holla at that judge. She the one making all the rules; I'm just trynta play by 'em," she said as the elevator dinged and a door opened. It was packed, but Lachez squeezed herself inside and offered James and me a three-finger wave before the doors closed.

✪ ✪ ✪

"Roxy?" Parker was snapping his fingers in my face. "You wanna join us?"

I shook my head. This shit was getting the best of me, too. "Oh, I'm sorry, baby. I've got a lot on my mind. I hope this works."

"I have a good feeling about it," Parker admitted as we piled out of James' truck.

"We gotta go get one of those mini voice recorders; then it's on our way to the north side."

I didn't want to be Debbie Downer, but I wondered, what made them so sure this girl was gonna act right or even do right?

After my brief encounter with her, I had no reason to believe she would care about anyone's plight other than her own. And considering there was money involved, I really had a feeling we were gonna leave her place disappointed.

But I figured I'd just follow the fellas' lead on this one.

JAMES

Parker knocked on the door while Roxanne and I stood off to the side. I wasn't sure if Lachez would even open it, but she shocked us all.

"Hey, short-timer," she said, smiling until she realized he wasn't alone. She glanced at Roxanne and then at me. "Oh, I see the whole gang is here." She laughed. "Now what the hell do y'all want?"

"Mind if we come in?" Parker asked.

She looked at him, me, and then Roxanne. "I don't know if I want her ass in my house."

Roxanne sighed hard, but she didn't say a word.

"We come in peace," Parker assured her.

Lachez eyeballed him for a good minute, and then glanced at me and frowned at Roxanne.

"Look, I may have been born yesterday, but, baby, I've been up all night," she said.

This was one hip white girl, was all I could think as she stood there trying to check us.

"We just wanna talk," Parker pleaded, using a soft voice; although I could imagine how pissed he was on the inside.

"We can talk right here," Lachez snapped, now pulling the door shut around her body. "'Sides, I ain't got shit to say to y'all!"

The next voice we heard turned all of our attention away from Lachez.

"Oooh-wee, I told you she'd be at the house, even though it's a Friday night," a woman said to another one.

In an instant, alarm settled into Lachez's face. She pulled the door open and said, "Y'all could come in but just for a hot second. I need to talk to these two." She all but ushered us into her place. "Junie!" she turned and yelled. "C'mere, we got company!"

As we walked in, a boy came running up the hall.

"Make sure they don't move," she instructed before she stepped outside and slammed the door closed.

"I ain't got no damn cigarettes!" I heard her say before the door closed.

As we stood near the doorway, we couldn't help but hear the argument taking place on the other side of the door. It was obvious the women owed Lachez money, but were trying to buy something from her and she wasn't having it.

Soon, she rushed back inside and slammed the door shut again. This time though, there was banging on the door.

"Why you acting all brand-new?" a female voice yelled from the other side. "You know I'm good for it, Chez!" she yelled again when Lachez didn't acknowledge she had even spoken.

"Okay, what y'all want?" She turned to the boy. "I got it from here." The boy turned and ran to the back.

I was tripping off of her place. For a hustler on welfare, she was living damn near better than the rest of us. She had plush shag carpet, a massive big screen TV that was hooked up to a surround sound system that any man could envy. Her leather furniture didn't look cheap, and from the bottle of Hpnotiq sitting on the coffee table, it was obvious her good taste didn't stop at her lavish furnishings.

The music playing from the TV indicated she either had cable or a dish service. This place was nothing like I had envisioned a single mother of three on welfare would have.

"What you doing? Casing the joint?" she asked.

"Oh, shit! Nah, nothing like that," I said.

She kept eyeballing me as if she wasn't sure allowing us in was a good idea. I liked her spunk. Parker had started the recorder before we knocked on her door. The look on his face told me he was getting mad all over again.

I took the lead. "Look, the reason we're here is simple; really. You saw what happened in court. That judge ain't trying to hear what anybody has to say. So my boy here is planning to file a lawsuit against everybody involved." I could tell we had her attention.

"A lawsuit? What's that gotta do with me?" She raised her eyebrows.

"Well, that's why we're here. I told him, dude, she may be willing to help us if we approach her right. You can understand how pissed he is, and he's ready to sue all of you, you and your girl, but my thinking is, we don't even really know the extent of your involvement."

"You know what a lawsuit would mean, right?" Roxanne tossed in.

Lachez looked at her and frowned. "I ain't got shit, so I guess y'all could sue me if you want."

"You got three kids, you got some kind of money coming in; that's something," Roxanne countered, and glanced around. "And you sure do have a lot of nice stuff in here."

Lachez frowned at her, then turned her attention back to me.

"So what would I have to do? You know, to avoid this lawsuit y'all talking about?"

"Well, all we wanna know is what happened. All you gotta do is tell us why you guys picked my boy here. How you did it and all the details we need to know."

She looked at Parker, back at me and then at him again. "Why you so quiet? You making me nervous."

Parker stared at her. At this point, he was also making me ner-

vous, but for other reasons. I wasn't sure if he was near the edge
and about to crack.

"Hey, Lachez, remember, I'm the one trying to work this thing
out. My boy here, he's had enough, and he's ready to get the ball
rolling on this lawsuit. You gotta understand how mad he is right
now," I said.

"Well, he ain't got no right being mad at me; I ain't done shit.
Like I told y'all, it's the judge you oughta be harassing; not me!"
She pulled her gaze away from Parker.

We all stood around looking at each other for a while before
she spoke again.

"So lemme get this straight, if I tell y'all everything, when you
file this lawsuit, you'll leave my name out of it?"

"Yep, that's what we're offering, but you've gotta tell us the
whole story. Don't try to bullshit us or anything like that, 'cause
we'll find out."

She looked like she was contemplating what to do. I was hoping
she'd make the right decision, because truth be told, none of us
had even thought about a back-up plan. I think we all had the feeling that this had to work.

"Hmmm, I'ma need something in writing; something saying
we've got a deal," Lachez said.

"Then you'll also write something for us?" Parker asked.

She looked at him suspiciously. "I see the cat ain't got your
tongue after all, huh? Yeah, it's a deal," she reluctantly agreed.

PARKER

The day after we got the goods from Lachez, I still couldn't believe what she had said. Thanks to James, we had both a written statement and a recording of the entire conversation. This Kelly girl was way out line for this shit, and although I wanted to march right over there and wring her fucking neck, James thought we needed to think about what to do next.

"We don't want to mess this up. We got the story now, so let's play our cards right. The last thing we want to do is slip up with her," he said.

He was right, but that didn't stop me from wanting to kill her ass. Even though I agreed to wait a few days, there were times when I literally had to stop myself from going up to her job in a fit of rage.

It was Sunday night and the thought of waiting another day to confront this counselor was too overwhelming. I had to drink to keep my nerves calm. James said he wanted to run a few things by his lawyer first and begged me to give him some time. The plan was to call her job and see if she was at work.

I sat in bed, thinking about this while Roxy was in the shower.

I never even heard the shower go off, but my eyes couldn't believe the vision in the doorway or our master bathroom.

Roxanne stood in a sheer black teddy with a small patch covering the area between her thighs.

"I wanted to take your mind off of our troubles," she cooed.

That got my attention in more ways than one. I placed my drink on the nightstand and watched my wife, longingly.

"Wow, that's good, um, I mean, you look good."

She pranced over to the bed and stood in front of me. I wanted her so badly it hurt. I took her into my arms and we exchanged a long and heated kiss. When she pulled away, our breathing was out of control.

"God I've missed you," she huffed.

"I've missed you, too." I reached for her shoulder, and urged her to turn over. "I want you from behind," I said, nearly begging.

I watched as she climbed on the bed onto her hands and knees, and then eased back a bit. She looked over her shoulder, and smiled. Roxy wiggled her hips in anticipation of what I had to offer. I palmed her hips and pulled her closer. Our lovemaking was so passionate and intense. When I felt her body quiver, my movements intensified. I grabbed her shoulders, pulling her closer.

"Oh, yesss! Oh, yes…Parker!" I missed the passion in her voice.

"Yes, Roxy?"

"Oh God, Parker!"

"Yes, Roxy?"

"Oh, I'm cumming, baby, I'm cumming!" Roxy cried.

Suddenly, I stopped moving, and collapsed onto her back. We both lay there, panting; our bodies covered in a thin layer of wetness. After a few minutes, I kissed her moist back and we tumbled onto the bed next to each other.

"I love you, Roxy," I whispered.

"I love you more, Parker."

✪ ✪ ✪

Morning came quickly. When I woke and realized I was alone, panic raced through my veins until I remembered the night before and smelled bacon. I closed my eyes and pondered the idea of lying in bed a bit longer. Just as I turned onto my side and opened my eyes, Roxy appeared in the doorway with a tray of food. I pulled myself into an upright position and smiled.

"What'd I do to deserve this?"

"You're asking, after the way you handled your business last night?" she mocked, smiling.

"Oh, *that* was all you, baby," I cheered, ready to dig in. We ate, had round two, and then went back to sleep.

I woke when she moved. "Hey, where you going?"

"To shower."

"Can I join you?"

"Mrs. Redman, if you don't start nothing, there won't be nothing," I teased. She was hot on my heels before I could make it into the bathroom.

LACHEZ

"Girl, what the hell am I gonna do?" I cried into the phone. I had told the entire story from beginning to end and was still at a loss when it came to figuring out what I should do to protect myself and my kids.

"What *can* you do? Sounds to me like you gave them what they wanted. I don't think they were after you. Let's face it. If they were, do you really think you'd still be at home with the kids?"

"What's that supposed to mean?" I asked Toni, not liking her answer one bit.

"Can't you go to jail for shit like that?" she asked.

"I dunno but, girl, speaking of the kids," I said. "Toni, that bitch said they could take my boys. I didn't know anything about no damn paternity fraud, any kind of fraud for that matter. Girl, I can't go to no damn jail!"

"I think you should calm down," Toni said. "I'm the one who should be worried. Girl, I missed my date for that damn DNA testing. Now they probably sending a warrant out for my arrest." She sighed hard.

I hated having to put her all up in my business, but I really had no choice. I didn't have another living soul that I could talk to about this shit. But as usual, Toni had a way of turning my drama around and making the conversation about her. I wanted to guide the conversation back to me and the issue at hand. But my mind was racing so fast, I sat there as she went on and on about how most men were such dogs and why she needed that money.

"Ah, Toni, this is not about you," I said.

She laughed it off a bit, but I was so dead serious.

"So she picked you, just like that?" Toni asked, now trying to dig even deeper into my business.

"Well, not really, girl. She basically asked if I could use some extra cash, told me a friend of hers needed help getting back at this guy. They didn't really tell me all the business up front, but basically they said my case was the kind they were looking for; said in order to get the money, I had to trust her. You know me; I ain't the one to run from money. Besides, she told me I wasn't really doing nothing wrong. It's no secret that I really don't know who these kids' fathers are, so why not try to come up?"

"Girl, you know I feel you, I really do. But what's up with Julius now? I mean, him and dude showing up like that, did you get flashbacks of the Johnny incident or what?"

My silence must've told her she had gone too far, because she quickly said, "Ooooh wee, girl, you know I don't mean no harm; I'm just saying."

Now I was sorry I had even called to confide in Toni in the first damn place. She knew damn well I didn't like to even mention Johnny's name. That was way back in the day when a bitch was living lovely for real. I had no reason to think my dudes would ever meet up and compare notes, but that's exactly what had gone down. And unlike the other three dudes I was stringing along, Johnny had a fierce temper.

I coulda died from the beating he gave me. I spent a whole damn week in the hospital, Darlene's nosey judgmental ass had to come stay with the kids, and CPS was talking 'bout taking my boys. Now, I didn't even like being reminded of Johnny, even if it was by accident.

"Bitch, don't let any more slips of the tongue happen," I warned

Toni. Sometimes, she would be bringing that shit up simply to fuck with me.

"You ain't gotta go all psycho on a bitch; I made a mistake," she said, sucking her teeth. "'Sides, I ain't the one threatening your ass with no lawsuit either."

"See why I don't like telling you shit, Toni?" I screamed.

"What?" she balked.

"You know what, nothing. Look, I need to go. I'll holla at you later," I said, and then hung up the phone before she could get another word in.

I didn't know what to do, but something told me I needed to do *something*. The last thing I wanted was to wind up in jail, sued, or have someone trynta take my kids.

I had to try and think. And more importantly, maybe I needed to get Kelly and her friend before they tried to pin this shit all on me.

"You know what, I think that's exactly what I'm gonna do," I said, already feeling better about my decision. As always, I decided to stroll to the mailbox, hoping it would clear my mind. When I did, I thought again about the first time I saw that damn white van. I should've known then that something wasn't right.

"Damn, why didn't I see this shit coming?"

I shook it off, and collected my junk mail, for once relieved that there was no letter from the AG's Office. When I got back to the apartment, my world really flipped from top to bottom, then back up again. The stack of junk mail fell from my hands.

"What the fuck are you doing here?"

"Junie called me."

I looked at the two strangers standing next to her and my heart threatened to stop beating right then and there.

"It's over, Lachez."

"What are you talking about, and who are these people you got all up in my house?"

"This is Jill Valdez and this is Heather Rice," she said, turning to each woman she introduced. "They're with CPS."

I blinked back tears. But what I really wanted to do was slap the piss shit out of Darlene. She knew better; that's why she brought back up.

"We're about to talk to the kids; I've already talked to Julius. These ladies say if you cooperate, this will all work out fine," Darlene said.

I could hear myself breathing hard. You didn't want to display violence in front of CPS workers, but Darlene had to know I'd get into her ass eventually.

"Ma'am," one of the ladies said to me.

Most of the rest of her little speech was a blur. The other lady went into the back to talk to the boys. Of course Darlene led the way. Before I knew what was happening I was being read the details of the investigation and being told how long I'd be without my kids.

When Darlene and the other woman walked up front, the kids had bags.

"You should look at this as a good thing," Darlene had the nerve to say. "You don't have to worry. The boys won't be in the system; they'll be with me, and we just want you to get better, you know, get yourself together."

If looks could kill, Darlene would have been a dead bitch! I stood there wondering why, all of a sudden, everybody wanted to fuck with me.

I must've cried for hours after they left. I didn't stop until Drew called.

"What's wrong?" he asked.

"It's my kids; they're gone."

"What? I'm on my way."

Before Drew got there, I made a few other calls.

ROXANNE

When Kelly walked out of her office Tuesday evening, and glanced in our direction, her expression looked like she was curious about three people standing in the smoldering Texas sun talking next to a car. But she didn't break stride as she passed us.

"Excuse me, is your name Kelly Johnson?" Parker asked once she was a few steps away.

She turned and looked like she wasn't sure we were talking to her. She was wearing a sky blue velour sweat suit and I wondered how she wasn't hot in that outfit, but didn't ask.

"Yeah? Who are you?"

"He's my boy," James jumped in. "You know, Parker Redman; the one you've been hitting up to pay for Lachez's baby even though you know damn well he's not the father."

She looked mortified.

At first she looked like she didn't know what she should do. Her eyes traveled from one to the next.

Before we could start questioning Kelly, she broke down and admitted everything! She even implicated her friend, Serena, who was the mastermind behind the whole plan. Kelly told us everything, answered all of our questions, and even agreed to do what she had to to stay out of jail. Apparently, because Serena had helped her get the job, Kelly admitted she had felt obligated to help Serena get the revenge she was after.

✪ ✪ ✪

"Oh, let me guess; you forgot something?" Serena snarled when she opened her front door to let me in. What she didn't count on was me bringing company, not to mention a crap load of misery to her front door.

Before she could shut it, Parker and James pushed their way inside. The cynical smile on her face suddenly disappeared.

"What the hell is this supposed to be?" she asked with much attitude.

"Your gig is up, bitch!" I said, much to the astonishment of everyone in the room. Serena frowned, and then dismissed me with a hearty laugh.

"Lookie, lookie, lil' Ms. Prim and Proper is trying to act tough all of a sudden. Go sell that shit somewhere else, 'cause I ain't buying!" Sheer evil was shining through her eyes. I never knew a woman who could go from pretty to downright ugly in a matter of seconds like Serena.

"We know what you did," I said, not the least bit daunted by her macho display.

My words bounced off her like she was innocent and ignorant to whatever it was I could've been talking about. She definitely knew how to put up a good front; that I could say for sure.

"I haven't done shit, and if you thought bringing Curly and Moe here was going to change that, you and these two suckers wasted your time, but you damn sure won't be wasting mine."

James looked at her, with disgust written all over his face. "You got a whole lotta nerve!"

Serena didn't hesitate to get in his face. "Nerves? No, darling, it's called balls! Something neither of you know anything about. I suggest you all get the hell out of my fucking house before I call the police. I ain't got time for whatever it is you all think you're here to prove."

She and James were in a stare-off, mad-mugging each other until Parker pulled James back.

"Let's stay on course," he said to James.

"Yeah, do that and get the fuck out!" Serena added.

"Oh trust, we're not going anywhere until we get to the bottom of this mess you've created," I said to her. Still Serena stood there unmoved by my accusations, and or the fact that it was three against one.

"First of all, I don't know what the hell you're talking about, nor do I care. Secondly, y'all don't come bustin' all up in my house, like you paying any fucking bills around this camp, and thirdly, I'ma give the three of y'all five seconds to get the fuck out or I'm calling the damn police!"

She marched over toward the phone and stood next to it with her hands planted firmly on her hips. "Now, unless you left something here when you packed your rags, I suggest you all beat it!"

Parker looked at her. "So you don't even want to listen to the evidence we have, right?"

Serena's eyes narrowed, but she seemed to dig her feet in. "Read my lips! I don't give a fuck what you have! I don't wanna hear shit from none of you! Now get the fuck out!"

James looked at her and said, "So you just want us out, right?"

"That's what the fuck I said," she snapped with her neck twisting.

"Well, before we leave, why don't you answer one question for me," James said.

Serena sucked her teeth and rolled her eyes. "I don't have to do a damn thing! I don't have to listen to shit, and I don't have to answer to nair-one of you!"

"You don't but you might want to, because paternity fraud is a serious crime. Not only can you lose your job, but you can wind up behind bars and, if that's not enough, my boy here can sue you for everything you got!" James threatened.

To my shock, Serena looked at James, a grin curling at the corners of her mouth, and then she said, "Paternity fraud? Puh-leeee-asse!" She turned to Parker and shouted, "Is that what they're calling it now? Paternity fraud? Is that what y'all are here to talk about? Fraud? Well then, Parker, I guess you told your wife and your best friend here about *us* then, didn't you?"

The temperature of my blood shot from normal to boiling in less than a second. I could hear my heart booming in my ears and I suddenly felt my throat closing in on me.

Serena took one look at my face, and then snickered. "Oh, from her reaction, I can tell she doesn't know anything about *us*, so I hope that's what you meant when you came here to accuse me of any kind of fraud. Because we all know, Parker, you're the biggest fraud of all!"

When Parker didn't deny her words, I stormed out of there before I lost it.

JAMES

Her words hit me like a bulldozer. My head was spinning from what they implied. After Roxanne ran out of the house, Parker lunged toward Serena and I stood as stiff as a concrete pillar, unable to move.

"Parker and Serena?" I whispered almost to myself. I couldn't even fathom the idea. He wouldn't, she wasn't even his type. He hated her; always had. She wasn't his type.

"Get the fuck off me!" Serena's voice broke my trance. I rushed over to the corner, where Parker was on top of her, his hands clutching tightly around her neck. She squirmed beneath him, her legs kicking and her hands clawing at his.

"You fucking bitch! I can't believe you did this shit to me! You've ruined my life! You ruined my life!"

I grabbed Parker by the shoulder with a little too much force and he released her. When he turned to me, I saw the fire in his eyes. He would've killed her, no doubt. It was as if he'd come to his senses. He eased up off of her. Serena was on the floor, coughing and choking.

"I'm having your ass thrown back in jail, you bastard! You must've lost your goddamn mind! You don't put your fucking hands on me!" She scrambled to get up off the floor.

I stared at Parker. I wanted her words to not be true; I wanted him to deny what she had said. I couldn't believe it. Actually, I didn't want to believe it. How long ago was it? Had they been creepin' all along? I was sick with this, and he wasn't saying anything; nothing I wanted to hear anyway.

"Man, I hate this bitch!"

"Yes, you've told me over and over again," I said somberly.

"Oh, you think you hate me, wait 'til I have your ass sitting up in jail for assault. You don' fucked with the wrong one! I'ma see to it that your ass is under the jail cell!" Serena screamed. She was now looking in the mirror; she must've been inspecting her neck to see if there was any evidence of Parker's attack.

"Man," Parker began. "It's not like she said; it's not all she's trying to make it out to be. Nothing happened," he finally admitted to me. "She's trying to fuck with your head."

"You're my dawg," I said to him. I didn't want to believe her; I knew how she was and how she could be.

"Dawg, I'm sick of her and sick of all this shit. I want you to tell me, you didn't fuck my wife?"

But before Parker could say anything else, Serena jumped in.

"Fool, please, you wish I was still your wife," she barked.

"Shut the fuck up, Serena!" Parker screamed.

The next words from her mouth, made me lunge for her. "Tell him, Parker, how you had to step in and father his child 'cause he wasn't man enough!"

Next thing I remember, Parker was pulling *me* off of Serena.

PARKER

I wasn't expecting to see Roxanne when I finally made it home because she didn't give me a chance to fully explain. I wasn't sure if James and I were still cool, even though I told him that Serena was just trying to get under his skin again.

When I unlocked the front door and saw Roxy sitting there like she was waiting, she looked like she was in another world, and capable of just about anything.

"You made such a fool out of me," she said in a voice that sounded like she was in some sort of trance.

"I didn't; you didn't let me explain," I said softly. I didn't want to speak too loud or even too quickly because I didn't want to do anything to trigger her temper.

"You had me befriending someone who you knew good and well you were fucking! That to me, makes me a fool," she said.

Roxanne was talking so calmly, she was scaring me to death. I didn't quite know how to handle her, except gently.

"Roxy, just hear me out."

"Hear you out? For what? So you can lie to me again, so you can lull me into a false sense of security with you?" She shook her head. "NO, I'm tired, Parker; I'm really, really tired. As if this shit with Lachez ain't enough, I have to learn that you've been fucking your best friend's wife?"

"It's not what you think?"

"Oh, so now you know what I think," she said sarcastically. But still, her voice was calm; too calm actually. "Let's see, did your dick enter her body in any fashion at anytime whatsoever?"

"Let me explain."

"That's the only explanation I'm interested in right now. Did you fuck her or not? It's a simple question. Either you did or you didn't, Parker?" Roxy was staring me straight in the eyes. She never flinched as she waited on me to answer.

"Technically, I did not sleep with her. But I did meet her before James. We didn't hit it off. I wasn't in to her. She was persistent, but then she vanished," I tried to explain.

"So why did you let her stand there and say something happened when it didn't? That makes no sense at all!" Her eyebrows met in the middle of her face. "Wait, is that why you called her house? I thought James told you I was at Serena's but he said he didn't know, then you call out of the blue? It all makes sense now!" she screamed.

When she raised her voice, I stopped talking. I wasn't trying to push her even closer to the edge. I wanted to try and explain what had happened between Serena and me and offer up the reason why I didn't tell her, or James. He didn't want to listen to me either. He brushed it off, said it wasn't a big deal, but I'd known him long enough to know he didn't mean it.

"Roxy, it's not what you think," I tried to say.

"Oh, it's exactly what I think; you were calling her house to talk to *her*, not me!"

"Yes, I was; you're right. I was calling to talk to Serena—"

"Oh God!" Roxanne cried.

"Whoa, hold up; wait a sec. Hear me out. I did call to talk to her, but only because I wanted to tell her ass off for what she had done to James; that's it. Remember, their daughter, or Semaj, is my goddaughter, or at least she was supposed to be."

I never cheated on you. I never cheated with Serena or anyone else. The only reason I didn't tell you in the first place was because James seemed to be pushing a friendship with you two, so I figured she either didn't remember or she also agreed that it was no big deal since nothing really happened between us, I just thought it didn't really matter."

I noticed the instant change in her expression. She wasn't completely on my side yet, but she couldn't hide the relief I saw.

"Baby, I love you. That Serena situation was a huge mistake that snowballed out of control. You know she's not my type. When James introduced us, I couldn't believe it. I had no idea she was the woman he had been bragging about. At the time, the person he described was friendly, outgoing and always had a smile on her face. Now, you tell me, is that Serena?"

"Friendly?" she asked, cracking an attempt at a smile for the first time since Serena had dropped the bomb.

"Yes, friendly, and always had a smile on her face."

"Wow! Did she ever pull the wool over his eyes?" Roxy chuckled. "That girl's been tragic since the day I met her."

"I agree, so when he finally introduced me to her, I was baffled. I remember thinking quite surely this isn't the chick he was describing all along, but they seemed happy. Remember, in the beginning, all hugged up and stuff? There was no way in hell I was about to ruin it for him."

"Yeah, but Parker, you should've said something. You definitely should've said something before now. She has him thinking you two have had a thing going all this time. Hell, even I thought you did," she admitted.

"But you should know I'd never cheat on you. What for? You mean everything to me," I said sincerely.

"I'm not completely ready to forgive you for this little mishap, but I am glad to know she was lying when she said you two slept together. The bigger issue is what do we do next?" Roxy released a sigh and looked at me. "I don't know how we're gonna fix this whole mess. And then to find out why she did all of this? She did it because she obviously wanted more between the two of you and felt like you rejected her? The girl is a sack of mixed nuts!"

I sighed. I'd never thought about it like that.

"What did James have to say about all of this?"

"You know how men are. We don't harbor things like y'all." I shrugged. "He says he's cool with it all, I mean, I should've told him, but really nothing went down, so I'm hoping he really is cool."

"So you explained to him, about the fact that she was lying and nothing really happened?"

"Well, I tried, but she tried to keep it going. But I think he believed me," I said.

"Oh, by the way, what happened when I left? And how'd you guys get home?" she asked, changing the subject for me.

ROXANNE

P arker and I had been through so much over the last few months that I started daydreaming about the good old days, or even the days when we might have gotten past this whole mess.

I started telling myself things were near an end. Everything was coming out now. Serena was behind this, and we knew why; now it was merely a matter of figuring out how to clear it all up.

"Let's go grab some dinner," I said as Parker walked into the kitchen.

"Yeah, that sounds like a good idea." His voice was clear, but something told me dinner was the last thing on his mind.

I got up and followed him to the kitchen. "Everything okay?" I wanted to pull the words back as soon as they had fallen from my lips. Parker gave me a knowing look.

"You know what I mean. What's wrong now?"

"What if none of this matters? What if none of this works? We can do all of this shit and the judge still says, oh well, too bad, keep paying."

"You can't think like that," I told him.

"I can't *help* but think like that. Let's go over all we've already gone through. I told them it wasn't me, and we still had to pay so I could get out of jail. I finally get out, we find out who this person is, she doesn't show up for a court-mandated DNA test, and nothing happens to her. Better yet, after she fails to show, the judge yells at me, and reminds me that if I don't pay, I'll go back to the slammer."

My eyebrows rose high; I realized where he was going and I understood. He continued.

"Then I hire a private investigator, we find her, I confront her, we get her to show up in court, and I know she didn't say I *wasn't* the father, but honestly, the judge didn't even care to ask that question. That's the real question she *should've* asked. But the point is she didn't want to hear anything even resembling the truth. And, get this." Parker turned. "So now, we've gone through all the hassle of getting her to lay out the plot, tell us all the details, confronted Serena and, although she didn't deny any involvement, we all know she's guilty, we know she is behind all of this, but again I ask, what difference will any of this make to the judge?"

I definitely agreed with him. Deep down inside, I knew there was no way none of this would move this judge. I didn't have the heart to tell him so.

"I say we wait and see, and not make any rash judgment. Let's believe that we're doing the right thing. Let's believe that once we contact her job and let them know what's been going on, and let them know about their possible liability, that they will definitely do something."

Parker was shaking his head. He had no reason to believe. Hell, I didn't even believe, but we had to try and hang on to some hope.

"Listen to what I'm saying. If need be, we can threaten to sue the company Kelly works for. Somebody has to do something about this. You're not Lachez's kid's father, so while the courts milk you for every dime we have, some guy is running around out there avoiding his responsibilities. It's gonna work, because it simply has to!" I said with such finality that I even started believing it myself.

JAMES

Last night, I talked with Honey about everything that had been going on. We'd been spending lots of time together lately. She told me something that really messed my head up.

"I know you're hurt by what your ex did, but I'm not sure cutting off your daughter is the best thing to do."

"I don't have a daughter," I said.

"Yeah, but a few months ago you didn't know that. And if you loved her then, how did you just suddenly stop loving her now?"

Honey was making sense, but there was still so much resistance in my heart because of what Serena had done.

"All I'm saying is, you could, and maybe you should, still have a relationship with Semaj."

The conversation ended when I told her I'd think about trying to visit with Semaj, but deep down, I felt like it would be too much drama because I'd have to deal with Serena the Sicko.

After Honey left, I started going over the plan. I still thought we were on to something, and regardless of what had happened between Parker and Serena's ass, I wanted to see her fall for once and for all. I could have killed that bitch. She had shown no remorse over what she had done to me, and she wouldn't even fess up to what she had done to Parker.

"What the hell was I thinking when I hooked up with her ass?" I questioned aloud, even though I was alone.

When the phone rang and I noticed the Redmans' number pop

up, I didn't hesitate to answer. But it was Roxanne's voice I heard and not Parker's.

"Hey, how are you holding up?" she asked the minute I answered.

"Holding up? Shit, I'm straight. Why you ask?"

"Well, Parker explained everything to me about him and Serena but I know he didn't get a chance to tell you. It happened before the two of you met, and it's not like he *actually* slept with her," Roxanne explained.

"Like I told Parker, I'm not even tripping. At this point, I just want to make sure she gets hers, so when I tell y'all I'm straight, I really am. Serena had me fooled, she did, but I'm not tied to her in anyway whatsoever, so I'm cool. I say we stick to our plan, and get this shit done!"

"Yeah, about that," Roxanne said. I hoped she and Parker weren't about to back out; we needed to get this counselor and Serena's ass. If I knew her, she wasn't done with any of us quite yet. "I wonder what you think about the plan."

"What do you mean?" I wasn't sure where Roxanne was going. I heard hesitation in her voice and I wanted her to spit it out; get to the point.

"Where's Parker?" I asked.

"He went to meet with his lawyer. But I wanted to let you know that Parker is kind of unsure about whether this will work," Roxanne said reluctantly.

"Well, check this. I called Kelly's job and asked who I would file a complaint with. They gave me all the information I needed. Also, I asked hypothetically what would happen if someone did half of what we suspect Kelly of, and the guy told me there could be criminal charges."

"Really?" Roxanne asked excitedly.

"Yeah, and you know what that means. I think we can get Kelly to roll over on Serena. There's no way a judge, any judge, even his, would be able to let a crime slide."

"That's a good point, but how long will all of that take? Seriously."

"If you can think of a way to speed this up, be sure to let me know, but so far, I think this is the best option."

"I'll have Parker call when he gets back from the meeting. Okay?"

"Yeah, that's cool," I said.

"Oh, and James, thanks, for everything," Roxanne said before she hung up.

Once we got off the phone I thought back to the shit Serena had tried to throw in my face. I was glad to know Parker didn't hit it, but I was still sick to know she wanted him to. But I shook it off; nothing Serena did surprised me anymore. And we would soon find out that she wasn't nearly done with us, me or the Redmans.

LACHEZ

I sat by pissed, but helpless as two strangers helped Darlene remove my kids from my home. It was a trip, listening to one of the women talking about it being best that the kids spend some time with Darlene. They didn't know Darlene like I did, but I wasn't about to go there.

I didn't act the fool either, but Darlene knew good and well that I was through with her ass.

By the time they left, I was a mess, so when Kelly thought her tough-girl street talk was going to scare me into changing my mind, I already knew I had made the right decision when I told Parker and his friends exactly where to find Kelly.

Thinking about the call that led me to that decision still pissed me off now.

"You fucking bitch! After all I've done for you?" That was Kelly's response after I told her I was about to turn State's evidence, because I wasn't being named in anybody's lawsuit.

"You are trippin'. You need to get your girl on the phone 'cause I'm not about to go down for you or her," I told Kelly.

"Listen, I need to know who you've been talking to and what you've already said," Kelly said. She sounded more scared than I felt, but I didn't care; this was too much.

"You know what, Kelly, if this friend of yours is worth your job, that's fine, but I'm not about to go to jail, be sued, none of that. I'm just warning you so you can warn her. Actually, I don't care, you ain't gotta tell her anything. I just want y'all to know, I'm out!"

"Wait, Lachez, hold up. Let me see if I can get in touch with Serena. Don't do or say anything yet; give me a chance to get her up to speed on what's going on."

"Why can't you call her now, while I'm on the line?"

"She's, she's going through a lot. Give me thirty minutes and I'll call you back."

"You got fifteen."

"I don't even know if I can get her," she said.

"I don't care. If I don't hear from you in fifteen, I'm gonna do what I gotta do."

About ten minutes after I hung up with Kelly, my phone rang.

When the caller ID showed "Private," my heart nearly skipped a beat. What if this was that man, his wife, and whomever else they've turned me into?

I took a deep breath and picked up the phone.

"Hello?"

"Lachez, it's Kelly, and I've got Serena on the line. We, well, *she* needs to ask you a few questions."

"Oh?"

"Listen, Lachez, I really don't have time for this. But if you keep your mouth shut, everything is gonna be fine."

"Keep my mouth shut?"

"Yeah, that's how we're gonna handle this. If you don't talk, there won't be a problem."

"Oh, we're way beyond a problem. These people are threatening to sue me, my kids are gone, and I could go to jail."

"Hold up, first off, nobody's going to jail. If Parker and his flunkies came to talk to you, they're bluffing," Serena said.

"I'm not about to find out. I'm sick and tired of this mess anyway, always looking over my shoulders. It's not worth it."

"Listen, have we not done everything we said we were gonna do for you? Maybe not in this particular situation, but over the years, did you get paid? You're in this more than you think."

"I don't care what y'all say," I said.

"Besides," Serena said. "I really don't have time to sit here and convince you that you should keep your mouth shut. And trust me when I say, my word against yours, honey, you don't stand a chance."

"Oh, you got the wrong number, baby. You think you can call me up with your little meaningless threats and expect to put fear in my heart? Bitch, please; you bes' check yourself!" I snarled at Serena.

"Oh, you think your little hoodrat antics are scaring me? Baby, I grew up in the Fifth Ward! You ain't saying nothing over here!"

"Good, then you know exactly where I'm coming from when I put it to you like this. If you ever call my fucking house yelling and screaming like you don' lost your damn mind, don't be shocked when you wake up one night and find me hovering over you in the comfort of your own fucking bed. You don't know who you fucking with. You may be able to scare everybody else with all your rusty street talk, whatever you think you can still remember from your Fifth Ward days, but you shouldn't forget, while you reminiscing, I live in the trenches every damn day! And I won't hesitate to come and work your ass over."

"Bring it, bitch!" she challenged.

"Oh, you ain't said nothing but a word. I can show you a whole lot better than I can tell you, baby. You better watch your back and your ass. 'Cause by the time I'm done with you, you'll wish they'd gotten your ass with that lawsuit."

When they finally hung up, I knew what I had to do.

I couldn't believe that bitch. After all she'd gotten me caught up in, now she wanted to throw around some threats? She better ask somebody. I started tearing my place apart, looking for the card I had gotten from one of the guys who had come there asking about her. But I couldn't find it to save my life.

That bitch really had gotten me fired up; she didn't know what she'd started by fucking with me. I was determined to talk to somebody. I sure as hell hoped they were going through with that damn lawsuit. I remembered his attorney's name, but I didn't know what firm he was with and I damn sure couldn't call information asking for Mr. Smith's law office.

I eased back onto the sofa. "Bitch got me all twisted."

I called that guy Parker to make sure they found Kelly and to tell him what all they needed to say to get to the bottom of this mess.

The knock at the door pulled me back from those thoughts. I nearly forgot Drew was on his way. It felt good knowing there was someone in my corner after all. I just hoped he'd still be there when all this shit cleared up.

SIX MONTHS LATER

PARKER

This time when I went to court, I had to admit that I felt somewhat better, but I was still uneasy. After spending so much time trying to secure another emergency injunction to show the judge the evidence we had, still nothing had happened until we did something I would've never considered.

It had really been Roxy's idea, but it worked. We did what we needed to do to bring Serena's involvement to her supervisor's attention. Surprisingly, when Lachez was contacted, this time she didn't hold anything back; she told the whole story about Kelly, and how Serena put them together. Both Kelly and Serena had been suspended pending the outcome of an investigation.

I wasn't sure if either was facing criminal charges, because this thing had taken on a life of its own, going in a direction none of us expected.

Three nights earlier, Roxy and I had watched as Channel 11's investigative reporters highlighted my story on the evening news.

"Can you believe it?" she had asked as we watched the 11 News Defenders Report.

And I couldn't. But what I couldn't believe was the snowball that happened after the story aired. My lawyer, who approved the interview, called to tell me that we had suddenly received that emergency hearing. The station had been flooded with phone calls from other men, their wives, mothers and sisters and so forth.

When the reporter called to tell me, he said, "You will not believe what's going on around here!"

"What's up?" I asked.

"This story has really started something. Calls keep pouring in, and you won't believe how many other men are going through the same thing!"

"What?"

"Yes! My news director wants to do a series; we'll be in touch about that later. But the reason I'm calling now is because we want to go to court with you when you get a date."

"Really?"

"Yeah, if that's okay. Are you cool with that?"

"Sure, but it's just strange. The night after the story aired, my attorney called and said the judge's clerk had called, notifying us of an opening on the judge's docket. Seems she finally wants to hear us out."

"Funny how a little publicity can change things, huh?"

"Man, you just don't know. We've worked endless hours to try and get this thing in front of her."

"Oh, trust me, I see it every day. But we wanted to know if we could come to court, if you wouldn't mind talking to us after the hearing. We're gonna try and pull a few more stories out of this. Also, once the series is completed, we're looking at calling one of our local congresswomen. I'm thinking Shelia Jackson Lee; she loves the press, but she also knows how to get results."

"Wow, this thing is taking on a life of its own," I said, still stunned by his news.

"Yeah, I'll admit, we've heard tons of stories since we aired yours. But yours, with the counselor and her colleague in on it and everything, it's still paternity fraud, but your case has exposed so many flaws in not just the family law system but also those in charge of handing out our tax dollars to so-called welfare mothers."

"This is all a bit overwhelming. I was just trying to bring some attention to something I thought was beyond wrong," I said.

"Yeah, well consider your job accomplished. Now, when is the court date? We'll call the court and get permission to be there and we'll see you there."

"Hey, thanks," I said before hanging up.

✪ ✪ ✪

Now as we entered the courtroom, with the reporter right behind us, I wasn't sure what to expect. The cameraman had to stay out in the hall, but I hoped their presence would make a difference.

On this day, Judge Brock appeared with her hair curled, she wore contacts instead of glasses, and her eye makeup stood out. Actually, for the first time, I realized her entire face was made up. I told myself that I was imagining things.

"Mr. Smith, I understand you and your client have been busy at work on this. While I appreciate all of your time and effort in this matter, I truly regret to inform you there's still nothing I can do."

"Your Honor!" Smith began.

She hushed him with one hand.

"I'm not finished. I also have been busy. I've been looking up similar cases and they're on the rise all over our country. But unfortunately, until the Texas Legislature does something, there is nothing I can do. As I mentioned on so many other occasions, because your client missed his opportunity to challenge the suit, there's no way for me to intervene."

I was even more stunned by her tone of voice than her appearance. She was mild-mannered and spoke as if she felt some empathy. I didn't know what to attribute her new attitude to, but I was grateful for it.

"But, Your Honor, are you aware of the possible charges pending against a Kelly Johnson and Mrs. Serena Carson?"

Again, she raised her hand. This time she nodded.

"Mr. Smith, I am fully aware, and all I can tell you is once charges are filed and they are convicted, then you may revisit this court, but for now, I must uphold the law." She looked at me. "I have nothing personally against your client. I believe he is not the biological father in this case, but the bottom line is I'm bound to follow the law. And the law here in the State of Texas, as unfair as it may seem, says if you miss that deadline to challenge paternity, you assume responsibility. Unfortunately, our age-old laws have not caught up with technology, or the times. There are no provisions in the law for cases like your client's. Who knows, maybe this will set a precedent, but until then, my order stands."

I released a heavy breath. I couldn't believe in this day and age, in the U S of A, I was being forced to pay for a child that I did not father.

"Now, I wish you and your client luck with this, but my hands are tied until the laws are changed."

Despite my not so happy ending, after the hearing, I did the interview and, this time, I stressed the importance of meeting those deadlines.

"So what's next?" the reporter asked.

I looked straight into the camera. "We go back and regroup, but this fight is far from over. There has to be justice out there for men who have fatherhood forced on them. We're going straight to the Legislature; somebody in the state of Texas can fix this. And if I die trying, I'm gonna make sure I get this law changed."

"And we'll be with you each step of the way," the reporter said before signing off.

When I walked out of the courthouse, hand in hand with my wife, I thought about all we had been through, and even though it wasn't over, I still felt some sense of vindication. That damn judge had admitted what we all knew. I didn't do it. Now, I just had to force lawmakers to listen and take action.

ABOUT THE AUTHOR

By day, Pat Tucker Wilson works as a radio news director in Houston, TX. By night, she is a talented writer with a knack for telling page-turning stories. A former television news reporter, she draws on her background to craft stories readers will love. With more than fifteen years of media experience, the award-winning broadcast journalist has worked as a reporter for ABC, NBC and Fox affiliate TV stations and radio stations in California and Texas. She also co-hosts the literary talk show, "From Cover to Cover," with ReShonda Tate Billingsley.

Known as one of the fastest writers in the country, Pat has wowed editors with her ability to turn out five to ten thousand words a day. But it's not just quantity that has Pat at the top of her game. The quality of her stories is what keeps the readers coming back. A much sought-after ghostwriter, Pat gets her greatest joy in creating her own stories. She is the author of six novels and has participated in three anthologies, including *New York Times* Bestselling Author Zane's *Caramel Flava*.

A graduate of San Jose State University, Pat is a member of the National and Houston Association of Black Journalists and Sigma Gamma Rho Sorority, Inc. She is married with two children.

Visit the author at www.authorpattucker.com.; Facebook-Pat Tucker; Fan Page-Author Pat Tucker Readers; Facebook-Sylkkep PL Wilson; Myspace-Author PL Wilson; Myspace-Author Pat Tucker; Twitter-cauthorpattucker; www.fromcovertocovershow.com.

READER'S GUIDE

1. If your spouse were suddenly arrested for nonpayment of child support, would you stand by his side?

2. How did you feel about Lachez's many ways to beat the system and make money?

3. Serena was bitter because men constantly cheated on her. Do you think her attitude impacted the kind of men who mistreated her?

4. When Parker and Roxanne first dated, he was upfront about other women. What did you think about the fact that she didn't seem to mind sharing him?

5. Would you agree to wipe out the family's savings to pay for a spouse's debt accrued before your time?

6. What did you think about James' relationship with Semaj and how should he have handled things when he learned about the results of the DNA test?

7. What do you think about the rule that only gives men thirty days to challenge paternity?

8. Should a man have to pay, even if DNA proves a child isn't his, when no one knows who fathered the child?

9. What would you have done if, like Roxanne, you discovered a friend had been envious of you all along?

10. What did you think about Lachez using the ADHD diagnosis as a means to get money?

11. After what he experienced, how did you feel about James going to a strip club because he was lonely?

12. What did you think about Parker's selective attitude regarding women he dated?